unborn

By Amber Lynn Natusch

Unborn

The Caged Series
Caged
Haunted
Framed
Scarred
Fractured
Tarnished (novella)

Light and Shadow Trilogy
Tempted by Evil

Undertow

unborn

AMBER LYNN NATUSCH

47NORTH

Published by 47North, Seattle

www.apub.com

Amazon, the Amazon logo, and 47North are trademarks of Amazon.com, Inc., or its affiliates.

ISBN-13: 9781477824290
ISBN-10: 1477824294

Cover design by Damon Za
Cover photo by Dannielle Gleim Damm

Library of Congress Control Number: 2014932943

Printed in the United States of America

To Shannon Morton,
who truly understands the need for a fictional bad boy.

PROLOGUE

It was not time for me to go yet—I had only just returned home.

The fiery pits I flew past blurred in my vision, painting everything around me the most vibrant orange. It was often said that there was nothing beautiful about my home, but I disagreed—vehemently. I much preferred it to where I was headed.

The unseen force that held me hostage moved me through the air at incredible speed. His attempt to pull me from the depths and eject me as quickly as possible was nearly accomplished, though the reasons behind his mission remained completely inexplicable. I had five months left before I was to leave—why had he come for me? Even more baffling was why *he* had come at all. The transition was never supposed to happen that way.

I knew the Dark Ones were fearsome creatures, capable of traveling between worlds, but, in all my centuries, I'd never seen one. *The Fallen,* Father called them, warning me of their merciless nature. For that reason, he'd kept me well-hidden from them—at least until that day. Even Father had been powerless to stop the one who ripped me from his protective hold.

"I feared this day would come," he yelled as his grasp on my arm gave way to the strength of the one sent to take me. "Take her where he won't find her. You owe me that much!"

Those were the last words I heard before the sound of the Dark One's wings drowned his wails completely.

I will miss him, I thought.

He loved me so.

Water from the Acheron boiled and spit, stinging my face as we crossed it. I knew it wouldn't be long before the familiar light of the world would start to permeate the darkened tunnel we were rocketing through. I'd never seen spring before; that was never part of the deal. The favored one spent the fertile seasons on Earth, and I the seasons of death and darkness. I wondered why I did not pass her on the journey—it was the only time I ever saw her.

When the Dark One broke through to the world above, my hopes were smashed. The eternal cold of my existence was not to be broken; spring was not awaiting my arrival. Instead, the bitterness of a lingering winter surrounded and engulfed me, magnified further by our blistering rate of ascent. As the air thinned around me and the chill burrowed deeper, the irony that I was always cold struck me. I never understood how a person could be so perpetually frozen, even when surrounded by fire and flame. Father wondered if it was because I did not belong in the Underworld—that my soul repelled the warmth that the torment of the damned provided.

When I snapped my attention back from my wandering thoughts, I saw that I wasn't being taken to meet my mother at all. I would normally have been entrusted to her care upon entering the earthly realm, delivered to where she always stood waiting, but never with open arms. Instead, I was being flown far and fast in the opposite direction, and, as my body shook and my breathing failed me, a faint sense of calm overtook me. Wherever I was headed, whatever fate I was destined for, I reveled in the knowledge that I'd finally be rid of her.

And that was a fate worth dying for.

////////////////////////////////////

1

The stench surrounding me when I awoke was insufferable. It coated the inside of my nose so thickly that I thought I could taste the rotten decay that made me want to retch. My eyes were clouded and heavy, my body catatonic. My mind was fuzzy, and I remembered little of the journey I had been on prior to my passing out. I did recall thinking I was destined to die. In some ways, that would have made my current situation far easier.

I felt like those I had spent half my life surrounded by: the lost, the broken—the damned. My body was as cumbersome as theirs, moving awkwardly as I attempted to pull myself up to stand. It would not comply with the majority of my commands. When I finally managed to force my eyes to take in my surroundings, my heart stopped, if only for a moment.

Where am I, I wondered, the words a whisper in my mind. I looked around, breathing shakily in the cold night air—and it was night, wherever I was. Either I had been unconscious for longer than I could have imagined, or I was somewhere so far away that the sun rose and set on a schedule much different than the one I expected.

I also was not expecting to see snow on the ground. The green of spring should have been emerging from the deadened earth by then. *What place is this that remains so barren and lifeless long after its time?*

I brought my focus to the claustrophobic setting I found myself immersed in. Towering walls of untextured concrete entombed me and paved the road beneath me. *A city,* I thought. I'd seen countless images of them in my life but had never been in one; I was far from impressed. I did, however, find comfort in the familiar gray shades of the buildings. They reminded me of the rock that housed the Underworld.

A sudden gust of wind blew down the alleyway, tossing my long auburn hair in my face. While I unsuccessfully willed my arms to untangle and retain the wild and unruly waves, a voice called to me softly. I almost missed it.

"Are you lost?" he asked, approaching me slowly. The light from the street behind him cast a glorious glow around his form but darkened his features entirely. I could not see his face.

My body still refused to move, so I stood firmly affixed to the snow-covered spot I had awoken in. I was not afraid of death. Father always said there were fates far worse.

Unable to find my voice, I merely stared at him blankly as he methodically advanced toward me. His moves were not cautious, but calculated, indicating that nothing about our encounter was friendly or chance. He had sought me out.

"Can I help you?" he asked as he stopped only feet away from me. I saw his hand draw slowly behind his back while the expression on his face warmed slightly—a ruse. He was a warrior for certain. "Tell me your name."

My tongue lay limp in my mouth, unable to move. Whatever had happened to me before I landed in this godforsaken place had rendered me utterly useless in every way. My body remained unreactive when he presented a knife far larger and blacker than any I had ever seen, and I silently cursed, knowing that I would die without properly saying good-bye to my father. He had always maintained that I would never go to him when I died—convinced my soul was bound to a lighter place.

When I did not respond, the warrior's expression darkened ever so slightly.

"You shouldn't have let them take it all," he said mysteriously, drawing back the blade.

I did not flinch when he lunged at me.

The dagger danced before my face, closing in for a killing thrust, before it suddenly stopped. My attacker's hand encircled my left arm, tightly holding me in place, and his grip shook violently.

"You can't be . . ." he whispered to himself. I knew not of what he spoke, nor did I have the ability to speak myself, but he did not appear to be looking to me for answers. His eyes were far too wide and unfocused for that. When he regained his composure, his jaw tensed harshly, scowling at me for a moment as if deeply contemplating his next move.

As he continued to stare at me, his curious expression bleeding slowly to one of disbelief, the oddest sensation coursed through me. I felt I knew him, though I could not explain how. What I did realize was that the longer he held my arm, the more I seemed to regain command of my body. I delicately pulled my feet off the ground one at a time, then turned my head from side to side. I flexed my hand as I bent my arms upward. He looked on silently as I did.

"Khara," I replied with the slightest of slurs. He looked at me strangely in response. "You requested my name. It is Khara."

"You're not an Empty?" he asked, expression unchanged.

"I do not know what you mean by an 'Empty,' but I do not believe I am one."

"Do you know who you are . . . *what* you are?"

"I am Khara, adopted daughter of Demeter and ward of Hades," I told him, regaining more clarity of speech. "And who are *you*, warrior? Why have you not finished your task?"

He released his hold of me, looking pained, then did the strangest thing of all. He embraced me.

"There has never been a female born of him. Not since . . ." he said disbelievingly as he pulled away from me just enough to look into my eyes. "And yet here you stand. We must go tell the others."

"What others?"

"Your brothers," he replied with a wink.

"And what will we tell them?" I asked, feeling as confused as I had when I first regained consciousness. A genuine smile broadened across his face, softening the harshness in his eyes. He was happy—truly happy.

"We will tell them that Ares was wrong," he said. "We will tell them they have a *sister*."

2

He gently draped his coat around my shoulders, adjusting the substantial amount of fabric to his satisfaction. As he did, I assessed him. Tall and formidably built, his dark blond hair was a tad unkempt, hanging over his eyes slightly while he fastened the top button. Crystal-blue eyes then met mine, and he nodded once in approval before taking my hand in his, leading me out of the alley and onto the adjacent street. I trailed him silently, processing all that he'd just told me.

I have brothers.

My father is the god of war.

Why had Hades never mentioned them or my father? How was I kept secret from them for so long? And why, presumably out of nowhere, was I suddenly dropped into my brothers' city—and into their lives?

"Your name, warrior," I asked again, remembering that he had successfully evaded my earlier question. He looked over his shoulder at me, as I trailed behind him slightly, and smiled yet again. He was the happiest person I had ever encountered—at least after deducing who I was. I wondered what gave him such occasion to smile.

"Drew," he replied, still grinning. There was something most pleasant about his face when he wore that expression. "And it's brother, not warrior, to you."

"You said that I am the daughter of Ares?"

"You are."

"And you are his son?"

"Yes, all of the brothers are, though we come from different mothers."

"And where, Brother Drew, are we meeting these other brothers of ours?" I asked, trying to look straight ahead and avoid taking in too much of my urban surroundings. I found it overwhelming to be dwarfed and hemmed in by the buildings around me, which was ironic given that my favorite place was miles below the surface of the earth, with only one way in or out.

"A club. It's not far from here," he replied, slowing his pace slightly. "Are you cold? Do you need to eat something? Would you rather I just take you home to rest?"

Home . . .

"I cannot return home. I have no one to take me," I explained as though that fact should have been painfully obvious to him. As his expression hardened, I saw that he was starting to comprehend my point.

"Did Hades cast you out?"

"No. He would never do such a thing. I am his dearest . . . he adores me."

"Then how did you come to be here? It's not like someone can come and go as they please from the Underworld . . ." he said, sounding uncertain, as though he wanted affirmation of his statement.

"A Dark One," I said, watching his eyes widen instantaneously. "He came for me. I do not know why."

A growling sound came from deep within his chest.

"And he just left you here?"

"So it would seem, though I do not know where 'here' is, geographically speaking," I replied.

"You don't even know where you are?" he asked, coming to an abrupt stop. "The Dark One said nothing about where he was taking you?"

"His grip on me was such that I could not see him, nor easily speak to him. He had me by the throat, though not tightly enough to harm me."

Again, he made a low, rumbling noise. I was uncertain how to interpret it.

"Detroit," he said, pressing his eyes shut while he breathed in deeply. "You're in Detroit. It's in America."

"I know where that is. Though my experiences in it are limited, I am not uneducated about the world above," I said defensively. I had not realized that I would be offended by such a comment.

"Sorry," he said, starting to guide me back through the city. "I wasn't sure . . . I didn't know."

"You did not know what I knew of the world above. That is understandable, given what little you know of me. I am certain you meant no offense."

He flashed me another smile.

"So you never answered my question before. Do you need to sleep? Eat? Warm up?"

"I am fine, thank you."

He searched my face for something, waiting for a sign of sorts. Eventually his smile faded, and he brought his attention back to where he was taking me. Had he wanted a smile in return?

I had never had much cause for overt affection in my life, though it was not completely foreign to me. The few times I could recall had involved Hades. His station was one that demanded the respect of all who surrounded him, and over time that hardened him into a militaristic leader—the god of the Underworld. It was only with me that a softness in him emerged—with me and with his bride.

Hades had not asked for me—never chose to have me in his life. Instead, I was thrust upon him, though, once he met me, Hades easily made amends with the situation and accepted me without prejudice. He raised me as his own. My only fond memories were of him and me together; now, I feared that I may never get to see him again.

And there were few things in life I feared.

We were deep in the heart of Detroit when we arrived at our destination. The buildings had grown ever taller and closer together, and there was an element of danger in the darkness around us. I had seen such places in periodicals and read about them in books, but I had never been to one in person. It was seedy, shady—criminal.

The façade of the club we entered was nondescript, just a redbrick wall with a heavy metal door—no demarcation of any sort to denote to a passerby what waited within. Drew tucked me in close behind him as he pushed us through a crowd of humans huddling near the entrance.

"Stay close," he told me under his breath before he dragged me into a cramped and poorly lit foyer. All that stood before us was a steep stairwell descending into a black abyss. It seemed to go on infinitely.

I had a sharp pang of longing—the black and claustrophobic nature of the hallway reminded me in the smallest way of home.

"Are you okay?" he asked as I hesitated at the top. "Maybe I should just take you home; you've had a long—"

"No," I protested. "I would like to meet my family. Besides, I enjoy the feel of being underground."

"Then I guess you're going to fit in around here just fine." He was smiling again. I failed to see what he found so joyous.

I had heard virtually no noise when we stood at the top of the stairs, but as we descended the music started vibrating the walls around us. By the time we made it to the true entrance of the club, we were easily fifty feet below ground level—I had an excellent sense of depth.

He swung the door open wide, and I was instantly assaulted by the cacophony and heat that the steel barricade had withheld. Before me was a massive open space full of humans, writhing and undulating shamelessly as one, hundreds, maybe even a thousand, deep. That was only the first level. As I inspected the establishment further, I saw that this den of sin had another floor that encircled the main area, also populated by dancing bodies. Lastly, I saw a raised section off to our right, which was devoid of the chaos and commotion that had overtaken the rest of the establishment. From where I stood, this section appeared completely unoccupied, though its purpose was plain. It was for those who wished to enjoy the debauchery from afar—on high.

It was for spectators.

The bass pulsed through the building, making the entire place vibrate softly while the sheer volume of the music was near deafening. I hadn't heard Drew talking to me while I inspected the club.

"Over there," he indicated, pointing up to the balcony for spectators. "Let's go."

He took my hand, yet again, and wove me through the gyrating mass, toward the stairs that I assumed led to my brothers. I wondered what they found so appealing about that vantage point. Did they like looking down on others? Did they rule them as Father ruled the condemned? Who were these sons of Ares I was so soon to meet?

Cresting the last few stairs, we came to stand in a sparsely inhabited area, furnished only with plush sofas and armchairs in dark shades of gray. Occupying the vast space were four males and two females. I knew the females to be human. The males were not.

"I didn't tell them we were coming," Drew whispered in my ear. "I was supposed to be patrolling tonight. I wanted to surprise them . . ."

"Surely if what you said is true—that I am one that should not be—then they should be surprised regardless."

Another smile. His ability to find joy or humor in all things was confounding.

As we stood, conspiring by the staircase, we were easily spotted. Neither Drew nor I was startled by the approach of a tall, raven-haired man. His build was solid but graceful, just as Drew's was. Another warrior.

"Shucking your duty tonight for a little grab-ass fun?" the man asked, both his tone and expression playful. "I didn't know you had it in you, Drew. But she's totally hot. I would have done the same thing." He turned his gray-blue eyes to me and smiled. "Feel like sharing?"

"Kierson," Drew started in a tone very similar to Father's when he was exhausted by the stupidity of his minions. "You're going to wish you hadn't said that in a few minutes."

Drew dragged me beyond the nuisance and toward the others.

"Everybody, listen up," he shouted over the resounding music. "This is somebody you have to meet."

All the men immediately fixed their eyes on me. All but one.

The group of them was sprawled out across the various sofas, lounging and drinking, except for the one who looked away from me. He was tucked back in a darkened corner, reclining in a chair against the wall. Upon him sat two women—women built for servicing. His eyes refused to meet mine just as his lips refused to meet theirs, pushing them away from his face to other more important tasks. They worshiped him like a god, and, though I knew of all who had reigned on Mount Olympus, I struggled in the darkness to recognize if he was one of them.

"Who is she?" another man called out from his station. He was methodically cleaning a blade while he stared at me intently, as though trying to ascertain what the great importance was.

"I met her tonight in an alley during my rounds," Drew explained. "I thought she was an *Empty.*"

That word again . . .

Whatever it meant, the term brought about their collective attention. Even the god's.

"I nearly had her head off, but when I grabbed her arm to steady her for the blow, I knew."

"Knew what?" the blade cleaner asked, his annoyance still plain. He wiped the dagger with such reverence, as though it were more than just a weapon—he treated it like a favored pet.

Another warrior.

"Her name is Khara. She is the adopted daughter of Demeter, raised in the Underworld by Hades," he said loudly, commanding their attention. "She is also one of *us*. Your *sister*."

The blade clattered when it hit the floor.

"Impossible," another of the men argued, coming to stand before me in an instant. "There are no females born of him, not since—" He stopped talking the moment his right hand cupped my jaw, turning it up to the scant light of the open room. "It can't be . . ."

"It is," Drew affirmed, gently removing his brother's hand from my face. "Khara, meet your brother, Pierson."

Pierson looked as though he had seen a ghost. It was an expression I was all too familiar with. Every time a new soul came to Father's domain it wore that very same mask—disbelief, shock, and mild horror.

While he stood dumbfounded, the man who had first approached us came near, pushing Pierson to the side slightly.

"Let me see." He took my hand, his eyes widening exponentially upon contact. There was a strange familiarity in his touch that I could not place, but it was oddly welcome. "I sure am glad you grabbed her before you lopped her head off, Drew," he said while continuing to stare at me, a look of disbelief still etched deeply into his features. Then, in the blink of an eye, his expression warmed. "So that's what's going on here," he said, grinning. "And I thought you weren't going to share because you were getting greedy in your old age, Drew."

Without warning, he crushed me into his arms, smothering my face as he pressed it tightly to his chest.

"Khara," Drew said with a sigh, "this is Kierson . . . our brother and Pierson's twin."

I fought to escape his monstrous show of affection and took a step back to take the two of them in. Though it had not struck me immediately, it was clear that they were indeed exact physical replicas of one another, though that appeared to be where all similarities stopped.

While Kierson behaved like a sex-driven juvenile, Pierson was positively serious in nature, his eyes analyzing everything around him.

While I assessed them, and they did me, the blade cleaner came to join us. He was slightly shorter and broader than the others, and he forced himself between the twins, violently casting the two aside. Neither one said a word in response. They looked wary of him, and, upon further inspection, I understood why. His nearly black eyes were sunk deep in his face, the rest of his features dominating. His head was smooth, with only a trace of hair shadowing the surface. His skin was lighter than the twins', which served to highlight the darkness in his eyes. To me, he wasn't fearsome, but he did appear far from friendly. I thought that had he been the one to fall upon me in the alley that night, I would not have likely survived.

"Casey," Drew said, stepping slightly in front of me to cut him off. "This is Khara."

He said nothing.

I returned the gesture and stared silently back at him.

"Do you fear me?" he asked eventually, his expression unchanging.

"Have you given me cause to?" I returned.

"Shall I give you cause to?"

"You offer violence in your glare," I said sharply, "but it is unoriginal—nothing I have not seen before. If you wish to frighten me, you will have to try much harder to succeed."

A wicked smile grew slowly on his face. It was nothing like Drew's or Kierson's. I had long known a warrior like Casey—one of Father's soldiers—who sought to terrorize me from the moment I set foot in the Underworld. He, too, wore that same smile often, and, for the first time since the Dark One came for me, I felt a twinge of fear. That smile promised pain and suffering at the enjoyment of he who wore it.

Casey said nothing else, but slowly walked back to whence he came, kicking his feet up onto his padded sofa after collapsing atop it. He collected his blade from the floor and continued to clean it silently.

I forbade the growing unease I felt in his presence to make it to my face. Centuries lived amid lies, deceit, and struggles for power served me well in that moment. Fear was a weakness that could not be publicly displayed without cost. Father had taught me that.

I longed to be near him again.

"Don't mind him," Kierson started, draping his arm casually around my shoulder. "He just needs to get laid. He'll come around eventually, but, until then, don't worry. He won't bite—not hard, anyway."

He ushered me to sit on a couch far away from Casey before dropping himself tightly beside me.

"You do realize that you can't sleep with your own sister, right?" a voice called from deep within the shadows to our right. "Incest is pretty low, Kierson, even for you."

I peered into the darkened area as the godlike man pushed his women aside and came to stand before me.

"Don't I get an introduction, Drew?" he asked, staring down at me wickedly. I did not enjoy the inequality of my position, so I stood, slowly raising myself from my submissive station. Something about him was different. The others all possessed a faint similarity—he did not.

"Khara," I said dryly, not extending any gesture of acknowledgment beyond my name.

His piercing brown eyes absorbed every inch of my presumably disheveled appearance. My hair was wild from the wind, and I still wore Drew's jacket. My pants had been torn somehow during my extraction from the Underworld, and I was certain my neck had been bruised, courtesy of the Dark One who stole me away. I felt small and weak—two things I abhorred—so I removed the jacket and stretched my frame to be as tall and intimidating as possible. If we were in a battle for power, then I would wield my sword as mightily as he.

"Oz," he said with a tight expression.

We continued to eye each other silently while Kierson nattered in the background.

"You are not my brother," I stated as fact.

"Not in the least," he replied, his voice low and menacing.

"Are you a god?"

"Hardly."

"Why do they service you if you are not?" I asked, gesturing to the women who waited mindlessly for him to return. They did not eye me favorably.

"Simple, new girl," he said, leaning in close to me. "Because I want them to."

He then returned to his post, letting the women fondle and worship him again. They wove their fingers through his golden-brown hair and kissed his face, his neck, his chest—but never his mouth. He sat between them looking smug and haughty, his deep brown eyes pinned on me for the first time since my arrival.

"*Sooooo*," Kierson drawled, looking around the group. "What do we do now?"

"Khara needs some rest. She's had a long night. She insisted upon coming here first before heading home because she wanted to meet her brothers," Drew said, addressing them. "I'm going to take her home. Anyone coming?"

"I'm in," Kierson replied, pulling me against him. "Khara can stay in my room."

"She's your *sister*," Pierson groaned, looking as though he wanted to tear his hair out in frustration.

"I didn't say that I was staying in there with her, did I?" he snarled in return.

"Fine," Drew conceded. "Grab your stuff so we can go. Anyone else? Casey?"

"No. I'll go finish your rounds."

"Pierson?"

"No. I'll go with Casey."

"Good idea," he said with a nod. "And be careful. There's something in the air tonight. I don't trust it."

"Aw, Drew. Aren't you going to ask me to come with you?" Oz mocked from his shadowy den.

"No, Oz. You look to be plenty occupied at the moment. We'll see you later . . . unfortunately."

Oz laughed the way Father did when he meant to put on a show of indifference. It seemed quite a show indeed.

"True," he scoffed. "Later it is then. Much, much later."

He shifted his gaze to me again, addressing me specifically.

"See you tomorrow, new girl."

His mockery earned my indignation, and I left without bothering to reply. I knew his sort; Father was surrounded by an army of them. Over the years, I molded my behavior to draw as little attention from them as possible. Silence proved their least favorite response.

Drew, Kierson, and I left together, all three of us making our collective way to a black monstrosity of a vehicle—a Suburban, they called it. It seemed large enough to transport an army. Perhaps that was precisely what it was designed to do.

Traveling quickly through the city, we soon found ourselves in what appeared to have once been a stately neighborhood. The houses, however, were now vacant, windows boarded up with brightly colored markings on the exteriors. Kierson explained the reason for the abandoned nature of the area, telling me about the collapse of the housing market and the outsourcing of industry jobs. Apparently, when the factories closed, people just walked away, leaving their homes behind. As the city deteriorated, those with the wealth and the power left, too, unable to protect what was theirs in the hostile climate that brewed as a result. In that moment, I found his inane ramblings irritating, though they did illustrate the reasoning behind the dilapidated buildings we had seen at the end of the drive home.

"And then we ended up here," he continued, oblivious to my desperation for him to stop talking. "The city was the perfect place to corral them when they started to infest other major cities. It was the best solution we could come up with at the time."

"Who?" I asked, thinking that perhaps he had finally said something worth listening to.

"Who what?" he asked, confusion in his voice.

"Who is it that you corralled?"

"I think," Drew started, cutting Kierson off before he could explain anything else, "that is a discussion for tomorrow, once you're fed and rested. You've had your fill of evil with the Dark One today. There is no need for you to dwell on it further tonight."

Kierson wheeled around in his seat to look at me as I sat behind him.

"A Dark One? You were brought here by a Dark One?"

"Yes."

"But how?"

"He flew me out of the Underworld."

"Wait . . . you came here from the Underworld?"

"That is where Hades lives, is it not? Drew did say that he was my adoptive father."

"Right," he nodded, mentally placing that information in a more accessible place for another time. "So what's that like? The Underworld? It has to be a totally messed-up place to grow up."

"You have not been there, I assume," I stated, knowing that it was a destination virtually inaccessible to all in existence—apart from the dead.

"No. None of us have."

"It is where the unsavory go when they perish—for punishment," I replied, thinking my answer should suffice. My brothers may not have been there in person, but surely they would have heard tales of Hades' realm in their lifetimes. If they had been alive as long as I had, the odds that they would be completely ignorant seemed miniscule at best.

"Maybe Khara doesn't want to talk about that right now, Kierson,"

Drew suggested. He was correct. Though the Underworld had consumed my thoughts since my arrival, I had no desire to explain my home. Especially to those who could not possibly understand it.

"Okay, that's fine. But can we get back to the part about the Dark One? Are you saying that he just swooped down to the Underworld and grabbed you, then flew you out and dumped you in this shithole of a town?" He looked dismayed, eliminating his previous childlike curiosity about my home.

"Yes. Essentially."

"Whoaaa," he said, sinking back into his seat to face forward as we pulled to a stop in front of the only habitable-looking home on the street. "That's intense."

"It was unwelcome and unwarranted," I replied. "It was also completely mysterious. Father yelled something about fearing that this day would come as the Dark One took me away. I have no clue what he meant by that statement."

Drew turned to look at me as he turned something with his fingers, making the car go silent and still.

"We will figure out what happened, Khara. On my honor, you will see your father again, and you will get your answers. But, for now, we need to get you rested and fed. Tomorrow we can sort through the details of this mess."

"Are you gonna call Sean?" Kierson asked him, a hint of concern tainting his words.

"No," Drew replied with an ounce of hesitation. "I have made the decision to hold off on that for now. He has his hands full out east. I see no reason to burden him with this as well, especially when there is nothing to report other than her existence. What he is dealing with has potentially far more disastrous implications than learning he has a sister. I do not think he needs a distraction to derail his focus."

"You mean further derail it, don't you?" Kierson asked with a tight laugh.

"I would suggest you keep your thoughts about her to yourself in his presence, Kierson. Sean is rather sensitive about that particular matter."

The two exchanged a knowing glance before opening their respective car doors to get out. They ushered me out of the vehicle and into their house within the abandoned neighborhood. While it was in a far better state of repair than the surrounding buildings appeared to be in, I couldn't help but think that it was in dire need of attention. The detailed exterior appeared to be of the Victorian style. Faded yellow paint flaked off the wooden siding, and the shutters hung askew around the few windows that still maintained them. The others were completely unadorned. Inside, there was a grand staircase leading up from the entryway to the second floor. It cut through the spacious living room, which was furnished modestly and contained enough seating to accommodate the crowd that lived there. There was little to no decoration of the space; no personalization that I could see. It was the pinnacle of practicality while maintaining a pleasant and quaint quality.

But it was not home.

"So," Drew started, leading me through the main level of the home. "We have a small issue we need to address tonight before you can get that rest I keep promising you."

"What is the issue?"

"We are short a room for you." He looked uncomfortable admitting as much to me. "If it would make you happy, I would give you mine. Or Kierson can give you his. Neither of us would mind sleeping on one of the cots in the basement—"

"The basement? There is a bed there?"

"Yes. We have extras there in case we have others coming through."

"I should like to stay there."

"Khara . . . it's really not very suitable for you."

"I would like to see it."

With a sigh, he led me to the door that opened to the cold, dark basement below. As if it called to me, I flew down the stairs as quickly as possible to see what I knew was destined to be my room. Drew followed close behind me. A rock foundation, little light, and a musty, putrid smell welcomed me, and, for the first time since I had arrived in Detroit, I truly felt like I had discovered a piece of home.

"This is perfect, Drew," I said, moving toward one of the rickety-framed beds. "I will stay here."

"Khara—"

"Truly. I am fine here. There is no need to change your arrangements." He looked confused by my choice, but let me be.

"Are you sure you don't want to share my room?" Kierson asked, coming downstairs to join us with a plate of food piled high enough for five of Father's men to eat from.

"This will be satisfactory, Kierson."

"Do you want some food?"

"No. I think I will sleep now. I've had so little recently that I may not wake for days."

"Then we will leave you to it," Drew said softly, pulling a blanket off a nearby shelf and handing it to me. "Sweet dreams, sister." His confounding smile appeared again, and I was as at a loss as ever how to respond.

"You as well, brother."

Uncomfortable with his engagement of me, I turned and walked to the bed, lying down while I tried to unfold the blanket and arrange it over me. Thankfully, they left without any further display of joviality. Perhaps they knew it made me uneasy.

I was not accustomed to such warmth from others, and, in the chill of my new room's air, I realized that I was about to be surrounded by it on a very consistent basis until I found a way home.

Perhaps Oz and Casey's surly ways would prove more welcome than I had originally assumed.

3

When I awoke the next day, I had no concept of time. The exhaustion I felt infiltrated every ounce of my being, and it took me three attempts to raise myself from the bed before I succeeded. With a sluggish gait, I made my way to the stairs that would lead me up to the main part of the home, the light, and my new family.

"She's up!" Kierson cried when I slowly opened the basement door. "I got you some stuff while you were sleeping. I figured you didn't have anything with you other than what you were wearing and thought you might like some fresh clothes."

Before I could object, he thrust a bag of sorts into my hands—he seemed overly pleased with himself. Surely procuring garments was not a difficult task in the city. I rummaged through the noisy bag, pulling out various shirts and pants, all of which were black in color. As I eyed them, he looked on, attempting to read my reaction. Was he waiting for a particular one?

"Thank you, Kierson. I am certain these will serve their purpose well."

"I figured you liked black since it was what you were already wearing."

"I do. It's highly practical."

A smile overtook his face at my reply.

"Go try them on," he encouraged, ushering me into another

room. A bathroom of sorts. "I think I got the right sizes . . . I know a thing or two about a woman's build."

"That's because you've seen thousands of them naked. You should have learned something by now," Pierson groused from the other room.

"Ignore him. He's just grumpy. You try them on and see what you think."

"I really don't see the need to—"

"Just go," he said with a tiny shove, closing the door behind me. Thankfully he was on the other side of it once it shut.

I sighed, already more exhausted than I had been in decades. I lacked the energy necessary to placate the childlike being awaiting my emergence from the bathroom. Knowing that there was no alternative, I pulled on an outfit from the bag he provided and availed myself to him. His smile was still in place when I opened the door, and it grew impossibly larger upon seeing me.

"Like a glove," he exclaimed, forcing me to turn around once for his inspection.

"Are they not too tight? They feel rather restrictive . . ." I replied, looking down.

"That's how the ladies wear them."

"And what if I should like to actually move in these pants? I feel as though they are in great jeopardy of tearing."

"Nope. I thought of that and made sure to get you jeans that had a little spandex for stretch. Stick with me, kid. You'll be well dressed *and* able to fight."

"I do not see how that is possible, but I shall take your word for it. For now."

"Ah, fuck," Casey lamented from the other room. "She's already buying his bullshit."

"Screw off, Casey. I don't see you being especially helpful to her at the moment."

"I'm not trying to sleep with her," he quipped in response. Kierson seemed offended by the remark and stormed into the living room where Casey presumably sat sprawled across some piece of furniture as he had at the club. I followed, if for no other reason than to observe their interaction. I needed to learn as much as I could about those who were housing me. My brothers.

"Just because I'm trying to help her doesn't mean I want to sleep with her, I'll have you know."

"And how many times did you think of her naked last night?" Casey asked from his reclined position on one of the two dark leather couches, just as I had envisioned him.

"Twice," he blurted out in response before wincing at his own admission. "But that's not entirely my fault. I'm not used to having a sister. Especially not a hot one. I'll get my head around it soon enough, asshole."

"I'm more worried that you're going to get your head *in* it . . ."

"Enough!" Drew yelled, descending the stairs from the second floor to join us. "You will not disrespect your own flesh and blood in my presence or hers. Is that understood?" His cheeks were flushed as he spoke, and his eyes were sharp and hardened. There was a prickle of energy in the room, making the tiny hairs on my neck rise only slightly. Drew was clearly angry with them, though over what affront I could not tell. "Is that understood?" he repeated, stopping to hover over Casey.

Casey shrugged in the most ambivalent way. I wondered if he had spent time in the Underworld. His actions and mannerisms would have been beautifully suited for a life there.

"And you?" Drew asked, staring Kierson down. "Do I need to be worried about your antics?"

"No," Kierson replied quietly. "I was trying to help. It's not my fault she's really pretty. But I get it, I get it," he said, his hands flying up in a gesture of surrender. "I get that she's family. I don't *really* want to sleep with her; it's just . . . well, you know. Old habits die hard."

"Well, see that they do die, and quickly, Kierson. I have no patience in this matter."

Kierson nodded once, his head hanging lower than normal. He, unlike Casey, would not have survived long in my father's home. His emotions would be perceived as a sign of weakness and would have been exploited at every turn. To survive in the Underworld, one could show no vulnerability.

I had mastered the art of indifference centuries ago.

"Khara," Drew called, softening his tone slightly. "Are you hungry?"

"I am."

"Kierson, why don't you go make her something to eat while Casey and I fill her in on a few things. She's going to have questions, I'm sure, so we might as well start with the basics and go from there."

"How come Casey gets to do that and I have to play housewife?"

"Because you make a way better bitch than I do," Casey purred.

"I'm going to beat your ass," Kierson spat, lunging toward an utterly unfazed Casey. Drew jumped in to stop the fight before it started. I looked on, thinking that it was a familiar scenario, yet another reminder of the Underworld. Fighting and violence had been the way of life for those I grew up around. And though I may have been somewhat protected from the bulk of their barbarity, I was not immune to it.

Both found me often enough.

"If this is how it's going to be now with her here, some of you are moving out. I will not have a complete breakdown of order," Drew warned, still holding Kierson back from Casey.

"Fine," Kierson snarled, yanking himself out of Drew's grip to stomp past me toward the kitchen.

"That goes for you too, Casey."

"Whatever you say . . ."

"And Pierson, you're not exempt from this either," Drew continued. Pierson merely looked up from whatever he was reading in acknowledgment, then dropped his eyes back to his thick and weathered book.

Drew once again turned a softer expression to me and gestured for me to come and sit beside him on the sofa. As I did, he launched into an explanation of anything and everything I could have possibly wanted to know about who I was, who they were, and what exactly it was they did—who they hunted.

"I didn't wish to overwhelm you last night with details, but you need to know more about who we are," Drew informed me, turning slightly to better face me. "You called me a warrior last night. That's exactly what I am. What we all are, you included. We were born of Ares, all of different mothers, to form what we now refer to as the PC, which stands for Petronus Ceteri, or the protectors of others. Our sole purpose is to maintain the balance between the natural and supernatural worlds. And that's exactly what we do."

"So I, too, am a warrior?"

"It is your birthright," he replied, looking less sure of himself than he had previously. "But there's really no way to be certain. We've never had a sister before. There's no way to ascertain what traits you inherited." Drew paused a moment, allowing me to process the information he so willingly provided. His transparency was disarming. I was not used to important details being so freely shared. "I know you were tired when I found you last night, Khara, so I don't know how much you remember of our conversations, but I mentioned something about there being no females born of Ares still alive. I feel I need to explain that further.

"Ares once had a daughter, Eos. She was his everything: a fearsome war goddess, ruthless supporter, and, from what has long been rumored, his lover as well. When she died, part of him changed, or so I was told. I was not alive when this occurred, but some of the others were. They said he was never quite the same after he lost her. From that point on, he declared that no female born of him would ever be suffered to live. That none shall walk the Earth when his beloved Eos was unable to.

"At first, we all took this to mean that he would somehow make it impossible to create a female. However, it came to light a few centuries ago that this may not have been the truth . . . that, more likely than not, if a female was created, she was immediately destroyed. This, Khara, is why you should not be," he continued, hesitating slightly before delivering his final statement. "You should have been killed at infancy—most likely the day you were born."

"But I was not," I offered, stating the obvious incongruity in his story.

"Clearly," he said with a grin. "What I cannot understand is *how*. How did you escape him? If there had indeed been others before you . . ."

"They were found and destroyed," I said, saying what he so clearly did not want to.

"Precisely, though not by Ares' own hands. He lost the ability to kill long ago, but he is still cunning and ruthless. He finds ways around the rules when it suits his purpose. So that leaves me to wonder exactly how you escaped his all-knowing radar."

"The parents I have always known were not my own. Perhaps my mother gave me to them to keep me from Ares, therefore preventing my otherwise imminent demise."

"That is the assumption I am making as well, but someone out there has to know more about the who and why in order for that plan to have worked. That concerns me. Loose ends make for messy situations, Khara. If you are to survive, we need to tie them up."

"I do not know if Father is fully aware of my parentage, but he is not a concern. He loves me in his own way. As for Demeter, I cannot be certain. We do not talk much, though I would wager she knows more about this than anyone else."

"We need to find her . . ." he said, his eyes willing me to see the depth of his plan.

"You would kill her if she knew how dire my circumstances were?" I asked, my voice emotionless. He did not answer. "I do not believe that she knows anything. She would have been rid of me by now if she had. I am nothing but a burden and a bargaining chip to her. She would, however, sell me out if it would get her what she wanted most. Unfortunately for her, she's already gotten all that she can in that regard, so there is no more to be done. She needs me, and she knows it. My death would only ensure the loss of her daughter. That is not something she would risk."

"How can you be so certain?" Casey asked, leaning forward as though my words held an interest to him that hadn't been present earlier.

"Because I am her ticket to Persephone. Without me, Demeter would never see her again. I am the reason she is able to leave the Underworld at all. For six months of the year, Persephone is traded for me. I stay underground while she and her mother walk the fertile earth, enjoying spring and summer. When her time is up, she is brought to Father and I am ejected into the death and cold of fall and winter. Demeter's sadness causes the change in the weather. I would watch as she wept and wallowed, her depression shaping and fueling the harshness of those seasons. She does nothing but pine for the day that the daughter she lost to Hades can once again return home.

"Her life would be intolerable without those six months she shares with Persephone. She would not risk losing them. Demeter is many things, but careless she is not. Had Hades not agreed to take me in trade for his beloved Persephone, I do not know what she would be like now."

"So she leveraged you for Persephone . . ." Drew said, his mind clearly working to put the pieces of the puzzle together. "How could we not have known this? Persephone is a wretched being who loves nothing more than to gossip and meddle. How has she not spread this information? Even if she didn't know who you were, she would surely say why she was let out," he contemplated aloud. "It was long thought that Hades eventually saw her for what she was and wanted to be rid of her, but Zeus would not allow it. He made him keep her, the concession being that Hades could be rid of her for half the year."

"She is unable to say anything. That is why you do not know the truth," I replied simply. "She is bound by whatever agreement was made. If she breathes a word about it to anyone, it is forfeit and she is relegated to the Underworld forever."

"Then how is it that you can speak so freely of it?"

"I am not bound by it as she is. As Father explained to me, it was not a condition put forth. It matters not at the moment, anyway. I fear that the agreement has been nullified in one way or another, as I am here and she is there—neither of us where we should be. Spring is my time to return to Father. That was taken from me by the Dark One."

"The Dark One?" Casey asked, his eyes widening to bottomless pits of black.

"She was taken by a Dark One and abandoned in the alley I found her in last night," Drew explained. "He probably left her for dead. Who knows what information he was privy to before her abduction. Perhaps he knew that she had never been left to fend for herself. That may well have been his intention."

Casey's chest rumbled violently.

"I should very much like to meet this winged one," he grumbled, his low, menacing tone promising pain. "I have a blade I would like to sink deep into the cavern where his heart should be."

"What do you know of the Dark Ones?" I asked earnestly. "Father would never tell me details, only that I should avoid them at all cost and fear them terribly. I did my best to comply."

"Too much. I know too much," Casey returned, offering nothing further.

"That is yet another discussion we will have when the time is right," Drew said, changing the subject. "There is no need to inundate you with anything more at the moment."

"What do you know of this agreement?" Casey asked, his brows furrowing in a suspicious manner. "Who is it with? Who governs it?"

"I do not know."

"Who is left to enforce the consequences if it is broken?"

"I do not know."

"How was it broken?"

"I do not know."

"What *do* you know?" he asked, his frustration growing. Casey suddenly seemed far less composed than he had proven to be. Something about the Dark One and my circumstances had him agitated.

"I am afraid I know too little to be of any help."

"Did the Dark One say anything to you?" Drew asked with far more tact than Casey.

"No, but Father said something strange as I was taken from him. He said that he feared that day would come—as though it wasn't a question of if but *when* I would be taken from him." I directed my response to Casey, hoping he would see it as something of worth.

"Sounds like maybe it's a meeting with Hades we need to arrange," Casey muttered.

"That is my wish," I replied, "but I am not certain how it can be achieved. I cannot travel to the Underworld any more than you can, unless you are withholding your ability to do so from me, and it would not be safe to send word to him. Messengers are unreliable, and their favor often lies with those who may benefit from the message the most in the moment. I think it unwise to attempt such correspondence."

"Agreed," Drew concurred.

"Maybe we can get him to come to us somehow," Kierson offered, entering the room with four gigantic plates full of various foods. I had almost forgotten him entirely in his absence.

"That would be highly unlikely," I replied. "In all the years I've known Hades, he has only left once, and that was the day he came to escort me personally to the Underworld—though he will be beside himself with grief, knowing that he cannot come to find me."

"But you just said that he technically *could* leave." Kierson looked befuddled as he tried to sort through things he could not possibly understand.

"He may leave, but it is not wise. The chaos that ensued after his short absence before took an extraordinary amount of time to right. He can go, but what he would return to would be unthinkable. He is not the horrible and cruel god others think him to be. He does, however, have a job to do, and it requires a commanding presence. Even the Underworld needs order, Kierson. Possibly more so than anywhere else."

Casey scoffed at my words.

"You clearly haven't spent enough time in Detroit. You might revise that statement once you have."

"We shall see. I think you underestimate my home, Casey."

"And I think you underestimate mine."

We engaged in another contest of wills, both staring the other down, waiting for the other's gaze to falter. Neither's did. Drew interfered eventually, purposefully diverting my attention to the food before me.

"Khara, please eat. I don't know what you're accustomed to, but, if you tell me, I will be sure to have it on hand for you."

"I require no special attention, Drew. What you have shall be sufficient." With those words, I took a cluster of grapes from one of the platters and plucked them off one by one, eating them methodically as the others looked on. I seemed alien to them, as though they were not certain that I required food at all. As I ate with their full attention on me, a door opened somewhere in the house, crashing closed with a thunderous noise.

Oz entered the room in the same clothing he had worn the night before. Given that all the others had changed, I assumed his behavior was not typical and wondered if he had returned at all that evening.

"I hope you all didn't wait up for me," he sneered, his arrogance stifling. Eventually his gaze landed on me, looking down his perfectly constructed nose in my direction. "Morning, new girl."

"Khara," I returned, fighting the urge to rise and stand firmly against his ego. Instead, his mockery would only invite my indifference. To be so easily baited would only further make me a target of his.

"Right," he drawled dramatically. "*Khara . . .*" The skin on the back of my neck tingled as he spoke my name. He reached over me to the plate of food beyond, his face and body brushing my hair along the way. As he pulled back, he stopped beside my ear while I remained perfectly poised and unmoving.

"Guess I'll see you later, new girl," he whispered, purposely reverting back to his preferred name for me.

"Fuck off, Oz," Kierson growled. "Go sleep your night off."

"Jealous, are we, Kierson? It's not an attractive quality. You should really work on that," he said as he retreated to the higher levels of the house. I was pleased to see him go.

"You really have to learn to ignore him," Kierson informed me, wrapping an arm casually around my shoulder. "He's a wicked pain in the ass."

"He is not one of you. I do not understand why you tolerate him as you do."

"One of *us*," Drew corrected, grabbing a strange-looking article from one of the platters. I had purposely avoided it, not fully comprehending what it was. "And Oz can be extremely helpful in a battle, if it suits his purpose at the time."

"What is he, exactly, that makes him so lethal in battle?" I asked, curious how he could be so helpful. He seemed positively repugnant to me.

"An angel," Kierson blurted out of a mouth filled with food.

"An angel?"

"Yes, as in from the heavens above." He dramatically looked up with his arms wide, making a production of his explanation.

"But the only angels Father ever spoke of were the Dark Ones. Are there others? Certainly Oz is not a Dark One . . ."

"Oz is somewhat of an exception," Drew corrected, eyeing Kierson tightly as though he had said more than he should have. "He was an angel, a Light One, but he turned away from that. Nobody knows why. He never talks about it."

"Nope. Instead he whores around and acts like a real prick all the time," Kierson added for clarification.

"Says the walking hard-on," Casey groaned.

"A Light One?"

"Yeah, you know . . . God's favorites? The good guys? The complete opposite of the Dark Ones?" Kierson rambled, hoping something he offered in explanation would sink in. "It's that whole yin and yang thing. The Universe has to have balance." He looked at me quizzically for a moment before continuing. "How can you not know about them? Seriously . . . I mean, you've been around for a while. I would have assumed you knew more about that kind of thing."

"If Light Ones are God's creatures, then I hardly see where I would have crossed paths with them. The Underworld is not a place that the virtuous would visit."

"Fair enough," he replied with a shrug.

"So, if Oz is an angel, then where are his wings?" I asked, thinking that was a perfectly reasonable question. As far as I knew, angels had them.

"No clue. We've never seen them and never asked. Oz isn't really the forthcoming type, Khara. He does what he wants, when he wants, how he wants. If he feels like telling you something, he will. If not, you will never know. That's just how he is."

I sat silently, mulling over what Drew had said. I had never known that one could be unbound in a way that allowed such freedom. The implications overwhelmed my mind so much so that I was having a hard time processing them all. To live in a way that had no boundaries was beyond perplexing. I did not know one could exist like that.

"Well, I have something to do in town," Drew sighed, stretching as he rose from the couch. "Will you be all right here without me?"

"I shall be fine."

My reply was met with a small smile.

"I knew you'd say that."

"I'm coming with you. I need to find that blade I lost the other night at the club," Kierson added as he pushed off the couch beside me. "I'm sure one of the girls on the cleaning staff will let me in." He couldn't hide the satisfaction in his voice, alluding to the fact that his charms could get him almost anything he wanted. Perhaps it was his boyish nature that won others over so easily—or maybe he had slept with all of them.

"Fine," Drew replied wearily. "Let's go. And, Casey . . . do not make me regret leaving you here."

"I wouldn't dream of it." His words were for Drew, but his dark stare was all for me. My hair prickled lightly as I reminded myself that he was not the one I feared. It was the one he reminded me of—my father's soldier—that elicited that response from me.

"Pierson," Drew called, pulling his attention away from his book momentarily. "Keep an eye on him, would you?" An absentminded nod was all he received in response. Drew muttered something under his breath about being stuck with the most insubordinate brothers as he made his way to the front door.

"I am still tired," I announced, taking a piece of pita off the plate. "I will be downstairs resting, if anyone should need me."

Without a word, I removed myself from their collective presence and tucked myself away in the confines of my underground room. The comfort I found there still surprised me. I thought of all we had discussed and came to the only conclusion I could: There was no way to get to my father or for my father to come for me. I was trapped in a world I did not wish to be in, with a strange family that I was struggling to get to know and understand.

The Underworld was no longer my home.

4

Hours later, a ruckus on the floor above me jarred me from my rest. The sound was an all-too-familiar wake-up call. Wanting to see what the trouble was, I made my way up the stairs while I tried to discern who was shouting.

When I opened the door, I saw yet another standoff that day, only between two very different men. Oz and Drew stood toe-to-toe at the bottom of the stairs, only the narrowest of margins between their faces. The second they realized I was present, the fight appeared to be over. Oz stormed out the front door without so much as a word.

"I interrupted," I said apologetically.

"No, of course not, Khara. We already finished our discussion. And, besides, you need not walk around on eggshells here. This is your home, too."

"For now," Pierson added, getting up from the armchair in the far corner of the room and walking past Drew to go upstairs. I had not even seen him there, his quiet nature allowing him to easily go unnoticed when it served him.

"For as long as she wishes to stay," Drew countered, his tone less than friendly.

"If my being here is a problem, I am happy to take my leave and go elsewhere."

"You are not going anywhere, especially not until we know more about why you came here in the first place. I do not trust Ares, nor do

I trust whoever put you in this bizarre situation to start with. Something about it does not add up, and until I know you're no longer in danger I would prefer you stay right where you are—where we can keep you safe."

"If you deem it best, I will stay. For now."

"Good. We are just about to head out for the evening. If you're finally feeling rested, you should join us."

"But you said to stay right where I am . . ."

He laughed heartily.

"Not literally right where you are. I meant I would feel better if you stayed with us."

"Oh."

"Go change. We'll leave when you're ready."

"Is this not acceptable attire?" I asked, looking down at the tight black clothes Kierson had procured for me.

"I think he picked something else out for where we're going. You saw the Tenth Circle last night. It's a little interesting . . ."

"The Tenth Circle?" I repeated, unsure of what that referenced.

He laughed in response.

"The club I took you to. It's a play on Dante's *Inferno* . . ."

I stared at him blankly, unfamiliar with his reference.

"It's not important. The point is that I don't want to draw any more attention to you than you'll naturally draw to yourself. We're trying to make you blend in a bit more. I think that would be safest for now."

"I have spent a lifetime blending in. This should not be a challenging task."

I made my way to the bathroom where I had left the rest of Kierson's purchases. Rifling through the bag, I searched for whatever items looked out of place. They were easily spotted. I took out the leather pants and pulled them up with a struggle, wondering what Kierson had been thinking about when he purchased them. When I found what could be passed off as a top, I stared at it for a long time before I could even figure out how to put it on. The straps and intricately woven strands had me perplexed.

By the time I emerged from the bathroom, Drew was standing just outside the door, preparing to knock on it. His eyes widened exponentially before narrowing tightly.

"I think perhaps Kierson got a tad carried away. Is there a jacket in there?" he asked, moving past me to look through the bag. "Here. Put this on." He tossed a short black leather coat at me and ushered me toward the front door.

"Where are the others?"

"Pierson just left, and the rest will be there already. Let's go. It's time for you to see just what your brothers do."

5

"So you police the supernatural?" I asked as Drew drove through an even more destitute section of the city. "I did not know such an organization was necessary."

"We do, and we are," he replied with a furrowed brow. "There must be order kept amongst them and a clear line between the human world and ours."

"But we occupy the same world as the humans. Surely your task is an impossible one, is it not?"

"There have been . . . *situations* to deal with over the centuries." His jaw flexed furiously, as though he'd fought to get his statement out.

"With the humans?"

"Yes."

"And how does my brother deal with such an occurrence?"

"Swiftly and quietly," he replied tightly. "Though not without remorse."

His words were quiet and distant, his expression pained. His distaste for aspects of his job was plain and not entirely dissimilar to that of my father. Perhaps I understood his plight far better than I ever could have imagined.

"Your responsibilities do not sit well with you always," I said quietly, stating my observation rather than asking.

"I have respect for all life, Khara, which is ironic given my parentage. I find no joy in taking one, human or otherwise. The fact that my station demands that of me is something I came to terms with long ago. But do not mistake my acceptance for apathy."

"I've never known someone to kill with a conscience. It is a concept as foreign to me as the life I've been thrust into here with you and the others."

He narrowed his stare at me across the massive vehicle, ignoring the road entirely.

"How much violence has befallen you in your time below?" he asked, his even tone belying his growing rage.

"As much as one should expect, given the circumstances."

"And Hades did not protect you?"

"He did what he could for me. But he had a job to do. He was my ward, not my constant companion. When I found myself alone, I was not immune to the evil surrounding me. I was a beacon to some of them—a plaything they could not resist. For that, I suffered, though over time I learned to adapt. The Underworld taught me much."

"Have you killed? To protect yourself?"

"Have not we all?" I replied, unfaltering.

"You have enemies there . . ." he inferred, realizing that I could not have possibly eliminated every threat ever posed to me.

"Of course."

"Hades knows this?"

"He knows of some. Others create a difficult situation for him. I choose to keep those to myself. He cannot possibly be troubled by things like that, and he is unable to keep some offenders away from me when I am not with him. It would only torment him to know. He has a kind heart where I am concerned. I do not wish to exploit that."

"Who are they?" he demanded in a harsh and commanding voice.

"It matters not. You cannot stop them any more than I can—"

"*Who?*" he pressed, his tone strange and commanding. I felt compelled to answer him, inexplicable though it was.

"There are many, but only one I fear. He is a thing of nightmares. A true predator."

"His name . . ." he continued, unsatisfied with my response.

"Deimos," I replied quietly. His name brought a shiver from my core.

An unfamiliar cracking sound echoed throughout the interior of the vehicle. I looked over at Drew to find the wheel he grasped in his hands nearly snapping under the pressure. Knowing it could not sustain much more, Drew was forced to pull over, needing to get control of his emotions before he destroyed an integral part of the Suburban.

"You should have told Hades . . ."

"Deimos is one of his chosen few. I did not dare disturb his inner sanctum—"

"He is nefarious, Khara: terror and torture incarnate. If he has his sights set on you, you are in more danger than you could possibly imagine."

"More than you have already told me I am in? More than I was in when I was constantly in his presence?" I countered. "I am exposed here; I fully understand that fact. What you fail to understand is that Deimos is obsessed with me. He does not wish to kill me. He desires to make me his own."

"Which is far worse than him wanting to kill you," Drew interjected heatedly. "What you fail to understand is that he is terror-inspiring for a reason. That is what he was created to do. He is of another realm, neither human nor god, living nor dead. He is the in-between, and, because of that, nearly impossible to stop." He paused for a moment, collecting himself before he continued. I had not known my brothers very long, but Drew had always presented himself in such a calm and controlled manner. To see him slowly unraveling as he spoke was disturbing. "He is Eos' brother, Khara.

One of the original three. To this day, nobody knows for certain how Eos was killed. Do you understand what I'm saying to you?"

"Of course. You are reiterating the presumed severity of the situation that has not presented itself to us yet."

"No. What I'm saying is that I don't know how to kill Deimos. No one does. We cannot protect you from him."

I pondered his concern for only a moment before replying.

"He does not know where I was taken, Drew. I do not need protection from someone who does not currently pose a threat. He is a concern for another day."

Drew's brow furrowed as he stared out at the road ahead. He said nothing, but it was clear that he was weighing the veracity of my statement with the accuracy of his. Deimos may not have known where I was at that moment, but, when word of my abduction reached him, he surely would leave the Underworld in search of me. He, too, was one of the few that could.

If not of his own volition then by my father's orders, he would hunt me down in an attempt to bring me back. Though he could be used as a way to return home, it was not an attractive option. Every second spent with him seemed like a century—one I would choose to forget, if possible.

"Tell me everything you know of him, Khara. Anything that could be deemed valuable in a combat scenario."

"I have nothing to tell you," I replied truthfully. "Nothing that you don't seem to already know."

"There must be something, a weakness of some kind or another that we can exploit."

I turned to see Drew once again staring at me across the dimly lit vehicle, which still remained motionless. His expression begged me to give him an advantage—no matter how small—over Deimos.

"He does have a weakness."

"What? What is it? Tell me," he demanded, his tone suddenly hopeful.

"Me," I told him plainly. "His weakness is me."

My answer did not seem to please him.

"And that weakness is going to draw him to you like a moth to flame."

"Yes, it will. Eventually. And, as you said, there is nothing you can do for me when he comes, Drew. You or the others. I will go with him willingly. It will be best for all of us. He will take me home—"

"This is your home now, Khara," he snapped. "Until we have answers to the mysteries surrounding you and I know it is safe for you to be anywhere else, your home is with us."

He reached across the car and took my hand in his, a gesture completely foreign to me. He gave it a light squeeze before he retracted his, placing it back on the steering wheel. Drew's protective nature was so ingrained in him that I knew he would put himself in Deimos' path in an attempt to save me and would surely die as a result. Son of a god or not, Drew would not be able to survive his wrath. Coming between Deimos and me would be a death sentence for certain. I resolved in that moment not to allow that situation to come to pass.

The silence in the SUV grew heavy and thick while Drew's concern grew greater and greater. I felt a strange pain in my heart, one I had never experienced before. I felt something for my brother—a sharp pain penetrating my heart. *Sorrow,* I thought to myself. *This must be sorrow.* Seeing the trouble on his face at the mere thought of my endangerment pulled that emotion from somewhere inside myself that I had not known to exist.

The tightness remained. It was physically uncomfortable, and I clutched at my chest, rubbing it, but the sensation would not abate. I needed to find relief before the unwelcome emotion tore me apart inside.

"He is more beautiful than you would imagine," I stated abruptly, hoping that distraction might ease both the ache in my chest and the tension surrounding us. "But it is a harsh beauty that belies an evil unimaginable—a ruse for the unsuspecting. This seductive warning makes a woman either want to run from him screaming or fall to her knees before him. In my time, I have done both," I explained, my words vacant of emotion. Any I felt for Deimos had long been drained from me; my mask of ambivalence now remained firmly in place. I could not afford to show the fear I felt toward him while in his presence, so I had eradicated it. My mind perceived danger when I saw him, but I no longer let it outwardly affect me. I was the portrait of apathy.

When I peered over at Drew, I could see that my outburst perplexed him, but I continued on regardless.

"I have heard of the human 'fight or flight' response, but with Deimos neither is effective. You can run from him, but your efforts will be in vain. As I have said, he will find you if he desires to. And fighting him has thus far proved ineffective; I have tried that as well. I did not relish the outcome. But, if I were to play into his desires, no longer resisting him—"

"If you are attempting to assuage my concerns, dear sister, I can assure you that you are failing miserably," Drew growled from the darkness beside me.

"I am simply offering a viable strategy," I pointed out. "If we wish to avoid a war with him that we cannot win, then this is our best option."

"I will never run from battle," he snapped, pinning sharp eyes on me in the darkness. "And surrendering you is not an option."

"It is a means to an end, Drew—"

"It could be a means to *your* end," he shouted, cutting me short. "Deimos is Ares' son, too, though he is not PC. He was created long before we were even a thought, an idea. Has it not yet crossed your mind that Deimos may know precisely who and what you are? Who you were born of?"

"That makes no sense. Why would he not have used such information to his advantage by now? If he knew he could manipulate me into succumbing to his desires so easily, he would have."

"He is insane, Khara. Insane people follow no logic, save their own," he countered, his voice low and warning. "I've heard rumors about him that made my blood run cold. I don't presume to know the inner workings of his deranged mind, but I believe there is a distinct possibility that he may know far more than you think he does. You cannot go with him—under any circumstance. It is not an option, and I will not allow it."

"We will see how you feel when the time comes," I replied, holding his sharpened gaze without faltering. "And it is a when, not an if, Drew. Now, shall we go meet the others? I am far more interested in learning about what you do than discussing a future that is not yet upon us."

He said nothing in response, only exhaled heavily, staring fixedly through the windshield ahead of him as he did. Then, with the turn of a key, the Suburban's engine hummed back to life, and he pulled onto the road. Once again, we were on our way to the Tenth Circle where we were to meet the others. I had not put much thought into Deimos' likely reaction to my abduction until that conversation and didn't want to put any more thought into him at all that evening. He was an ambush waiting to happen. An unavoidable fixture in my life.

Drew had vowed that he and the others would keep me safe and hidden from Ares until they knew better how to proceed, but I would not let them die in the process, only to see them again in the Underworld under the most unfortunate of circumstances. Surely they would go there upon their deaths when so many had fallen because of them. I could prevent that fate.

My eternal torment for theirs seemed a small price to pay.

6

"What took you guys so long?" Kierson shouted over the infernal music that blared around me, shaking my insides.

"Car problems," Drew replied, eyeing me tightly. His look was a warning, though one I did not understand. If he perceived Deimos as an imminent threat, I could not fathom why he did not see fit to brief the others on all he had learned during the course of our drive. Before I could add to his explanation, he ushered me to the far corner of the upper deck that my brothers seemed to claim as their own whenever there. "Not now," he warned. "This is not something to discuss in public. Names like that of the one who will come for you have power around certain beings. We do not need to unleash that so early on." I nodded in agreement. "You wanted to see what we did tonight, and you will. But you will also see why we do it and who we do it to."

"Meaning . . . ?"

"Meaning there is evil crawling all over this city, Khara. It's overrun with it. I'm amazed the humans can even survive under such a cloak of darkness, but they do. Perhaps they're more resilient than we give them credit for," he informed me. "But more specifically, my point is that, because this evil is everywhere, you must use discretion when discussing matters of interest outside of our home or vehicle. Those have been protected . . . by magic. Pierson dabbles in it, though it is not his primary gift. Normally, you may speak freely if he is present. His paranoia, or what he prefers to call diligence, fuels his need to keep prying ears deaf to all conversations he is a party to. But in an effort not to tempt fate, we will not speak about the one who seeks you here, even though Pierson is present, understood?"

"Understood," I replied, ruminating on what he had told me. "You said that magic is not his primary gift. What would his primary gift be, precisely?"

"It would be a matter to discuss in the aforementioned safe places," Drew countered, a hint of his more jovial nature breaking through his armor.

Kierson bounded up behind us, throwing his arms around both Drew's and my shoulders.

"Seriously, Drew. You've been hogging Khara all night. When do we get to show her our stuff?"

"Must you constantly be reminded that she's your sister?" Casey lamented as he approached. "Your 'stuff' shouldn't be making any appearances in her presence."

"Don't be such a dick. You know what I meant!"

"See. You can't even go two seconds without referencing your anatomy—"

"I'm going to fucking whale on you," Kierson shouted, lunging for Casey, who stood there smiling as though he'd gotten exactly the response he'd wanted.

"Is this what I've come to witness, Drew? This is what you do to maintain the balance?" I asked, feigning complete confusion.

"No. It isn't," he ground out through gritted teeth. "But it seems to be how I spend the majority of my time lately." He flashed an intimidating gaze at the others. "You two, enough. Go back over to Pierson. Khara and I will be there in a minute."

Kierson looked like a scolded child while Casey continued to smile, hovering defiantly for a moment before he too made his way over to the couches where Pierson sat, poring over a book of some sort. Oz was nowhere to be seen.

Drew led the way over to them, indicating that I should sit down next to Pierson. As I did, Pierson did nothing to acknowledge me, his eyes never leaving the book in front of him. The writing was in a language unfamiliar to me, which was strange given that I had become versed in so many over the centuries.

"Khara," Drew called, breaking my focus on the foreign text. "Do you have a preference as to who you would like to accompany on tonight's patrol?"

I looked at the others as I assessed my options. Casey stared me down, looking every bit as hostile as I thought him to be. Pierson continued to ignore me. Kierson, however, looked at me with pleading eyes, begging for me to choose him. His enthusiasm was unwarranted and tiring, but I could not bring myself to choose anyone else when it was so plain that he actually wanted to be assigned the task of educating me on PC affairs.

"Kierson appears to want the job," I stated. "I shall go with him."

"Yes!" he shouted, jumping out of his seat. "Awesome. This is going to be a blast. You won't be sorry."

"I think she already is," a familiar voice purred from behind me.

"On the contrary," I rebutted, turning to see Oz approaching from the darkness behind me. "I am certain I will find Kierson's teachings informative."

"Ah, yes. Nothing describes a night on the town with Kierson better than 'informative,'" he mocked, coming around the couch to sit next to Casey.

"This is not a social matter. It is one of business, something I assume you know little about."

"Is that so, new girl?" he questioned, leaning toward me.

"Indeed." I leaned forward to mimic his aggressive posture, staring him down as I did.

"Why do I feel like I'm refereeing tonight?" Drew pondered aloud with a sigh. He stepped into my line of sight, breaking my eye contact with Oz. "I think you should head out. Remember, you are going out with Kierson so that he can both teach you and keep you safe. You are to do as he tells you. Any sign of trouble and I want you out of there, do you understand? You run until you get back here." After he was certain I had absorbed the full weight of his instructions, he pulled out a shiny silver device from his pocket and thrust it into my hand. "This phone has all of our numbers programmed into it. If you need us, just hit this button and say the name of the person you want to talk to. It will do the rest."

I turned the cell phone over in my hand, analyzing it carefully. I had heard talk of these devices before from Father's soldiers but had never seen or used one. My life had become a crash course in the unknown.

"And where will you be?" I asked, wondering what would happen if I were to need to retreat to the club. If there was enough danger in Detroit to not allow us to speak freely in the club, then there was enough there for me to not be alone there either, per Drew's own admission. He appeared far more concerned about my well-being than I was.

"Out. But Pierson will remain, should you need to return."

"And I will be here as well," Oz added unhelpfully. "But I will likely be far too occupied to be of any assistance to you. Unless, of course, you felt like joining in . . ." His heavy gaze eventually drifted from me to the dance floor, a clear indication of why he would be too busy to help me, should I have found myself in need. He was proving to be a creature of habit. One that I did not enjoy.

"Shall we?" Kierson prompted, extending a bent arm in my direction. I knew not what to do with it so I came up beside him, only to have him intertwine our arms before turning us toward the staircase that would take us down to the main area and the exit. I was growing more anxious to leave by the minute. "This is going to be so awesome, Khara. Hunting is such a rush . . . well, it is when you actually find someone up to no good, but that happens readily enough to keep my spirits up."

His mischievous grin exposed nearly every tooth his mouth contained. It was clear that he loved his calling, though I still did not fully understand what that entailed. Finding evil and eliminating it did not excite me as it did him. Surely I was missing something.

Once we stepped out onto the sidewalk, he looked around until he located the colossal black vehicle I had just ridden into town in and made his way over to it.

"Can we not walk?" I asked, not wanting to admit that being inside that oversized contraption made me uneasy. There was something unnatural about it that did not sit well with me.

He shrugged ambivalently and conceded, redirecting us down a narrow passage between the towering buildings to a less traveled road. He explained along the way that bad things rarely happened in crowded areas. That concept made little sense to me—they happened everywhere in the densely populated Underworld.

"So what do you use to find scenarios that require the attention of the PC?" I asked while we made our way down the dark and rather malodorous street. Refuse was strewn about without concern, and people lay sleeping in the middle of the sidewalk. I stepped carefully over one that appeared to be lying in a puddle of his own bodily fluids. "Certainly you don't just wander aimlessly all night long in hopes of finding some nefarious creatures engaged in unsavory acts. This city is too large for that plan to be statistically advantageous, if one could call such a course of action a plan at all."

"Drew specifically told me not to go into too much detail about things, if you chose to go with me—at least not for now. He knows I can get a little carried away when I'm excited, and he doesn't want to overwhelm you. You've had quite a shock to your system as it is. We don't wanna blow a circuit, you know?" I thought I understood what he was saying and nodded. "But," he said with a shrug, "what Drew doesn't know won't hurt him, right?" Again, I nodded. "The truth is that, for the most part, each member of the PC can sense all types of supernatural, with very few exceptions. Unfortunately for us, most of those exceptions reside in Detroit. That's forced us to adapt over time," he explained, taking my arm as we crossed the street.

"Have you adapted as a whole or individually?"

"Both. We were each chosen to police this city and what roams its streets for a reason," he continued, his expression darkening momentarily. "Those of us still left were best suited for the task, I guess."

"Still left? There were more . . . *are* more? I have other brothers?" I prodded as we continued down the increasingly desolate street. Even those who had apparently taken to inhabiting them disappeared as I looked off into the distance.

"You have many brothers, Khara—*hundreds*, though those numbers dwindle over time as they fall. Our job is not without danger, nor are we immune to its consequences."

The immensity of his statement weighed heavily on me, forcing me to stop in my tracks and fully acknowledge it. I had more family than I could comprehend, and likely had lost even more than that which still existed. I wondered if I had passed them in the Underworld, not knowing who and what they were. They would not have known me either. The dead do not feel as the living do. They are consumed only by terror and pain—that was my experience with them.

That unwanted feeling in my chest was returning at the thought of my brothers facing an eternity of torment for their actions above. I needed to quash this feeling immediately.

"Are you okay?" Kierson asked, assessing me curiously.

"I am fine," I replied dismissively, continuing in the direction we had been headed. "So you have survived unscathed. What is your adaptation that serves you so well, since you implied that you were not one who could sense these few supernatural beings originally?"

"The answer to that lies with my mother—well, Pierson's mother too, obviously. Do you know of the Banshees?" He took my lack of response to mean I did not. "That's what she was. I don't know what

Ares was hoping to accomplish through that bizarre pairing, but he seemed moderately pleased by what it produced."

"Which was?"

"A strange bastardization of what our mother could do," he said, leading me down yet another dark and narrow way. "A Banshee's wail signaled an impending death, most often the death of someone in a prominent family. That's what our mother did, but our powers don't work quite like that. Alone, Pierson sees things, precognition, if you will, but his premonitions won't necessarily come to pass on their own. They are not always certain."

"So he can see where danger lurks and stop it?"

"Sort of." He looked befuddled, trying to explain whatever gifts he had received from his mother. "But not without my help. Have you ever heard about twins having strange connections . . . knowing what the other is thinking without saying anything? Feeling what the other is feeling, stuff like that?"

"No, I have not."

"Okay, well, this might sound weird to you then, but Pierson and I have that kind of connection. Like a strong one. When he sees something, I can sense it. I can't see it, but it's like he can direct me to it."

"This is why he is not out with us?"

"Pretty much."

"Does he not fight at all then? He has the same fierce look as Casey at times, the same that Drew wore before he nearly ended me. Is he not a warrior as the rest of you are?"

"He is, and don't ever let him hear you say that," Kierson warned, his playful demeanor quickly overtaken by one of caution as he caught my arm, demanding my attention. I stopped walking immediately. "He's a bit sensitive about that particular issue. He tries to make up for that with knowledge, hoping that if he appears superior to everyone else intellectually, he will not be questioned."

"Understood." My eyes looked down to where he still held my

forearm, and when his gaze followed mine down to his hand, he released me.

"Sorry," he apologized, looking sheepish as he did. "And, yes, he can fight. If a war breaks out, you want him on your team, that's for sure. He's nearly as cold as Casey, and that's saying something."

"How is it that you are so unlike him then?"

He shrugged, tilting his head to the side.

"He got the brains and the brawn," he said quietly, looking over at me with a smile that did not reach his eyes as all his previous ones had. "I guess I just got the good looks."

I furrowed my brow, not understanding his logic.

"But—"

"It was a joke, Khara. Get it? We're identical twins . . . we look exactly alike." When he didn't appear to get the response from me he sought, a look of exasperation overtook him. "I'm making fun of myself because it makes it easier than having others do it for me. Beat them to the punch, so to speak."

His words still perplexed me.

"You must have brawn if you're the one out here fighting while Pierson sits comfortably on a couch awaiting your return," I countered.

"I guess . . ."

"Do you kill with ease or not?"

"Well, yeah, but—"

"Do you hesitate when the time to strike comes?"

"Never," he said, looking offended by the question.

"And if something evil rounded that corner now and threatened my life?"

His eyes darkened slightly.

"I'd tear its fucking head from its body."

An unfamiliar tugging sensation plagued the corners of my mouth, and I could do nothing to stop it. What I could only describe as a faint smile ghosted my expression.

"You see? You have something that Pierson does not."

"Yeah? What's that?"

"Heart," I said plainly. "Loyalty. My father spoke of those traits often. One might assume that all who dwell in the depths are devoid of such qualities, but that is not the case. Hades has many who would do for him what you just admitted you would do for me. That cannot be learned, he would tell me. Someone is either inherently driven to serve in such a way, or they are not. Pierson is not. You, however, are. I see your heart as superior to his brains, and I have no doubt that your brawn is as well. Those who possess that degree of loyalty appear to be charged with something extra when they fight. I have witnessed it. It is a fearsome sight indeed."

His face had gone slack by the time I finished my explanation. For a moment, he did little more than stand before me and stare, silent for the first time since I had met him. Then, in what I deemed to be his true nature, he scooped me up in his arms, crushing me to his chest and burying his face in my hair.

"I'm so glad Drew found you . . ."

"Yes, as am I. I am not entirely certain what would have become of me if he had not. I may have been wandering the streets of Detroit still."

"That's not what I'm saying, Khara. I'm saying that I'm glad he found you because I feel like you fill a void that has been empty in me for longer than I can remember. It feels right having you around."

Again, I found myself trying to absorb the sincerity of his words. The result was astounding. Having directed my attention to it, I noticed that I, too, seemed to have something deep within me more at peace in his presence. It was strange to recognize the emptiness only after it had been filled, however slightly.

I had little time to dwell on this realization, though, before Kierson all but threw me down, his gaze snapping up to something in the distance I could neither hear nor see. To me, the street appeared vacant, aside from a single human passed out on the sidewalk, but as Kierson's body coiled to strike I knew that something ominous was present.

It was precisely what he had wanted to happen. A chance to show me what he and the others could do.

"Stay close, and *always* behind me," he said sternly, taking me by the arm and all but dragging me down the road. We were nearing a crumbling tenement at the end, with no light surrounding it and nowhere to go beyond it. It seemed as though the street just stopped completely before it.

Kierson slowed as we approached, casing the outside cautiously until a woman's scream broke through the silence. He leapt right through a broken window and disappeared inside, the darkness swallowing him within seconds. I jumped right behind him as I was told to. Dust and dirt blew into my face as I landed in a crouch, making it still harder to see.

"Let her go," Kierson growled from the far corner of the room. "You know the rules."

"I . . . I can't stop," a shaky voice replied.

"Last chance," Kierson warned.

I walked toward the voices, wanting to see just how the situation would play out. Would whatever creature Kierson pursued let her go, or would he face the wrath of my brother? Furthermore, I had a strange desire building within me that demanded to see just *what* the assailant was. I had not seen the evil that I had been so constantly told of since meeting Drew and the others. Curiosity got the better of me.

Just as I rounded a thick concrete pillar, I could see the three of them, though light was still scarce. A thin and sickly looking man held the young girl, her face cupped in his hands, mouths nearly touching. The second I stepped into view, his hollow, empty eyes snapped directly to me.

And they never left.

The tortured man leapt at me like a soul possessed, face contorted with a foul determination, though he did not make it far. Kierson, true to his word, severed the being's head from his body with one pass of his blade. Had he not already been holding the weapon, I was quite certain he would have used his hands, as he had earlier claimed he would.

While Kierson examined his kill to be certain it was thoroughly dead, I walked to the petite brunette with whom the being had been toying to see if she was all right. She appeared to be stunned and did not respond to my questions or move at all. I presumed that fear had frozen her in that state. Kierson, however, did not.

"Shit," he muttered under his breath when he came up alongside me.

"Shit?"

"He already got her. We're too late." His words were plain, but his tone and expression were not. They were saddened, a direct result of some realization he had when he looked at the paralyzed girl. "She's an Empty . . . I have no choice." He turned me around to face him, placing his hands on my upper arms firmly. "I want you to go outside."

"But you said I was to stay with you—"

"I know what I said, Khara, but this," he said, turning sad eyes toward the vacant girl, "this I don't want you to see. Just wait for me by the window we came in through. It won't take long."

I did not wish to prolong whatever suffering he felt, so I did as he bade me, walking away briskly toward our original entrance point. Echoing off the walls, I could hear a whisper of a song being sung. It held an eerie beauty. I felt lulled by it momentarily before it ended. Directly after that, Kierson appeared before me, attempting to wipe himself clean of the blood that his clothes were covered in.

"It's why we all wear black when we go hunting," he confessed, that same weak smile painting his expression with false happiness. "C'mon. We have to head back and check in with Pierson. I need to see if he felt what I felt."

"Did something go wrong? Were you not hoping you would encounter something like this? A way to display your skills to me?"

"I wanted to show you my mad skills, but not like that," he said, hopping out of the window. He turned back and reached for my hand, assuming for some reason that I was incapable of getting out of the very window through which I entered. Instead of refusing the unnecessary gesture, I took his hand and allowed him to guide me out.

"Should I then assume that something did go awry in there?"

"Yep. That's a safe bet." He reached into his coat pocket, producing the same style phone that Drew had given me. With the push of a button, he was speaking to him directly.

"We have a problem. Meet us back at the club. And call the others. This affects us all."

Whatever playfulness Kierson had exhibited prior to that moment was suddenly absent, leaving behind a warrior far more befitting of the title. We walked in silence to the Tenth Circle at an urgent pace. Not long after we arrived, the others filed in, all of us convening in the usual area upstairs.

"So what is this problem that so desperately requires all of our attention, Kierson?" Casey inquired, though he was clearly disinterested in the answer.

Kierson, who had remained silent until everyone arrived, shot a look to Pierson, the two of them appearing to have one of those wordless conversations he had earlier alluded to. Eventually, Pierson nodded in confirmation of something the rest of us had yet to be let in on.

"I killed an Empty tonight."

"*What?*" Drew asked, stepping toward Kierson. "Are you sure?"

"Of course I'm sure, Drew. Pierson will tell you the same thing."

"He did as he says he did," Pierson added. "I saw the event play out in its entirety."

"Where? How?" Drew pressed, desperate for answers.

"We were only a few blocks over. Khara and I were just walking along, shooting the shit, when suddenly I got that feeling I get . . . you know . . . the one I get when Pierson sees something."

"And?"

"And he led me to a Breather. When I got there, I thought he'd maybe taken too much from his victim, but it was dark and I couldn't quite tell. I told him to let the girl go, and it seemed like he really wanted to."

"But?"

"But . . . it was like he really couldn't. Like it was somehow out of his control."

"They all claim that when they overstep," Casey argued. "The greedy little fuckers have it coming."

"No," Kierson bit out harshly. "I'm telling you, this was different. You should have seen the look in his eyes. He was afraid and confused."

"If he was so afraid, then why didn't he listen to you?" Drew asked, confusion overtaking his expression.

"I don't know. That's why it's so weird. I really think he would have, but then Khara came around the corner, and it seemed to spook him. He went all crazy and made a play for her. I took him out instantly." None of the brothers responded to his tale. Instead, they all stood silently, staring at him. "So while I checked the body to be sure he'd been properly disposed of, Khara went over to the girl to see if she was okay. When I came over to join her, I realized what had happened. She was gone. Way gone."

"This just doesn't make any sense," Drew said, sitting down on the couch. "How long has it been since one of them has gone that far?"

"Too long for this to have happened without provocation," Pierson offered.

"Exactly."

"But I'm telling you the truth," Kierson declared in defense of his actions.

"I'm not saying you aren't; I'm just trying to sort this all out. When I saw Khara the other day, it took me a moment to realize that she might have been an Empty because it had been so long since I'd taken one out. I couldn't be sure right away."

"Turns out you were wrong anyway, Drew," Casey purred while he took a seat across from him.

"Obviously I was, Casey. I'm just trying to reiterate the point that we have not had issues with the Soul Breathers for an exceedingly long time. Why now? Why would one of them go that far now? Especially when they know that death is imminent if they do. It's suicide."

"Perhaps that soul was particularly tasty." Casey's lazy grin was starting to visibly rile Drew. Pierson stepped in to offer his intellectual assessment of the situation in an attempt to stop the fight that was brewing.

"There are too many unknown variables for us to make any sort of conclusion at the moment. What we need to do is better track the Breathers so that we do not have any repeats of tonight. We need intel. That should be our top priority at the moment."

"Agreed," Kierson said, coming to stand beside his twin. "I do not want to have to do that again. I don't like killing humans."

"I'll do it for you if you're too soft," Casey offered, repeatedly wiping his blade across his leather pants in a rhythmic motion.

"Must you?" I asked, my voice seeming to startle them all as though they had forgotten I was there altogether. "Kill them, I mean—the Empties. Must they die?"

"Yes. If they are not taken out, they will only take the soul of another to fill the void left in them. They have to. The very thought consumes their being, unrelenting until it is sated," Drew explained. "If they are permitted to do this, a nasty domino effect is set in motion that will eventually infect the city, a rampant plague of soulless beings overtaking the human population. They will leave nothing in their wake. Our job is to keep the balance and police the supernatural. In doing that job, we must keep the humans from knowing that otherworldly beings exist or from falling victim to them. If an entire city were to be robbed of their existence because the Stealers could not be contained, it would not go unnoticed. Once done, there would be no way to easily undo it without extensive collateral damage."

His explanation was thorough and compelling, but I was still confused.

"Stealers?" My look of confusion must have tipped Drew off to the fact that Kierson had explained nothing of what had happened that night. "What Kierson and I saw was a Breather. What is this Stealer that you speak of?"

"Soul Stealer, to be exact, Khara. They were one of the many evils that thrived in the New World. To prevent the potential debacle I just described to you, they were eradicated . . . in a fashion."

"What Drew is trying to tell you is that we came to terms with them—an agreement—that changed the breed, if they can be called that. Creating the Soul Breathers was the palatable solution to the problem. Because the Stealers sustained themselves on the souls of others, more precisely the light or goodness within them, humans were a readily accessible food source for them. The Stealers quickly became efficient at draining a person of their soul, and had no qualms about doing so," Pierson clarified.

"And that is what an Empty is? One whose soul has been taken?"

"Precisely. They are the soulless remnants of their former selves." A vision of the young female who Kierson had saved, only to have to slay, flashed in my mind before fading. "If an Empty could survive in that catatonic, questionably human state, perhaps they could be allowed to live, but that is not so. Nature abhors a vacuum, and so it must be filled."

"With another soul."

"Correct," Pierson affirmed. "The Empties will not rest until they have taken one. They know no restraint. They will take it violently, publicly, however they have to in order to sate the hollow cavern of darkness that remains deep within them. It is a liability far too great to be tolerated. I'm sure you can now see why."

"I do understand the need to kill them, but what I do not understand is how the Breathers factor into all of this," I stated, not seeing how that piece of the puzzle fit.

"Before the agreement was made, it was apparent that the Stealers posed an enormous threat to the balance. The New World was vast, and regulated by only a few of us. It took decades to see what was happening with them, and once we did it was obvious that they had run amok, infecting enough of the population to be of great concern to the balance and therefore the PC. When it became a war between the PC and the Stealers, whose appetite had grown larger than their restraint, it was clear that the war would not be easily won by either side. We could kill them easily once located, but they spread so quickly that for every one we took out, another Empty had already been created. In effect, it was an everlasting stalemate. Seeing the futility of an eternal battle, we had to look for other solutions that reached beyond our normal methods. In the end, we found a compromise. The Stealers were preservationists and saw reason when presented with an option that would prevent an eternal war."

"Or you could call a spade a spade and admit that we pussed out, Pierson," Casey countered, still methodically wiping his blade across his pants.

"Hardly, Casey," Pierson spat, his tightened features clearly displaying his disdain for Casey's analysis. "We took the most logical route and did what needed to be done to protect the balance. We allowed them to sustain their lives by taking tiny pieces of light from the humans, and their kind no longer spread like wildfire. This plan has been in effect ever since, and it has worked brilliantly—"

"Until now," Kierson said flatly, finishing his twin's sentence for him.

"And that is why you think there is a problem. You think this tenuous agreement that you struck with the Stealers has been dishonored? That what you've allowed them is no longer enough?" I asked.

"It's possible," Kierson replied. "That's exactly what happened tonight—he broke the treaty. What we have to figure out is why, if there is a 'why' at all. And fast."

"What were the exact conditions of the agreement you set forth with these Stealers?" I asked, curious as to how creatures so potentially dangerous to the balance could be allowed to exist at all.

"They had to willingly relegate themselves to one location; we chose Detroit for several reasons, not the least of which was its inherently seedy nature. They also had to agree to no longer remove an entire soul when they fed. Ever," Pierson informed me, his tone serious. "If they did not abide by those rules, the punishment was to be instant death. We would then make an example of their death to their fellow Breathers so that such an infraction would not occur again."

"That is all? Those Stealers still alive at the end of the war all agreed to those terms?"

"Most did. Those that didn't . . ." Kierson hedged.

"We made examples of," Casey sneered. He seemed more than happy to make that point clear. I assumed he had particularly enjoyed carrying out that punishment.

"So how do they survive now? They live on partial souls?"

"They take bits and pieces of their victims. Tiny parts of the light from each of them—a happy memory, a special feeling—not enough for that individual to really notice, although it seems whatever is taken is gone forever. I doubt the victims ever knew they'd had it to begin with. With all the darkness already in this city, we figured it was as safe a place as any to allow them to live, knowing that their food source would be scarce at best."

"Ain't much happy in Detroit anymore. It's a great diet plan," Casey drawled before getting up and walking away from our gathering altogether. Something appeared to be vexing him greatly.

"Until now, our agreement stood. The Stealers weakened over time to become what we now refer to as Soul Breathers, a sad and lesser version of their former selves. They look sickly from the lack of full and intact souls in their diet, their skin sallow and cheeks gaunt. Most humans assume they are either ill with a terminal disease or that they are junkies. Either way, they pass in society without scrutiny, and that is what we wanted."

"What will happen if tonight's occurrence is not an isolated one?" I asked, thinking that it was not an impossibility.

"Then," Drew started, walking toward me slowly, "there will be war in Detroit."

"How can we ascertain whether or not this is already the case?"

"We have ways," Pierson stated, his tone haughty and superior. It was clear that he was not about to elaborate on his statement, and I lacked the energy or desire to demand it of him.

Drew stood before me, his hands resting gently upon my shoulders. A smile painted his expression pleasant, though I could sense he found nothing enjoyable about the conversation. It was all a show for my benefit; one that was neither necessary nor appreciated.

"It will all be fine. We'll get to the bottom of this quickly so that we can get back to the bigger issue at hand here, which is figuring out what happened to you and how to keep you safe from whatever may be coming for you. Okay?" I nodded. "Good. Now I want you to sit and relax for a bit. I know you're no stranger to violence, but witnessing the taking of innocent life is never easy or pleasant."

"I didn't let her see," Kierson said softly. "I made her go around the corner. I just . . . I couldn't let her see."

"Good thinking, Kierson," Drew praised before turning to Pierson. "I need to make a call. I'll be outside for a minute if you need me.

I'm putting you in charge of rounding up intel on this. Don't let me down." With that, he left, walking toward the staircase as Casey had only minutes before, though it was clear Drew planned to return. Casey did not.

I looked around the vast balcony, only to see that the other member of our party, the one who liked to lurk in the shadows, was missing.

"What of Oz?" I asked, wondering if this was a matter in which the PC would find him useful.

"What about him?" Kierson replied, looking more perplexed than usual.

"Where is he? Should he not be a part of this?"

Kierson shrugged.

"Oz does what he wants, when he wants. There's no counting on him for anything—other than being a bastard most of the time." He smiled at me deviously, leading me to believe he was pleased at the insult he'd slung at Oz, who was conveniently not there to defend himself. I nearly returned his expression.

"So what are we to do in the interim while we await word from Drew?"

Kierson's smile spread wider, containing more mischief than it had only moments before. His eyes betrayed him as he glanced over the railing to the dance floor below and the undulating mass of bodies moving with the pulsating rhythm that seemed to enliven the entire building.

"I do not like what you are insinuating," I warned, taking a step back from him.

"C'mon, lighten up a bit. It's not like we can do anything else about this debacle right now, anyway. Let's have a drink. Relax. You know, have fun?" But I knew not of the fun he spoke. It was not a part of my life, and, judging by his response, that fact was inevitably written across my face. "Ugh . . ." he sighed, his shoulders rounding in defeat. "Fine, at least come get a drink with me at the bar. I need to unwind a bit."

I watched as the sadness he held deep within surfaced, flashing in his eyes for only a second before it withdrew yet again. If companionship was what he needed, I could give him that much. He may have saved my life that night. For that, I would reward him with what he requested.

"A drink," I replied tightly, making sure he knew that dancing or any other such nonsense was not going to occur.

"Excellent." Taking my arm in his, he led the way to the stairs, not bothering to acknowledge Pierson before leaving. It appeared that he was busy anyway. "What's your poison?" he asked when we reached the bottom of the stairs.

"Excuse me?"

"Your drink of choice? What will you have?"

I was uncertain how to answer him. While in the care of both Demeter and Hades, I primarily drank water and, on occasion, ambrosia. Nothing more. However, I was under the distinct impression that he was not suggesting either of those.

"You may order for me. Whatever you have will suffice."

Our destination was on the far side of the mob before us, and I cringed at the thought of having to navigate through them all, their sweaty stench already offending me from where I stood. Without time to relay those concerns to Kierson, he took my hand and pulled me behind him as he cut his way through the mass with ease. Though I was loath to admit it, there was something strangely appealing being surrounded by the dancing horde, swallowed up in their debauchery. I had not expected to find it so amenable.

It reminded me of home.

When we arrived, Kierson leaned forward against the waist-high barricade, and a scantily clad woman in black leather came over to him immediately, ignoring the protestations of the others attempting to procure a drink.

"How's it going, Special K?" She was intoxicated by him, his mere presence alone enough for her to nearly fall to her knees in service of him. When he winked at her in response, she bit her lip and inhaled deeply.

"I need the usual, Trina," he shouted to her over the music. "Two of them."

It was only then that her eyes fell on me, and the change in them was instantaneous. Seductive desperation turned to pure hatred. I knew that look well.

"Who's this?" she asked, barely able to keep the venom in her tone at bay.

"This? This is my sister, Khara."

Again, the transformation in her expression took only a second.

"Oh . . . it's nice to meet you, Cara," she replied with a disingenuous smile.

"It's Kah-ruh," I said slowly in the hopes that her tiny mind could process my words.

"Right . . . sorry. Two whiskeys comin' up!"

While she went about pouring the drinks, I turned my back to her so that I could better observe the crowd. I liked to know what was going on around me, and had learned long ago that it was best not to turn your back on the unfamiliar. It tended to have unenviable consequences. As I scanned the vast room, I saw Oz on the far end, making his way to the upper level. True to form, he was not alone.

I soured at the sight of him, still wondering what made him valuable enough to my brothers to tolerate his unwelcome presence. Everything about him was repugnant, from his disgruntled nature to his flagrant sexual exploitations. What made me wonder further was why his behaviors seemed offensive to me at all. I was raised around men like that. They were everywhere to be found in the Underworld, but there was something particularly off-putting about those behaviors when they came from him. Perhaps what caused them to be so disarming was the fact that they came from a Light One—a revered being, according to Kierson—who one would expect to be both noble and pure.

Whatever the reason, I did not enjoy the feeling at all.

"Here you go," Kierson shouted, handing me a tiny glass containing an amber-colored liquid. "Down the hatch." He lifted his strange little glass into the air before putting it to his lips and swallowing the contents of it in one drink. Sensing that it was a custom of sorts, I mimicked him, taking the entire mouthful of whiskey down in one swallow.

The fire I felt in response made me choke, gagging and fighting for breath.

"Jesus, Khara!" Kierson yelled, bending down to meet my face while I fought to purge myself of the liquid fire. "Have you never done a shot before?"

"Is that not obvious?" I wheezed between breaths.

I heard him bark at the woman behind the bar to get him some water quickly, and soon I found myself emptying the glass he handed me in only seconds. Feeling remotely better, I motioned toward the staircase that wound its way up to the second floor and started in that direction, pushing my way through the unrelenting crowd. The task seemed far more taxing than I had bargained for. Kierson had cut through it with such ease and grace; I, however, did not.

I could hear him shouting my name as he followed me, but I did not stop to acknowledge him. I felt ill and wanted nothing more than to go to the restroom and expel the foul beverage from my stomach. Waiting for him was not part of my plan.

Once I made it to the stairs, I took them two at a time, feeling the burning sensation start to rise in my throat. Pierson eyed me strangely from the couch as I sped past him to the private bathroom on the far end of the space. Kierson continued to follow me until I waved him off, insisting that I was fine. His guilt was nearly palpable.

Without hesitation, I burst through the bathroom door, my brow starting to sweat, and I turned right around the corner in search of a sufficient outlet for what was about to escape me. Instead, what I saw stopped me dead in my tracks. Though it should not have surprised me in the least, I still had not expected the scene that played out before me. How quickly I had become sensitized to the normalcy of the human domain. Had I stumbled upon sex of that nature in the Underworld, as I so often did, I would not have faltered. But that night, I did.

One sweep of the bathroom door had hammered me with reality.

I looked straight ahead, beyond the two fornicating against the sink before me, to find a pair of intense brown eyes staring back at me from the mirror in front of him. As Oz thrust himself repeatedly and unrelentingly into the female of the evening, his gaze remained firmly fixed on me through the reflective surface. Unmoving, I looked on as he punished his whore, slamming her hips into the cold porcelain sink. He pushed her face away from him as she craned her neck around, seeking his mouth.

Never the mouth.

Expressionless and brutal, Oz embodied his very essence even in his sexual encounters. It made something in the pit of my stomach seize. He belonged in the Underworld with the rest of the depraved souls that served my father; such brazen acts were rampant there. I knew much about them, having looked upon those activities from a very young age. At times, I found myself involved in them. But something was different this time—something unexpected.

No longer able to engage his stare, I turned and left the sobering sight, returning to find a seat on the couch next to Kierson. I sat in silence, my whole body sweating. As I tried to calm my stomach, I found myself unable to erase the vacant yet hateful expression Oz had worn in the bathroom from my mind. Something about it was inexplicably puzzling and uncomfortable. My cells felt discordant, out of harmony with their neighbors, and my skin prickled and burned.

I assumed it was an effect of the whiskey.

"Do you feel any better, Khara?" Kierson asked, putting his arm around me. "I'm really sorry about that. I figured since you grew up where you did that, you know, you'd probably had worse than a little Jack Daniels before."

"I am fine," I replied, my words clipped and abrupt. A direct effect of my battle with the alcohol, no doubt.

"Okay," he said cautiously. "But you don't look so good . . ."

"As I said, I am fine, though I think I would like to leave, if that is permissible. My head is throbbing, and that infernal pounding reverberating through this building is making it worse. I hardly see how you can tolerate it on such a regular basis, let alone once you have imbibed such a hideous drink."

"Take her home," Pierson ordered, tossing the vehicle's keys to Kierson.

"I'm on it!"

With more enthusiasm than the task warranted, Kierson bounded off the couch, extending a hand toward me, though it never made it to mine.

"I'll take her home," Oz purred from the darkness he seemed to shroud himself in wherever he went. Without awaiting a response, he stepped in front of Kierson, snatching the keys out of his hand. He loomed above me ominously, and when I stood up to meet him our bodies touched.

"I think I prefer Pierson's initial plan," I informed him, my face only inches from his.

"And I prefer mine," he retorted indignantly. "Let's go."

Taking my arm captive, he ushered me around Kierson and toward the staircase.

"I have seen where your hands have been this evening, Oz. I would prefer not to wear your whore, if it is all the same to you."

Again, my words were curt and heated. He seemed to find my tone amusing and let out a great laugh indicating so.

"I have the sneaking suspicion that you are not charmed by me, new girl. But how could that possibly be? I'm *irresistible*. You've seen the way women fall at my feet. Why should you be any different?" I could hear the mocking in his words. I would not take the bait.

"I'm weary of you already, Oz. Perhaps I should return and get Kierson so that I may at least have a buffer from your narcissism and inflated sense of entitlement."

"Kierson is likely busy with sloppy seconds at the moment. I'm afraid you will have to suffer my company for one car ride. Could you deign to endure that, or shall I leave you to drive yourself? I'm wondering if you could even figure out how to get the damn thing in gear."

"I find it curious that you think I have to suffer you at all. Suffering implies emotion—attachment. I possess neither of those things, especially not for you," I snapped, educating him on the reality of our relationship with heated words. "Present or absent, I care not. Drive the vehicle or don't; I shall find my way home regardless."

His expression darkened at my words.

"Eager to serve yourself up on a platter to the bowels of this city, are you?" he asked, halting our exit just shy of the door. "You think you would survive? Shall we test that theory?"

"I have survived worse, I can assure you."

"There are dangers in the unfamiliar, new girl," he said softly, leaning in to deliver his warning directly from his lips to my ear. "You would be wise to acknowledge that."

"And you would be wise to acknowledge that you are nothing to me. I neither want to fuck you nor heed your words. You have proven yourself to be little more than a self-indulgent leech that has attached itself to my brothers. They have honor—purpose. You have neither of those things. Why they tolerate you at all is an enigma. They claim you have skill as a fighter, though only when it suits you. I cannot imagine what scenario could inspire you to do anything more than unzip your pants and spread your seed."

A flash of anger burned in his eyes momentarily before a serpent's smile spread wide across his face.

"I think I will take you home, new girl," he drawled, his face still near my own. "I can't let you die just yet. You're far too entertaining for that." He pushed the heavy metal door open and led the way up the long stretch of staircase to the street above. When we stepped onto the street, the moon was still high in the sky. He looked at it curiously for a moment, inhaling the night air deeply. "Can you smell that?" I lifted my nose to the air in an attempt to re-create his gesture. I smelled nothing beyond the stench of the city. Again, he leaned in close, his breath tickling the skin on my ears. "Desperation. Fear. They're rampant in this hellhole, marking the path of evil. Learn the scent. Let it imprint on your brain so that it triggers the same response in you. If you're lucky, your recognition will keep you alive."

I pulled away from him and stared impassively.

"I am fluent in fear and desperation. It is the language of the Underworld. Do not presume to know how to keep me safe from what evokes it," I cautioned, my tone as dark as his eyes. "Only moments ago you were all too happy to leave me to my fate. I think I preferred that behavior."

"Ah, but I told you that I find you entertaining. I'm not ready for you to succumb to the city just yet." He turned in the direction of the vehicle and walked toward it, tossing the final words that he would speak to me that evening over his shoulder. "I'll let you know when I am."

7

I awoke the next morning to yet another heated discussion coming from the living room above. Unable to sleep any longer, visions of Oz in the bathroom still plaguing my mind, I decided to join my arguing brothers to ascertain what the problem was. I assumed that I was once again the cause of it.

"And they told you nothing?" Drew pressed as I quietly opened the door to the main part of the house. When I stepped through it, I found Drew staring Casey down, a clear and distinct tension having overtaken his reserved demeanor.

From Casey's usual perch on the sofa, he looked up at Drew as though he could not have been less intimidated.

"Nothing. Nobody knows anything."

The click of the door latching behind me alerted them to my presence.

"Khara, I'm sorry," Drew apologized, coming to greet me with a faint smile. "Did we wake you?"

"No. I was already awake."

"You got home all right last night, I see. I heard about Oz's theatrics at the club . . ."

"He is a nuisance, though utterly harmless. He delivered me home as he said he would."

"Harmless?" Casey baited. "Oz may be many things, but harmless is not one of them. Beware the fallen one, *sister*. He is far more than he lets on."

I considered his choice of words carefully before responding, having only heard the term "fallen" used to describe the Dark Ones.

"Fallen?" I repeated, asking for clarification. "Like the Dark Ones?"

Casey raised a brow at me curiously.

"I'm surprised he didn't tell you last night. He so enjoys talking about himself."

"We did not speak during the drive or after it."

My statement must have been far more scandalous than I could have imagined. Both Drew and Casey eyed me strangely, then looked at one another in an attempt to communicate something that I could not follow.

"Not a word? He said nothing?" Drew asked for clarification.

"No. He warned me about the city on our way to the vehicle. I told him that I did not require his guidance or input. That was all."

Again, the two looked to one another strangely before responding.

"And he didn't try to . . ." Drew's expression begged me to understand something in the subtext of his words, but it was lost on me.

"Fuck you," Casey interjected. "He didn't try to fuck you?"

"He did not," I replied, unable to keep the sourness I felt at the thought off my face.

"Well, I guess there's a first time for everything."

"Would someone please explain the term 'fallen' that was just used to describe him? If you are not referring to the Dark Ones, then I would very much like to know what you mean when you use that word. I have only ever heard it applied to them."

"Who have you heard call them that?" Casey asked, looking more interested in the conversation.

"My father."

"Then he is misinformed. Fallen means precisely what it implies," Pierson said as he descended the stairs from the second floor. "Oz has fallen."

"Fallen from where? And why?"

"From grace," Pierson clarified, looking pained by the task of having to explain himself. He continued through the living room to the kitchen, not wanting to frustrate himself with my ignorance any further.

"We told you he was an angel, Khara," Drew interjected. "He's just not a very good one."

"If he is evil, then why do you associate with him?"

"He's not evil per se," Drew sighed, gesturing for me to come join him on the sofa. As I did, Casey rose to stand and block my way.

"And not all of your brothers are good. It goes both ways." He pushed past me, he too making his way to the kitchen. His words were unnecessary; his true nature was hardly lost on me.

"Oz is . . . complicated," Drew started, running his hand through his hair, tugging on it slightly.

"I hardly see that. He seems quite predictable to me."

"Well, that's what he wants everyone to see. He wasn't always that way. He's devolved over time." Drew pressed himself further into the sofa, leaning back against it as though he needed to rest before telling his tale. "None of us fully knows why he fell. Like we told you before, he's hardly forthcoming with information like that. However, it seems pretty clear that he has no intention of trying to rise again. He likes what he has become."

"I fail to see what there is to like."

"I know, Khara. He seems to have been on his worst behavior since you showed up. But I can say that he has his moments, even though they are few and far between. Ask Kierson; he owes him his life."

On cue, Kierson made his way down the stairs to join the rest of us. He rounded the bottom step and said nothing at all, his normally goofy expression absent from his face when he turned to face Drew.

"Is that true, Kierson? Did Oz save your life?" I asked, ignoring the rising tension between him and Drew.

"I've got to go to the store," he replied coolly, looking past me to the kitchen. "You coming, Pierson?"

"Yes, I think that might be best," he replied, coming to join his twin.

"Drew, I think you oughta come, too. We need to have a little chat."

"Kierson—"

"Not here," Kierson growled. It was the most angry I had seen him. Not even when he had killed the Breather had he seemed so hostile. Whatever was behind it was clearly an unwelcome subject as far as Kierson was concerned.

The twins exited the front door without another word. Drew gave me a tight smile before heading out to join them. Their leave left only one remaining brother in the home—Casey—and I had no intention of joining him in the kitchen. Instead, I decided to take in my surroundings a little more thoroughly. Things had moved quickly since my arrival, not allowing me the opportunity to become comfortable with my new environment. In the past, I had the luxury of centuries to accomplish that task. In the present, no one knew how much time I had, so I chose not to waste any of it.

Essentially all I was familiar with in the three-story home was the basement—my room—and the first floor. I had yet to wander beyond that. Making my way to the staircase that led upstairs, I rested my hand on the newel post and looked up the steep and narrow stairway. It was benign enough, with weathered wooden risers, but it was where it would take me that gave me pause. Would my brothers not take kindly to my exploration of their home? Would it be seen as an affront of sorts? So many of their reactions to things were beyond my comprehension. I could not possibly presume to know how they would respond if they knew. With Casey home, it was even more disconcerting. He had only moments earlier admitted to being every bit as callous as I thought him to be. I did not wish to be on the receiving end of his wrath, if it could be avoided.

With a cautious glance over my shoulder to see if he was watching, I carefully treaded up the steps, trying my best to be silent. Once

I reached the second-floor landing, I looked to my left, taking stock of the rooms. There were four closed doors along the narrow hall—presumably my brothers' bedrooms—and one bathroom, whose door was slightly ajar. The patterned paper covering the walls was in tatters, pieces hanging and torn off along the entire hallway. I couldn't help but pluck a loose piece off as I passed, making my way to yet another narrow staircase at the far end of the hall.

Again I tread lightly on the stairs, attempting to make as little noise as possible while I ascended them. When I reached the top, I found a very different layout than the floor below. There was virtually no hallway at all, only a landing with a single wooden door. Turning the knob gently, I pushed it open to find a long, sparse, but tidy, bedroom. I did not wish to invade the privacy of whomever's space this was, so I turned to leave. But then I stopped. In the far corner of the room was a spiraling staircase leading into the turret I had seen from the exterior of the Victorian. There was a window at the top of it, letting in a glorious beam of light that diffused its way through part of the space. Wanting to see where it led, I crossed the room quickly and climbed the stairs, stopping to stare out the surprisingly large window that faced the backyard. From it, I could see the rooftop of the third floor in its entirety. It also had a view of the main part of the city just off in the distance, overlooking all the neighboring homes with their rows of decaying roofs clearly on display. I was intrigued by the sense of openness out there and found myself lifting the sash to allow myself passage.

Stepping out onto the flat, black roof below, I was greeted by the sun as it slipped from behind the seemingly ever-present clouds that shrouded Detroit. The solar warmth was familiar and yet not—oddly different from that of my home. The rays on my face pierced me deep inside, reaching to a place that nothing in the Underworld ever could. As though the fire in the sky commanded me, I tipped my chin up, allowing my hair to fall back, exposing my neck and chest to invite the heat. But before I had a moment to bask in the sensation, a gruff voice rumbled low in my ear.

"New girl, is there a reason you're intruding on my space?" I turned to find Oz uncomfortably near me. I looked him over slowly, wearing every bit of the disdain I felt for him on my face. My gesture was misinterpreted, judging by his amused reaction. "Or maybe you've finally come to your senses and came looking for me . . ."

"I thought I would explore the Victorian, in the event that I should need to navigate it under duress at some point."

"Sure," he mocked, stepping around my shoulder to stand before me, thereby blocking out the sun. "That seems a convenient excuse."

"I did not know that was your room. Now that I do, I will be certain to avoid it at all costs," I retorted. "I shall leave you to whatever it was you were doing." When I turned to leave, he caught my arm. His grasp was firm, but not uncomfortable.

"Running away so soon?" he asked, a mischievous look on his face. "You're already out here; maybe we should get to know each other a little better. I think we've been off to a rather rocky start."

"I know what I need to know," I replied. My response did nothing to derail him, so I tried another approach entirely. "Actually, there is something that you could familiarize me with."

"Really?" he replied, curiosity overtaking his tone. "And what would that be?"

"Kierson—you saved his life once. I want to know from what and how."

He tensed at my words, his grip on my arm tightening. His lips pressed together in a straight line, erasing any amusement his face had displayed earlier. My inquiry had affected him.

"Don't ask questions you don't want the answers to, new girl."

"I ask such questions because I want the answers they hold."

"Who told you about that?"

"Unimportant."

"Well, I can see that whoever did wasn't interested in letting you in on all the details."

"They all left before they could."

"Ha," he laughed, letting go of my arm and turning away from me. "They weren't going to tell you shit. Those assholes knew exactly what they were doing, which means it wasn't Kierson. He's too dumb to have thought of that. Casey doesn't give a shit—there's nothing in it for him to tell you. The only way he would have served me up is if he could have sat back on that fucking sofa and watched the chaos play out in front of him. No, this has Drew or Pierson written all over it."

For whatever reason, my question had rattled the fallen one. He continued to ramble on, muttering to himself about exactly whose ass he was going kick for alerting me to something he apparently viewed as confidential. Uninterested in his rant, I retreated back to the window into his room. It was plain that he had no intention of telling me what I wanted to know. Why no one would remained a mystery.

"Where do you think you're going?" he asked, stopping me just short of my escape with his words.

"Inside."

"No, I don't think so. Not until you tell me why you asked that question."

"I asked because I knew you would not answer. You were as forthcoming as I expected, which only further cemented my opinion of you. There is no point in us chatting. It will change nothing. I just wanted to illustrate that point to you, given that you seem oblivious to it."

His eyebrows rose momentarily. My explanation surprised him.

"Well played, new girl."

"You are not the only one well versed in games, fallen one."

The surprise washed from his face instantaneously.

"Careful, new girl," he warned, moving quickly toward me until he loomed above me as menacingly as the worst of the Underworld. "You don't want me to make this more than a game."

I saw no reason to respond. Instead, I turned around to continue my exit, stepping through the open window without looking back. He would stay true to his words or not. Either way, I had made my point: I was not a toy for him to play with.

As I made my way through his room, he made no attempt to follow. I had not paid much attention when I originally entered, the spiral staircase occupying most of my focus, but as I walked through, I couldn't help but notice how surprisingly pristine it was—clean, neat, and orderly. Everything that he was not. It seemed strange that someone who cared about nothing other than himself would bother to attend to something else in such a fastidious manner. Perhaps there was more to him than he let on.

Exiting his room, I quickly made my way to the stairs and down to the lower floor, wanting to be far away from him. When I reached the hallway below, I came face-to-face with Casey, who looked every bit his menacing self.

"Snooping around, are we?" he asked. His tone implied indifference, but it was plain that he was angry.

"No. I only wanted to see the home I now live in."

"I see you found Oz's room without much trouble," he continued, his eyes drifting over to the stairs I had just descended.

"That was quite by accident, I can assure you. Had I known it was his, I would have avoided that part of the house entirely."

His eyes narrowed, doing nothing to improve his expression.

"There's nothing up there for you," he said, leaning in closer. "Understand?"

"There's little up there for anyone," I replied, remembering how sparse Oz's room was. "But I have no intention of visiting there again."

He continued to stare at me silently, assessing something. Only when he turned and walked away did I assume he had found what he wanted in my words.

"Food's downstairs," he called over his shoulder.

Famished, I followed behind him until we reached the living room. He broke away to take up his station on the couch while I continued on to the kitchen. Alone, I searched the room, opening and closing cupboards and drawers methodically until I found the implements necessary to eat the food laid out across the counter. Once I served myself, I sat on the chair that had been tucked underneath the ledge of the vast rectangular surface constructed in the center of the room. As I ate, I questioned what had happened on the roof only moments earlier. Before now, I had never given any situation much analysis after the fact. For almost my whole life, I had taken most things at face value. Though the Underworld was full of deceit and various other machinations, I knew that was how it operated. There was no need for deep thought when everyone around you was evil and vindictive. Assuming the worst was a means of survival. But things in my new home were different. My brothers operated in such an unfamiliar fashion that I often found myself assessing every look, every question, every deed, for what might lie beneath it. Oz's confounding behavior took my analysis to an entirely different level.

He made me long for home.

But fate had demanded that I return to the surface before my time and to an unfamiliar setting, placing me in the hands of my brothers. There was a reason why, though none of us could fathom it. I chose to focus my energy on finding it. If I was ever going to return to the Underworld, I needed to discern why I was in Detroit. I also needed to procure a being capable of bringing me back from whence I had come.

A problem for another day.

8

"So I learned something interesting while I was out," Kierson mumbled, his mouth full of some type of edible concoction. His earlier irritation with his brothers seemed to have completely dissipated. Food also often seemed to be an easy distraction for him. "It sounds as though the Breather I killed the other night wasn't the only one seen hanging on by a thin thread recently. Very recently."

"Where'd you hear that?" Pierson inquired from across the kitchen table, his air of superiority firmly in place.

"I have my sources, same as you," Kierson fired back as he glared at Pierson. It seemed the brothers had parted ways not long after leaving the house, leading me to question if their investigative strengths lay in their individuality, not their combined forces. "Anyway, it sounds like there are a few of them staying together on the east side of the city limits in the old train depot, or what used to be the old train depot. At the rate that thing's falling apart, I'm not sure there's too much of it left standing."

"Why out there? There aren't humans living anywhere near that place," Drew replied, his thoughts flowing freely from him as though he had not meant to share them at all but could not stop himself. He also appeared unable to stop himself from pacing around the kitchen.

"Fear would be my guess," Kierson said with a shrug, resting back into his wooden chair. "If you knew that you were about to sign your own death warrant by crossing a line you couldn't come back from, wouldn't you stay as far away from temptation as you could?"

"That's hardly a relevant point, given that they will need to feed sometime," Pierson rebutted.

"True, but Kierson might not be entirely wrong." Drew stepped up to the edge of the kitchen table where the rest of us sat, placing his hands down firmly on it. "There is safety in numbers. Perhaps they are communing together to keep themselves in check. Keep themselves from falling off the wagon, so to speak."

"It's not fucking AA, Drew," Casey snarled from the far end of the table. "You're giving them way too much credit. My bet is that they're coming together for a common goal, and it ain't a good one." He stood and mimicked Drew's stance, leaning toward him. "Why don't we just march down there right now and take them all out. Quick and easy."

"We don't know that they've done anything wrong yet," Pierson pointed out.

"So we should wait until they do? Kierson saw what that one did the other night. Should we wait until we have an army of them about to rain down on the humans? I'm sure that would go unnoticed . . . Nobody would find it strange at all if a slew of Empties went shuffling their way through the city like the zombie apocalypse had finally come. Or maybe we should just say 'fuck it' to the treaty and clean this mess up like we should have in the first place. We're not fucking diplomats, and we're not fucking cops. There is no system of justice here. Our job is to maintain the balance at any cost, and, as far as I can see, having those loose cannons running around town is a risk we can't afford."

"What we can't afford is to behave like the days of old," Drew rumbled, the two staring at one another as though reliving a conversation they'd long ago had.

"I liked the old ways," Casey purred with a reminiscent smile on his face that reached his eyes. It gave them a menacing glint.

"As I recall, but that's not how we do things anymore. Not everything needs to be a bloodbath, Casey."

"Maybe," he sneered. "But it should be."

"All right, all right! Before you two start swinging, can we go see if my source was legit first? Then we can decide how to take them out if need be."

All eyes turned to Kierson. Pierson looked puzzled, Drew surprised, and Casey enraged.

"When will we be embarking on this mission?" I asked. "I would like to go, if for no other reason than to learn more about the enemy."

"They're not the enemy per se, Khara," Drew said, turning his attention to me. "They're no different than any of the other supernaturals that roam this earth. The Breathers are entitled to their survival just like the rest of them. But if they do in fact have plans to breech the confines of the agreement en masse, then they will pay with their lives."

"I am not concerned with how you classify them. I only wish to learn more," I explained from my station next to Kierson. "If I am to stay in this city, I think that only stands to reason."

His expression tightened, weighing my words carefully before he spoke.

"I'm not sure . . ." he hedged. "If things go south, I don't know that I want you there."

"If your mission is for reconnaissance, then I do not see the harm. And if I am truly one of you, was I not bred to do this? To police the boundary as you all do? How will I learn to do so if I am never exposed to the very situations I was created to mediate?"

He looked pensive for a moment before sighing heavily.

"This should be a relatively benign mission," he muttered to himself. "Fair enough, Khara. You make a valid point, though if you are to come, then it will be with all of us there to ensure your safety, should something unexpected arise. We still don't know where your strengths and weaknesses lie. You are a daughter of Ares, and that means something, but until we know where the other half of your lineage comes from, and what skills you possess because of it, we cannot take unnecessary risks." He walked out of the room, only to return seconds later carrying a long blade. "We have until nightfall. Let the training begin."

Hours later, the brothers had determined that I had no remarkable talents with either weapons or my hands. I was completely untrained, and I grew tired of being reminded of that fact repeatedly. My bruises attested to that on their own.

While they struggled to ascertain how someone so unskilled could survive the perils of the Underworld, they endeavored to provide me with the centuries' worth of training that I lacked. They were all so elegantly lethal in their movements, whereas I was anything but that. I soon found myself feeling something I never remembered feeling before: frustration. Had they not so ardently defended the veracity of our familial tie, I would have thought it untrue. To an outside party, the disconnect would have been obvious.

"Khara," Drew began before taking a long drink of water. "I'm starting to think this is a bad idea. You can't really wield a sword or dagger or blade of any sort. And your target skills with a gun were . . ."

"Yikes," Kierson interrupted, contorting his features into a hideous grimace.

"Inaccurate was the word I was looking for," Drew continued, sending a chastising expression Kierson's way. "My point is that you are more likely to be a liability than an asset in any fight."

"But you do not wish to fight them," I countered, recalling his earlier words. "Are we not going there solely to establish the truth of Kierson's claim?"

"Yes, but—"

"While I may not have the abilities that you all possess, I am not without them entirely. Is survival not a skill? Evasion? Are they not forms of defense?" I asked, advancing toward him. "You may find it hard to imagine, but weapons were scarce in my father's kingdom. And though brutality was rampant, I suffered little, comparatively speaking. Do not mistake that outcome for lack of exposure. I may have been Hades' ward, but for some that only made me more of a target, not less of one."

"Your point?" Pierson asked leadingly.

"My point is that I seem to have an uncanny knack for avoiding trouble even when immersed in it. Perhaps it is not a skill that you would have expected, but it has its merits nonetheless. Is it not possible that such an ability could be used to defuse the situation with the Breathers rather than escalate it?"

"Interesting theory, but would it not have worked while you were with Kierson the other night?"

"I was not given the opportunity to try."

"You weren't given the opportunity to try because you would have been killed if I had let you," Kierson argued, unable to conceal his overwhelming concern.

"There is only one way to find out," I continued. "Surely your gifts have been honed over time. If mine are not permitted to be, they will never advance and I will constantly be in the very situation you wish for me to avoid being in—at the mercy of those around me."

I scanned the faces of the brothers, finally landing on Drew's. A visible struggle within him plagued his expression. My words were getting to him, and he saw the validity of my claim, but it warred with his loyal and protective nature. He felt a deep responsibility for the lives of those he commanded, and he wanted to keep us from unnecessary danger, especially me. It was plain that if harm were to befall me his mind would never be at peace.

"I don't like it, Khara," he told me, his tone cautionary.

"Of course you do not. It goes against all you stand for to put me in front of a perceived threat, but you know that I am right."

He sighed heavily, his brow still furrowed with concern.

"Fine. But you aren't going out there unarmed, even if you can't use a weapon well." He reached around his back and produced a small dagger, one petite enough to conceal easily and withdraw quickly. "Change of plan. We're going to spend the next hour on one skill only: efficiently and effectively killing Breathers. Hopefully it's enough time to gain some proficiency in that endeavor."

"Hopefully she won't need to do it," Kierson added.

"Hopefully I'll get to kill those fuckers all by myself, making it a nonissue," Casey said with a malicious grin.

Perhaps he would.

9

"Your complete lack of fear is disconcerting," Drew mumbled as he drove into a darkened and seemingly abandoned part of the city. Night had fallen, granting us cover for the mission at hand. It was time to hunt down the Breathers.

"It serves no purpose, never changing the outcome that you are destined for," I replied. "I choose to focus on things within my control. Extenuating circumstances, by definition, are not."

Silence fell over the car for a moment while my words settled into my brothers' collective consciousness.

"You are one crazy bitch," Casey commented from his post in the back row of seats. When I turned to observe his expression, I found it to be nearly as impassive as always, though it held a hint of something new as well—amusement, perhaps.

"Not crazy. Realistic."

He shrugged in response.

"Whatever you want to call it."

"We're almost there," Drew called from the driver's seat. "I'm going to kill the headlights so we arrive in darkness. It's going to be hard to see since these streetlamps haven't seen a working bulb in years and the cloud cover has the moonlight kept to a minimum." He parked the car along a side alley before turning around in his seat to address us all. "I know this is more of a recon mission than anything else, but be on high alert. If things start to escalate, I want it shut down quickly, but only if we have to. Casey, that means keep your shit locked down until I tell you otherwise, understood?" Casey merely grunted his confirmation. "Okay then. Let's do this."

They all filed out of the Suburban, and I followed closely, as I had previously been instructed to. The area had a nefarious feel to it. My instinct was that Kierson's source was right. Had I been looking for a place to hide away from the watchful eyes of the PC, I would have chosen this location for certain.

"He said that they're on one of the upper floors of the old Central Station building," Kierson said as we all huddled together near the rear of the vehicle. "How do you want to do this?"

"Pierson, have you had any visions of this?" Drew asked.

"No. Nothing."

"Okay, we'll have to go in blind then. I think we should split into three groups. Casey can take the west entrance. Pierson and Kierson, you guys can take the east. Khara and I are going to take the main entrance and follow the grand staircase up. If there is any trouble, we regroup in what used to be the main lobby area. Got it?"

"Define trouble," Casey smirked.

"The kind that you don't start," Drew replied, pinning dead-serious eyes on Casey. "We've had this treaty for a long time now. Don't go fucking it up because you've got a hard-on for payback."

Casey stepped into Drew's space, thrusting his face into his.

"If you don't like how I operate, then send me somewhere else," he snarled, staring Drew down. "Oh, wait . . . you can't, can you? You need me, and you know it. Now, fuck off. I have things to do."

Without another word, Casey stormed off toward the station.

"We're going to loop around the block and go in from that direction," Kierson informed Drew while Pierson started heading down the side street we were parked on. He then turned his attention to me, placing his hands on my shoulders and bending down so that his face was near mine. "Be careful in there. Listen to Drew. And, if things go south, remember what I taught you: Stab those fuckers in the throat, then run."

"I will."

He flashed me a grin before jogging down the road after Pierson, leaving Drew and me alone. Looking over at my companion and brother, I could still see the stress lines on his face. He truly thought me incapable of what we were about to do. Fortunately for me, his lack of confidence mattered not.

"Let's go before I change my mind," he muttered under his breath.

With a nod of my head, we took off running slowly toward the abandoned building, keeping to the darkest shadows. If Kierson's source was correct, the term "abandoned" would prove to be a misnomer. Either way, I was intrigued to see what we would find when we arrived.

There was an open area surrounding the decrepit old building, presumably a once well-kept green area. I had never seen such an area before, and, even though the snow that had met me on arrival in Detroit had melted, the remnants of the dead seasons still lay below it. It was as though nature could not sustain itself in my presence.

We stopped in the doorway of the final building on the street before we crossed the deadened earth to enter the train depot. Drew pulled me near him to give me the directions he wanted me to follow.

"We're going to sprint to the front entrance and stop along the outside of it. Make sure that you press yourself flat against the concrete pillar on the right," he instructed, pointing to the exact place he wanted me to stop. "I'll stop just behind the one to the left. I want to see what I can hear before we enter. It's highly unlikely, but in the remote case of this being a setup of some sort I don't want to walk right into it."

"And if you hear nothing ominous?"

"Then we're going to go straight in through the foyer to the grand staircase beyond it and haul ass up those stairs to the next level. We'll be totally exposed at that point, so I want to get to the second floor where we can gain a little cover."

"Understood."

"You have your dagger?" I pulled it out to show him, the blade glimmering only slightly in the minimal light. "Good. I want it in your hand from here on out. If we're taken off guard, you may not have time to get it out."

I nodded, maintaining my grasp on the weapon provided to me.

With a grim expression, Drew nodded back, signaling our advance toward the building. We ran swiftly and quietly, hurdling over refuse and debris, both in the streets and the yard leading up to the depot. As I was instructed, I stopped alongside the farthest right pillar and pressed my back against it, looking over at Drew while he assessed the situation. After a minute, he seemed to be satisfied that there was nothing awaiting us. He flashed a hand signal, and we darted through the front doors that hung open and toward the massive staircase that was well beyond. Surprisingly, it was dwarfed by the magnitude of the lobby inside.

Though a small part of me wanted to take in the architectural nuance of the once-grand room, I instead continued up the staircase, taking the steps three at a time until I was beside Drew on the landing of the second floor. He quickly grabbed my arm and directed me to a hallway on our right that we could take shelter in. When we arrived, we found the twins waiting for us.

"Where's Casey?" Drew whispered. Kierson shrugged in response while Pierson shook his head slowly from side to side. Before Drew could lament Casey's insubordination, an echo from farther up the stairwell rang throughout the building. It was a singular sound multiplied by the poor acoustics in the cavernous building.

The three brothers took off immediately at lightning speed, nearly forgetting me altogether. I struggled to keep pace with them as they rounded the staircase with ease, taking flight by flight as they approached the top floor. Just before we arrived, a voice called out from the darkness.

"Well, what do we have here?" Casey's growl was unmistakable. "It's like a motherfucking convention for you sons of bitches."

Seconds later, the brothers crested the landing at the top level of the train depot with me only one set of stairs behind, blade in hand. When I finally caught up, I walked into a vast and open space, able to see the entire floor in one view. What inhabited that space was precisely what we had come in search of. Kierson's source was both reliable and accurate.

Hundreds of disheveled and crazed-looking Breathers stood in a wall formation before us. Casey stood paces in front of us, separating us from them and baiting them intently. He wanted a war, and it seemed that, if he continued his antics, he was sure to get one.

Drew, sensing the tension, kept me sheltered behind him, the twins flanking him tightly, but I could see all that was happening through the small spaces between their bodies.

"So, we hear you assholes have gone rogue as of late . . . not a wise choice," Casey chided. "Not very smart at all. But why would I expect anything less from you leeches?"

"Casey!" Drew called out sharply.

"They look extra hungry, don't they, Drew? That would make them a liability, would it not? And aren't we supposed to take out liabilities?" Casey taunted, his tone clearly displaying how much he was enjoying what the evening promised him.

Drew whispered something to the twins before looking over his shoulder at me.

"Stay here. Don't move. Anything comes at you, kill it, then run to the car." He handed me the keys. "You know how to unlock it?"

"Yes."

"Good. Run there. Lock it behind you and wait for us."

Without awaiting my response, the three of them advanced slowly on the horde, fanning out as they did until they met Casey. I stared at the Breathers, whom I could now see more clearly. All had their gazes firmly locked on my brothers—the clear and present danger in the room.

Then one turned his hollow eyes on me.

They widened instantly, and I could see his breathing increase while he licked his lips. As if that were a sign to all the others, they too fixed their stares on me, behaving exactly as the first Breather had. Seeing their change in behavior, the brothers all drew their weapons.

"Drew," Kierson called out, seeking instructions from his commander. He knew what was coming. He had seen it before.

"Steady . . ." Drew answered, surveying the posse poised to strike at any second. "We came to talk, to warn you about the one who was taken out last night. If you want to live, then stand down."

That same crackle of energy I had felt around him before spread through the room, but the effects were not the same as they had been before. The Breathers' eyes never left me, as if Drew had not addressed them. As if my brothers did not exist at all.

Those eyes were on me and me alone.

And they were coming.

10

I could see their attack with infinite clarity, as though their movements were slower and far more deliberate than they should have
been. When Drew looked back at me, yelling at me to run, he too
seemed to move at an unusual speed. I heard his order, the words falling on my ears with authority, but there were just so many Breathers
to fight. My brothers surely could not have fought them all.

That reality gave me pause.

An audience of one, I watched the wave of Breathers crash upon the
four warriors that stood between me and impending doom. I did not
run. I did not flinch. Instead, I stood stoically, knowing that if my fate
was to die that night, then I would in a way befitting my heritage—I
would die fighting. Perhaps I would even prove my father's theory
wrong. Maybe my actions would return me to the Underworld after all.

But the wave didn't reach me, not immediately, at least. Instead,
I watched my brothers fight with a lethal elegance, cutting through
the throats of the enemy easily, one after the next. Blood rained down
upon them, but they never faltered, their mission clear. They had a
threat to remove, and they would do so without fail. It was a morbidly
beautiful sight to behold.

"Khara!" Drew roared, his voice cutting through the cacophony
of battle and death. "*Run!*"

His words compelled me in a way they had not before, and I
found myself turning to do just as he bade me. Unfortunately, my

timing was poor, and I made it no farther than two steps before I felt a cold hand clamp down tightly on the back of my neck, flinging me around violently to face its owner.

"So sweet . . ." he breathed, pulling my face toward his. I felt paralyzed for a moment, staring blankly into his icy gray eyes, as though I wanted to freely give him what he intended to take.

"Khara!" Kierson screamed from across the room, having seen my captive state. His words were enough to free me from whatever trance had enthralled me. I felt my hand grip the hilt of the blade tighter.

"You should rethink this," I whispered, continuing to stare into his dead eyes, though no longer feeling the pull they had possessed.

"So sweet . . ." he repeated, licking his lips in anticipation.

"Wrong answer," I said, my tone laced with the indifference I felt.

Just as Kierson had taught me, I sank the dagger blade deep into his throat, withdrawing it with a twist. His body fell heavily to the floor, icy blood spraying me as it did. Whatever this strange being whose blood was as cold as the dead's was, I hovered over it, remorseless, wondering what had infected its mind so thoroughly that it could not see reason, nor impending doom, in my brothers' presence. Attacking my brothers and me appeared to be suicide, yet each Breather did it with fervor—marching to their death in an attempt to reach me.

I looked up to see how the others were faring against the force of the PC, but I was not afforded much time to do so. Several other Breathers had breached the wall that my brothers had sought to establish and were on a direct course for me. I stared them down, wiping the blood of their fallen ally off my blade and onto my pants, just as I had seen Casey do so many times. As they approached, they slowed slightly, fanning out to encircle me. My only way out was to retreat back down the stairs.

But I would not run.

I looked them all over with sharp eyes, flipping the blade over and over in my hand.

"You will not succeed," I warned as I stood firmly, prepared to take them on.

"Neither will you," a voice rumbled low in my ear. "Not on your own." I hazarded a glance over my shoulder to find Oz there, his eyes assessing the impending danger. "You guys never told me you were going out to have fun tonight. I feel so left out."

He feigned a pout.

"I care not of your feelings, Oz," I retorted, returning my gaze to those who were preparing to attack.

"We'll discuss that later, new girl."

Before I could argue, the Breathers charged us, descending upon Oz and me simultaneously. With my blade at the ready, I steeled myself for the first blow, but it never came. What did come was the wash of cold blood running down my face, soaking my dark clothes. Oz had slain them all before they were even within my reach.

As if unsatisfied with the depth of his involvement, he then joined the brothers, taking out Breathers at an alarming pace. In what seemed to be less than a minute, the battle was won. The five of them stood staggered throughout the room, surveying the carnage to assure that none of the soulless survived.

"Clear over here," Kierson cried from deep within the room.

"Clear," Pierson echoed from my distant left.

After they affirmed their victory, Drew turned cold and angry eyes to me.

"I thought I'd made myself abundantly clear, Khara," he said, his voice rising with every step he took toward me.

"I cannot explain, but I could not go, Drew. I felt compelled to stay," I offered in my defense.

"You should have felt compelled to leave!" he shouted uncharacteristically. "Why should you have stayed? For what? To die?"

"If that was to be my fate, yes."

"She really is one crazy bitch," Casey scoffed, coming to stand beside Drew.

"It felt wrong to leave—like desertion. I did not wish to run like a coward. I do not fear death."

"Yes, yes, we know you don't fear death," Kierson cut in, walking toward me. "But for fuck's sake, could you tap into some basic self-preservation instincts? You just stood there and almost let him suck the life out of you!"

I looked at him and felt that strange tugging sensation at the corner of my mouth.

"Almost, Kierson. Almost." The smile I could not explain only grew. "But it seemed far more sensible to stab him in the throat, just as you taught me."

A look of unabashed pride erased the fear and concern from Kierson's face.

"I guess lesson number two will be how to deal with multiple attackers at once then. Seems like Oz might have saved your ass on that one."

"Oz interrupted me. Nothing more."

The fallen one appeared entertained by my assessment of what had happened. He pushed off the blood-spattered wall to come and join the conversation, a smug expression marring his face.

"So your contention is that I didn't save your ass?"

"To be saved implies that one was losing in the first place. I was not."

"Cocky, aren't we, new girl?" he mocked, circling me from behind like a hellhound sent to cow the damned. "Should we see how you fare next time without my aid?"

"There won't be a next time," Drew barked, stepping between us. "Khara is officially off the hunt."

"I'm curious, Oz," I said, turning around to face him. "Why save me at all?"

"Like I said before: I'll keep you around as long as it pleases me. For now, it does," he explained with an evil smile. "But tomorrow is a new day."

"Enough, you two," Drew shouted. "I'm tired of your cat-and-mouse games, and we have a pile of bodies to deal with, in case you hadn't noticed. I'd like to get this crime scene cleaned up and get out of here."

Not knowing how one would even begin to sterilize such a tainted place, I looked around, surveying the magnitude of cleanup that was necessary. It was formidable, to say the least. My initial estimate of one hundred Breathers was sorely inaccurate. It should have been pluralized. Hundreds—possibly a thousand—corpses lay strewn about the room. Some were beheaded entirely; others had their throats sliced clean across, leaving a macabre smile where no mouth had previously been. Blood pooled inches deep in sections of the room.

"What needs to be done?" I asked earnestly. I was not above helping remedy the mess I had helped create.

"Pierson," Drew called across the room to the brother that had not been standing with us. He, too, was assessing the carnage in his own analytical way. "Can you do it, or do I need to call in some help for this one?"

"The Specialist will not be needed. I require about fifteen minutes and complete concentration, though. Leave. I will get back on my own," he said, never looking at us. His mind was too involved with solving the puzzle before him.

"If you don't require our help, then we'll go. Meet us at the Tenth Circle when you are finished. It's closer by foot," Drew replied before glancing down at his own appearance. He then assessed the state of the rest of us. "One more thing, Pierson. Can you take care of this?" Pierson looked up to see Drew indicating our bloodied appearances. With a put-upon sigh, he closed his eyes and muttered something low and guttural. I felt the prickle of magic along my skin, and when I looked down to see if it had accomplished what Drew had hoped, I saw not a shred of evidence that we had just been in a bloody battle.

"Thank you," Drew called to him as we headed for the stairs.

Pierson never responded, only knelt at the far left of the blood pool and started mumbling something that I could not quite discern. Drew had said he dabbled in magic. If he was capable of clearing that scene alone while only slightly skilled, it made me wonder just what he could do under the tutelage of the right mentor. The thought was awe-inspiring.

"Let's go then," Drew ordered, leading the way down the stairs. Kierson tucked himself closely beside me while Casey and Oz took up the rear, weapons still drawn. Though it was doubtful, there was still a chance that others remained, hidden deep within the shadowy building. An ambush would have been an unwelcome end to our evening.

"We can train some more tomorrow," Kierson whispered in my ear while we descended the stairs. "You did good, but your hesitation made me nervous. Kill or be killed, Khara. Truer words have never been spoken."

"Maybe she needs a different training partner, Kierson. One that can ensure she knows not to give the enemy the upper hand. I don't think that's been your strong suit, historically speaking," Oz mocked from behind us.

"That's not what happened, and you know it, asshole," Kierson argued, stopping midway down the second flight of steps to face off against Oz. "And we are *not* going to do this right now, got it?"

"Here we go again," Casey muttered, pushing past us.

"Aw, that's cute, Kierson. Don't want your girlfriend to hear about your ball dropping?" Oz sneered, moving closer to us. "Seems she already knows the outcome of the situation. Should we tell her the details?"

"I misjudged a situation," Kierson said flatly, his tone eerily calm. I knew that voice. My father used it often just before he raged.

"You thought with your dick, and it would have gotten you killed if I hadn't stepped in."

"That's your interpretation of the situation."

"Oh, bringing out the big words now, are we? 'Interpretation' . . . that's five whole syllables. Did you hurt yourself with that one?"

I watched as Kierson's jaw flexed violently. His anger was reaching a fever pitch, and I knew that if Oz continued to do what he did best and pushed Kierson's buttons further, yet another war was about to break out that evening. It seemed that Drew had come to that same conclusion, and he stepped in between them.

"Not. Now," he growled, using that same commanding tone in his voice that had brought me to my senses earlier in the evening. He was truly compelling when he chose to be.

I could see Kierson fighting Drew's orders, but he succumbed to them eventually, turning away from Oz. He took my hand and pulled me along beside him, leading me out of the building. The gesture felt odd, but I allowed it. He seemed to find comfort in the contact.

"Do not give him what he wants, brother. He revels in the misery of others. If you continue to fall victim to his tactics, you will never find peace in his presence," I said softly as we stepped into the night.

"One of these days I'm just going to clock him right in the face. Jack up all that rugged handsomeness he has going on. He's such a fucking prick," Kierson ranted as we made our way to the car. I looked behind us to see if Oz was enjoying Kierson's frustration but was surprised to see that he was no longer there. Drew alone followed us.

"If you are insistent upon that course of action, please be certain that I am present," I said, looking up to see his irritated expression. "I should like to see it."

Even in his flustered state, Kierson could not restrain his elation at my comment—he smiled uncontrollably. Letting go of my hand, he placed that arm around my shoulders, pulling me tight against his body.

"I don't know what I did before you showed up, Khara, but I know that I have no intention of letting you leave now that you're here."

I was uncertain how to respond, so I remained silent. No one had ever declared their affection for me so freely. Would it hurt him if I disappeared in the night, either of my own volition or if taken by one of the potential evils hunting me?

I would miss him, I thought to myself.

The feeling surprised me greatly.

11

We congregated on and around the sofas on what I had grown to believe was the PC's level of the Tenth Circle and awaited Pierson's arrival. Drew looked agitated and unsettled, pacing a path back and forth through the middle of the seating area. I watched as he checked his phone incessantly. He was worried.

There was an air in the building I had never noticed before. It had always been seedy and lecherous even at the best of times, but on that night it held something else—something different—a warmth that invited me in.

"I'm going back there," Drew said finally, pulling me from my thoughts. The tension in his voice illustrated just how anxious he was. His eyes constantly returned to the cell phone in his hand. "It's almost eleven. He should have been here by now."

"He's fine," Kierson protested. "You need to chill out and let him do his thing. I would know if something had happened to him."

"Then what's taking him so long? We need to regroup and sort this mess out. Once we do, I'll have to report my way up the chain."

"He'll be here soon. I'm sure of it."

As if his words were prophecy, in walked Pierson, looking every bit his normal, serious self and then some. When his eyes fell on me, that expression darkened. He approached Drew, leaning in to speak directly into his ear. The two of them then made their way into the shadows that were normally home to Oz and his harem. Oz, however, was nowhere to be found.

"I wonder what they're talking about," Kierson muttered to himself before getting up slowly. "Wait here. This doesn't look good." With increasing speed, he made his way over to the other two, interrupting their private conversation. Pierson looked none too happy about it. Casey eventually stood up and went to join the group as well. Whatever was being discussed seemed to only escalate with his presence.

It was clear that they did not want me involved, so I sauntered over to the railing and focused my attention on the crowd below. It was larger than usual, the humans packed together so tightly that I could not understand how they moved at all, and yet they did— writhing together in a tawdry synchrony. It was like watching a pit of snakes from above. I was utterly hypnotized.

And then there was the hum. I felt, not heard, it, but it was plain all the same. It vibrated its way through me in a way quite different from the blasting music. It was a rhythm all its own, and it called to me.

Unaware of how much time had passed or of Kierson's presence beside me, I came back to myself when he touched my arm. He had apparently been calling my name several times before I responded.

"Khara?" he continued while I fully regained my senses.

"Not a word, Kierson," Drew barked as he approached us from behind.

"She deserves to know," Kierson argued, his sad gaze fixed on me.

"I deserve to know what?" I asked, turning to look at Drew. Casey and Pierson followed behind him, their faces equally grim.

"Kierson has spoken out of turn," Drew said calmly, his voice narrowly restraining the anger behind it. "We don't know that there's anything to be concerned about."

"Bullshit!" Kierson snapped. "They had a fucking picture of her, Drew. A close-up."

"That doesn't mean anything—"

"The hell it doesn't! You saw what happened the second they laid eyes on her tonight. It's the exact same thing that happened when Khara went hunting with me. It didn't seem odd that he went after her that night; he was completely out of his mind. But when you factor in what happened when she came into their view tonight, it is impossible to ignore the fact that something about her is making them act crazy."

"You think I have inspired this madness?" I asked, turning to Kierson. I wanted his opinion on the matter. The others may have chosen to overlook him, but I would not.

"I don't know . . . maybe. I can't figure out why. None of us can. But I just know that something about this isn't right."

"Khara," Drew started, his voice soft and patronizing. "I'm sure it's nothing to stress over. We just need to get some answers regarding the matter."

I saw the photo in question pinched between Drew's fingers and reached for it, gently plucking it from his grasp. Observing it carefully, it was plain to see that Kierson's concerns had merit. The picture had been taken the night I arrived at the house. The night Drew happened upon me.

"How could they have procured such a detailed photograph while I was inside the Victorian? The house is warded, as you've said—safe from intruders. How could one then get close enough to have taken this photo?" I asked, holding the evidence in my hand.

"We're going to sort all that out. It could mean nothing—"

"Or it could mean everything. You do not know."

"Possibly," he agreed, his features tightening even further. "Either way, it's not safe for you to come out until we know."

"But it may not be safe for me to stay home either. You do not know if the wards were indeed compromised to obtain that picture."

"They were not," Pierson countered.

"But you are not certain of this?"

His eyes narrowed, but he said nothing in response. For the first time since I had met him, there was a hint of doubt in his eyes.

"We're not certain of anything, Khara, but we can keep you in the house and make sure that one of us is always present in the unlikely event that the wards have been breached," Drew interjected.

"I will be kept prisoner," I stated plainly.

"No, you will be kept safe."

I stared at him, a wave of frustration crashing through me. My growing anger only fueled it further. My life had been lived entirely under the watchful eyes of others, and I was weary of it. Being mysteriously emancipated from the agreement that tethered me to my revolving pair of homes had given me a chance to exercise some measure of freedom—no matter how small—for the first time in centuries. I had not been aware of how badly my soul craved this until it was threatened by a couple of overzealous siblings and their need to protect me.

"Can we speak of nothing else?" I snapped uncharacteristically. "Every day I am bombarded by warnings of the evil and doom that are surely coming for me—the death that awaits me at every turn. I am tired of being the ward of others. It is enough. If I am to be trapped in this godforsaken place, then at least let me be so in peace until I can find a way to return to the Underworld on my own terms and no longer be your burden to bear."

I pushed myself off the railing and headed for the stairs. I had never felt such heated emotion as I did that night and was uncertain as to why it took me over as it did. I knew that my brothers were only looking out for my best interests, but it was overwhelming, and I felt suffocated by their concern. It was too much.

I wanted to be alone.

I wanted to follow the hum that beckoned to me.

"Khara!" Drew shouted, presumably chasing after me. I did not bother to look back.

"I will be at the bar if anyone should care to talk to me and not order me about," I yelled to them.

With every step I ventured away from my brothers, my mood worsened, festering like an open wound. I had assumed that leaving would alleviate my anger, but it did not. That is until the wave of bodies enveloped me. It cleansed me as I navigated through far more easily than before, as though the crowd was parting for me, and only me, in the most subtle way. By the time I broke free of it, my mood had lightened significantly. How ironic that I had chosen to find space from my brothers by immersing myself in the masses before coming to linger tightly alongside the bar.

I leaned back against it and watched. It was not only the club itself that felt different that evening but also the crowd. I could not quite place it, but there was an apparent depravity to it that had not been present before, not to that degree. The foulness that pulsated through the building only fed the humans' lascivious behavior. Try though I did, I could not look away from them. I felt their dark desires call to me.

Utterly mesmerized, I hardly noticed the voice calling from beside me, offering me a drink.

"You look thirsty," he said, speaking just loudly enough to be heard over the music.

I turned to find a man who appeared slightly older than me—by human standards. His eyes were nearly as dark as his raven hair, which was pulled back, away from his face, and affixed somehow at the base of his neck. Something about him made me want to continue to stare and assess him. His features were stunning, if not slightly imposing. They reminded me a little of Oz's—angular and harsh.

"I am fine, thank you," I finally replied, letting my eyes fall back on the vulgar spectacle before me. It took some effort to accomplish that task.

"They're hard to ignore, aren't they? The show seems to be considerably more interesting tonight. Perhaps something here is inspiring them."

I turned my attention back to him, about to dismiss his theory, but I stopped when my eyes met his. If the crowd had just held me in a trance, looking at him had broken it. As I stared into the depths of his gaze, he offered me a short glass full of amber-colored liquid. Intoxicated by his appearance or not, if it was whiskey, I was not about to drink it.

"What is it?" I asked, my skepticism impossible to hide.

"Tequila. You looked like you needed one."

"Does it taste like Jack Daniel's?"

He scoffed in response.

"Hardly. Pure gasoline tastes better than that," he explained, reaching the glass even closer to my hand. "But there's really only one way to know for sure."

I eyed his offering for a moment before accepting it, gently lifting the glass from his hand. Our fingers brushed lightly as I did, causing heat to run through me instantly. I looked up to see his eyes widen, his reaction a telltale sign that he felt it too. Without reservation, I threw back the contents of the glass as I had the night with Kierson. Instead of falling ill immediately, I felt a warm and welcome sensation course through my body. It made me realize why humans—and Kierson—were so fond of drinking.

"Better?" he asked, seeing the satisfied look on my face.

"Much."

"Another?"

"Yes."

He leaned over the bar, gaining the attention of the scantily clad woman nearest to us. She nearly floated toward him, as though no one else was there. His eyes must have had an equally intense effect on her. I turned away while he ordered, looking up toward the balcony where my brothers were deeply entrenched in their discussion. The thought of constantly rehashing all the things that could possibly be out to get me was exhausting; I saw no use in it. Though I tried repeatedly to make that point known, they only ignored me. I was glad to be away from them.

"Round two, my dear," he said, obscuring my line of sight with another glass. "Cheers."

He tapped his glass against mine, then drank it down. I returned the gesture. Again, that warmth ran through me, shedding my psychological burdens. His hand fell upon my arm, pulling me toward him gently.

"You seem quite enthralled with the dance floor. Should we go there?"

I felt my eyebrows rise in a suggestive way.

"The dance floor?"

Enjoying the expression on my face, he leaned in so close that our cheeks grazed one another's.

"Or we could go somewhere else."

"Khara!" Kierson shouted, breaking me away from the unknown man beside me. "There you are. Hey, I know you're super pissed and all, but you can't just wander off like that. Especially not now."

"I can't?" I volleyed back at him. "You all seem to have my future planned out for me. I saw no need to stay when it was so clear that my opinions were not wanted—my presence not needed. I found something else to occupy my time instead."

"Aw, c'mon. Don't be like that. I came to you the second I figured out that they had no intention of telling you about the photo."

"Is that what you did?"

"You know it is," he replied, a look of consternation on his face. "You get me, Khara. We make a good team. I came to you because I wanted you to hear it from me."

"So tell me, Kierson, what is it you've come down here to do?"

"I want you to come back up there with me," he countered, pointing up to the balcony.

"And if I refuse?"

"You won't." His words and smile were playful, as though his charms alone were enough to invite my compliance. Perhaps they were.

"Fine. I will come with you, but I do not wish to hear any more about my in-home incarceration."

"Deal."

I turned to excuse myself from my strange courtier's presence, but when I did I found that he had already left, having slipped away quietly. Kierson could appear intimidating to a human. Perhaps he assumed that we were something other than siblings.

Kierson's eyes drifted to the empty glass I still held, causing a wry smile to cross his face.

"Giving good ole JD another chance, are you?"

"Tequila," I corrected, placing the glass down behind me.

"Atta girl! Don't let a bad first time keep you down. You must forge ahead in the name of having a good time."

With his arm wrapped around my shoulders, he ushered me through the crowd and up to the others who awaited my return. With every step farther away from the mob, I felt the draw back to them even greater. I wanted to submerge myself in their carnal rhythm, wrapping it around me until I was fully engulfed. Being away from it felt wrong in every way possible.

"Khara," Drew started as I approached him and the others, his tone apologetic.

I put my hand up to stop him before he could continue.

"You needed me?"

"Yes," he replied, his brow furrowed slightly. "Take a seat."

I did as he asked, sitting at the end of the couch nearest to the railing that separated me from the place I wanted to be.

"Have you calmed yourself down?" His tone was not unkind, though it carried authority. Had I said no, I do not think he would have been pleased.

"I am fine," I muttered, my eyes drifting off toward the balcony's ledge. "You can thank the man who purchased the two glasses of tequila I drank for that."

"You're drunk?"

"No. I am content."

"Good," he replied, eyeing me cautiously. "Then we can continue working out the details of your—"

His words delicately washed over my mind. I paid them no attention. Instead, the music that I would have normally found offensive sang to me, and I soon found myself lulled into a trance. With eyes closed, I fell back against the dark leather sofa, letting that warm sensation I had felt only minutes earlier bathe me.

"Khara? Khara?" I could hear Drew's calls, his persistence annoying me. I refused to answer him.

"I wouldn't bother her, Drew," Kierson interjected. "She just slammed those hefty tequila shots. Considering her lightweight status, I think our sister is in the throes of passing out."

"She looks high, not drunk," Pierson corrected from somewhere in the distance.

"Well, I didn't see her hitting the bong at the bar, but anything is possible in this place."

"Maybe someone slipped her something," he countered, starting an entirely new debate amongst them. Their incessant chatter was maddening, and I once again found myself wanting nothing more than to escape it.

Right at that moment, as if on cue, something moved me. Not physically, as the thought implied, but internally—ethereally. The bass pulsating through the building pushed me to my feet while a haunting voice drew me forward toward the railing and nearer to the writhing bodies below. The growing need to be with them was insurmountable.

"Seriously, can somebody please explain what's gotten into her?" Drew demanded, his voice barely audible over the music that beckoned to me. The irony of his question was not lost on me when it was finally answered.

It was never a matter of what had gotten into me.

It was a matter of what was about to be let out.

12

My body swayed gently at first as I closed my eyes and tossed my head back. I shook my hair loose from its binding, letting the mass of waves crash over my shoulders before tossing it around wildly. I felt free— truly free—for the first time in my life, and I wanted nothing more than to bottle that feeling and keep it with me forever, however long that might prove to be.

Suddenly, I felt restricted by my clothing, the tight nature of my shirt offending me. I sought to remove it as quickly as possible. I wanted to tear it off with my bare hands, but the fabric would not yield, so I yanked it up over my head as quickly as I could. The blast of air on my bare chest was exhilarating, and I paused in a state of half undress to enjoy the sensation.

The commotion behind me was an annoyance, a buzzing sound that served only to make me want to escape them faster. With one more tug, I was free of the strappy black tank that bound me, and my hair landed lightly against the skin of my back, tickling it slightly. The sensation was heavenly. I heard their voices rising, but I pushed the noise aside while I climbed the railing of the balcony. All I wanted to do was lean over and let the music carry me away. I had no worries, no cares—no inhibitions. The single thing that mattered to me was the call of the crowd below and the motion of my body.

Gathering my hair up in my arms, I turned my back to the mob I was soon to join, giving my brothers a final glance before I leaned back, ready to fall in a graceful dive. But I went nowhere. I saw Oz lunge for me, his arms catching me around my waist and legs. His grip was violently tight when he pulled me back to the floor on which he stood.

"What the fuck are you doing?" he snarled at me, forcing my arms into his jacket, dressing me frantically. I had no answer for him. I simply stared in response.

"What's going on, Oz?" Kierson shouted over the raging music.

"We need to leave. Now," he replied, shoving me in front of him. My footing was unstable as he felt it necessary to half push and half carry me out of the Tenth Circle, not waiting for my brothers' approval of his decision. They sounded less than pleased with Oz's rough handling of me and saw fit to tell him that as he continued, unfaltering on his course.

But they did not attempt to stop him.

"Oz," Drew said, his voice carrying a hint of warning. "Explain yourself."

"I can stop to explain this to you, or we can get her out of here unharmed," he said, grinding to a halt. "Which would you prefer?"

"Move!" Drew ordered without skipping a beat.

The brothers fell into formation around me and collectively we crashed through the crowd with the precision of an army, never slowing. Oz's harem of usual whores looked utterly abandoned as we barreled past them in our escape.

"If anyone comes near her, kill them," Oz said sharply.

"Why?" Pierson asked as he kept pace, flanking my right side.

"Because she just announced what she is to a veritable den of evil."

His answer proved to be more befuddling than enlightening, given Pierson's expression, but he questioned Oz no further. None of them did. For the first time since I had met them all, they respected both him and his authority. I was unsure how to interpret such a sudden shift, but my mind didn't linger on that long. The only puzzle it wanted to solve was how best to evade my captors and return to the call of the crowd.

The stairs to the street were taken at record pace and in total silence. For whatever reason, Oz's statement was taken at face value. I knew that answers were imminent, but not to be offered at that moment. Their first priority was once again my safety, though it seemed debatable as to what I was being kept safe from. To them, every evil entity within the city of Detroit was likely to be after me, a conversation that I had grown tired of having. What they were incapable of grasping was that I was raised in the Underworld—tempered in evil. Barring the Dark One who took me from my home, I'd never found the presence of malice to be cause for concern. Why being above, on terra firma, would so grossly change this fact was inexplicable to me.

My brothers did not appear to share my sentiments.

As we broke free of the building and made our way to the Suburban in continued silence, my curiosity became unbearable. Whatever epiphany Oz had thought he had had at the baring of my body was nonsensical to me. He ruined my feeling of freedom, and for no reason apparent to me. That realization is what tipped my scale from curiosity to anger.

"Get in," he snapped at me, pushing me into the back of their monstrous vehicle. He got in directly behind me, coming to sit practically on top of me. The others filed in around us, with Drew in the driver's seat.

"Will the house be safe enough?" he asked, looking over his shoulder to Oz.

"As far as I know, your wards should hold against anything that might follow us," Oz said tightly. "But until we arrive there, she isn't safe. We need to get her back to where she can be protected easily."

"And why this sudden urgency from you to keep her safe?" Casey asked from a seat behind us. "She is born of the PC—one of ours, not yours. And I am not convinced that she does not possess that which makes us lethal and hard to kill, even though she seems unable to call upon it easily."

"She may be born of Ares, making her PC, but that shared blood that courses through your veins and binds you together is not the cause of her danger. It is the blood you do not share that does."

"Her mother . . ." Drew whispered, now driving intolerably fast through the city.

"Yes," Oz ground out as though it pained him to answer.

"Am I missing something here?" Kierson asked, leaning over me to look at Oz. "Why are you totally freaking out about this? What exactly did she do to have you thinking she's set off all kinds of alarms? So she flashed her tits at the bar—what's all the excitement for? I mean, they were nice and all but—"

"She's your *sister!*" the others shouted in chorus.

"I know, I know!" he yelled, cringing away from me. "It's easy to forget that sometimes."

"Well, start remembering," Drew warned.

Oz snorted in obvious frustration.

"You want to know why her flashing her tits at the bar was basically as good as putting her head in a noose?" he growled, before unzipping my borrowed coat and turning me to face him. He sheltered my chest with his body, pulling me close so that the others—especially Kierson—could not see it. "Because the second she pulled her shirt up over her head, she exposed her secret, which she then quickly displayed for all below to see." As we pulled into the driveway of the house, he slid the coat off my shoulders. Running his hand through my hair, he collected it all before sweeping it up to bare my back to the brothers. His touch was surprisingly gentle. I could not see their faces, only Oz's chest as it pumped rapidly, his breath coming hard and fast. "These are why we had to leave."

I felt his finger trail along my left shoulder blade, then the right.

"What are they?" Kierson asked, with childlike awe.

"The question is not what they *are*, Kierson," Oz said, clearly annoyed. "The question is what are they *for*."

"They aren't scars?" Casey asked.

"No," Oz replied grimly.

I heard movement from behind me as yet another brother pressed closer to look at what I could not see.

"Wings . . ." Pierson whispered. "They are for *wings*. But how? They're so faint. They look nothing like your markings, Oz."

"And that is why she needed to get out of there as quickly as possible," he stated, sounding as disgruntled as ever. "Her markings are not like mine, because she and I are nothing alike." His body tensed, his grip on me tightening. "My wings unfolded long ago, but hers have never seen the light of day." Pausing yet again, he seemed unable to say the words he needed to. His disbelief was plain. "She is not a Light One, as I am . . . or was. She is *Unborn*."

13

"What is the meaning of 'Unborn'?" I asked when I heard the collective gasp echo throughout the vehicle at the mere mention of what I was.

"An angel who has not yet birthed its wings," Oz said, pushing me away from him to speak to me directly. His gaze only faltered momentarily, taking in my state of exposed flesh. "There has not been such a creature earthbound in centuries," he continued, zipping up the coat he had given me. He looked away as he did. "They cannot survive on their own. Without their own kind to protect and raise them, guiding them through their metamorphosis, they perish."

"So I am an oddity?" I asked plainly.

"Not an oddity—an *impossibility*." His tone was flat, but there was something in his eyes—a sadness. A disbelief.

"I cannot be an impossibility, for here I sit in front of you, as real as anyone else in this vehicle."

"But the Unborn are children. You are not a child," he said, his own confusion growing. "And they haven't set foot on Earth in longer than I can remember, primarily because they evoke the response that the Breathers had toward you. To them, there is no tastier morsel."

"Inside," Drew barked from the front seat, his unease with the situation growing. "I want her inside quickly. We can sort this out from there."

Without pause, Oz jumped out of the SUV and quickly disappeared around the side of the house. The others unloaded me from the car and whisked me through the front door, all on high alert for anything strange that could pose a threat. Oz was still nowhere to be seen.

They searched the house, all calling out "clear" when they felt their area was secure. While they did, I stood alone in the middle of the living room, trying to make sense of what I had learned. The others no longer viewed me as Khara, but instead they saw me as a thing—one that required a label. This revelation only fueled their paranoia.

Amid the ruckus around me, a lone low voice called out to the group, halting them all instantly with a single realization.

"Her mother is an angel," Casey said slowly. "And her father is Ares."

I watched as the four of them descended upon me, staring at me intently. They all turned a shade paler than normal.

"Her eyes," Pierson whispered, taking a fraction of a step closer to me. He reached out and cupped my chin in his hand gently, angling my face up to the light to analyze the emerald shade of my gaze. "How did we not see the resemblance sooner?"

His question fell unanswered as they all gaped at me with blank faces.

"We have to call him," Drew uttered. "Now." The four of them silently shared grim expressions at Drew's words until Oz's gruff voice broke the heavy quiet surrounding us.

"The perimeter of the house is clear," he reported, coming down the stairs. "The neighborhood is clean, too. I did a quick sweep just to be sure we were not followed . . ." His voice trailed off as he took in the sight before him: four solemn warriors staring deep into my eyes. "What's going on?" he asked, stepping closer to me. "And who is it you have to call?" When no one answered him, he moved toward them slowly, coming to stand by my side, his arm grazing mine. "I don't like having to ask twice, Drew. Who do you have to call?"

He was unable to mask the growing irritation in his voice. I imagined he did not like being uninformed of things, nor was he used to being so. Yet there he stood beside me, his ignorance only fueling his anger until it was virtually palpable. He, like me, was in the dark.

And he was not pleased by it.

"Sean," Casey finally replied after acknowledging that Oz would not let the issue go. Oz tensed at the name. "She is his sister. His *true* sister."

"Fuck," Oz sighed.

Casey smirked at his response, something about it amusing him greatly.

"That's exactly what he's going to say when he finds out."

I took refuge in my underground sanctuary, not wanting to listen to the one-sided conversation that was taking place in the living room above anymore. I had only heard of Sean once, on the night I arrived in Detroit, but, even from that brief mention, I could tell he was highly esteemed by the others, if not feared by them. That thought weighed on me. I did not need another overprotective brother in my life, so I was less than enthused about having to potentially meet one.

Stretching myself across my borrowed bed, I lay in the darkness and waited for the chaos to pass. Eventually my mind wandered off, wondering how Father was and if Persephone had indeed been taken back to him in the Underworld when I had been removed from it. Their relationship perplexed me—such passion and such hatred. It was impossible to make sense of his desire for someone who despised him so, and yet he pined for her desperately in her absence. If my abduction led to a breach of the agreement, she would be forced to stay with him permanently. He would be elated. She would be inconsolable.

Before I could contemplate matters further, the basement door opened, spilling light into my shadowy home.

"We need to talk to you before he gets here," Drew said from the top of the stairs, his silhouette framed beautifully by the brightness behind him. "Prepare you, as the case may be."

"Prepare?"

"Yes. There are things about the PC that you still do not know. I think it will help make your meeting go as smoothly as possible if we inform you of them beforehand."

"Smoothly?"

Drew sighed lightly, descending a few steps before answering.

"Sean can be . . . *tricky*, Khara. He is guarded, in much the same way as you are, but I imagine your reasoning for that quality is vastly different than his."

"Understood," I replied, making my way up the stairs to join him. Before I could walk through the door, Drew stopped me by placing a gentle but firm hand upon my shoulder.

"He gave nothing away on the phone, but I don't think this news has pleased him. His tone was cool and unreadable, which is never a good sign with him. He will be here soon. In the meantime, I need you to know that no harm will befall you."

"You have said as much before, Drew. There is no reason for me to doubt you in your promise. Your honor is plain. It is a part of who you are. Fear not, brother, for I feel none."

The smile that perplexed and pleased me grew wide across his face. Try though I did, I could not look away from him when he wore it.

"Well then, sister . . . he will be here shortly. Let me give you a crash course in all things Sean."

14

My brother's words rang true in my mind the second Sean set foot in the house. Everything about him screamed power, danger, and vengeance. His soulless black eyes pierced mine, looking for something that I was not sure they could find. But that apparently would not stop him from trying.

Kierson seemed agitated by his presence, fidgeting mindlessly beside me with the hilt of his dagger as the dark-eyed one approached. Casey and Pierson remained on the couch while Drew stepped forward to greet Sean—their brother. Their leader.

"This is Khara," Drew said, extending an arm toward me. I stepped forward so Sean could examine me more closely.

"And how did you come upon her again?" Sean asked, still standing feet away from me.

"I nearly killed her," Drew admitted with a hint of sadness in his voice. "At first, I mistook her for an Empty. My surprise by her appearance forced me to action, but once I touched her I knew."

"An Empty? How interesting," he said, his words devoid of emotion. "Remind me again, why this is the first I'm hearing about any of this." His expression was pleasant, but it was a ruse. To me, it belied his true irritation.

"I knew that things had been taxing for you out on the East Coast. I did not wish to burden you with something that we had under control for the time being."

"Implying that it is no longer under control."

"No. There seem to be some complications."

"I see," he replied, turning his bottomless black eyes to me. "We can discuss your failure to report later, Drew." Everything about his delivery of that statement told me that Drew was not likely to enjoy that conversation. "Now, Khara," he said, looking at me. "Let me see if Drew's words are true, if you are indeed one of us."

Without hesitation, I advanced toward him, stopping only inches away. I looked up into his eyes and watched as he reached for my arm, his gaze never leaving mine. The second we connected, I felt it, and it was apparent that he did as well. His eyes slowly but unmistakably lightened to the very shade of my own and his expression softened. He knew then that what Drew had said was true. I was his sister.

"I can feel it. She is one of us . . ." His words carried an awe that I had only heard on rare occasion. It was beautiful.

"I am," I replied softly. "And above that, they say I am your true sister, both of us born of the same mother."

"And who is your mother, child?"

"I do not know for certain. I have never met her. She left me as an infant in the care of another. Drew and the others presume that she did this to keep me safe."

Sean growled.

"From Ares." He looked to the others momentarily, his eyes distant and harsh, but there was something else in them as well—pain. The kind of pain that only unwanted knowledge could bring. Father had that look often. "And with whom did she entrust you?"

"Demeter, goddess of the earth and harvest."

"And she has kept you hidden all this time?" he continued with dubious inflection. "How? How is that possible?"

"I do not know how. Our brothers concur that, because I am a daughter of Ares, I should not be—that my death would have been swift had Ares had any knowledge of my birth. But why would he search for something that he did not know to exist? Perhaps it was far easier to keep me safe than you imagine."

"But where did she keep you? Surely she did not hide you in plain sight. That would be madness, and I know that I have never come upon you before at her home."

"The woods. Somewhere deep in the woods where others rarely, if ever, ventured. Her earthly magic proved helpful in camouflaging me there," I explained. "And the rest of my time was spent in the Underworld."

His eyes blackened instantly.

"The Underworld?" he spat, his jaw clenching wildly. "How did you come to live where the damned roam free and torment reigns?"

"Through a transaction—a barter."

His nostrils flared.

"Explain. *Now.*"

"Hades agreed to take me in trade at Demeter's suggestion. It was the only way she could see Persephone. She thought if she were to provide him with a savory alternative to her daughter that he would release Persephone from her imprisonment in the Underworld. Demeter's plan did not work out as she had hoped, but Hades did agree to take me, for what purpose I still do not know. In bringing me to his realm, Demeter was granted six months of the year with her daughter. The other six she had me, a burden that she grew to despise over time. She always wished that Hades would have grown to desire me instead of her own child, and reminded me of that hope unrelentingly, but he did not. Persephone is his obsession, explainable or otherwise. He loved me as a father should love his child. Nothing more. Nothing less."

"Interesting that Persephone has never made that fact known," Sean muttered under his breath. He was perplexed by what I had told him.

"She could not have told you even if she had wanted to. Her knowledge of what had been done was not to be shared without great consequence, as I understand it."

"Fine, but then who would sanction such a depraved agreement? Surely it took more than Hades' compliance in this trade to bind you to the Underworld and demand Persephone's silence. An outside party would have been required."

"I do not know."

He exhaled with frustration. It appeared as though Sean was not used to being without the crucial information others were so often denied. A similarity he and Oz shared.

"Fucking Persephone," he growled, clenching his fists tightly. "Trouble is never far when she is involved." After exhaling slowly in an effort to calm himself, Sean continued. "It matters not. Not at the moment, anyway. I am more interested in sorting out who your mother is and how you came to be here."

"Agreed," Drew concurred, still by my side.

"How can we be certain that she is my true blood? Ares has only once mated with the same female twice to create particular progeny: Jerzyr and Jaysen. It would be uncharacteristic for him to have done so again. Do we know that you were born of an angel as you were told?"

"Khara," Drew prompted. "Let him see the markings."

I nodded, pulling my shirt up over my head while I turned to expose my back to Sean. I felt him delicately brush my hair aside before his fingers lightly traced along the silvery white lines etched into my skin.

"The Unborn," he whispered. I was not certain he knew the words had escaped until I answered him.

"Yes. Oz said that is what I am."

"She said I must find you," he continued without pause. "That you were not safe now. You, Khara. You are whom she spoke of. She was warning me about you." His voice was thick and heavy when he spoke, and I turned to see him staring at me, green eyes nearly glowing. "You truly are my sister."

"Who, Sean?" Drew asked softly from beside me. "Who said Khara was not safe?"

Sean's eyes softened in the slightest way.

"Her mother. *Our* mother."

"But I thought you'd never met her," Kierson inquired, confusion lacing his words.

"And I still have not, but I received her message nonetheless through another channel. A channel that I would never question. There was little doubt that it was her at the time, and there certainly is none now."

"So you do not know her either," I asked plainly.

"No. She abandoned me to Ares right after I was born."

A voice called from the stairs as Oz sauntered his way down to join the group. Sean bristled at the very sight of him.

"Well isn't that interesting," he drawled as he descended the last step.

"*Ozereus*," Sean uttered with utmost disdain. "I am uncertain what it is you find entertaining enough to drive you from your typical sullen solitude."

"And I am uncertain as to why you are devoid of emotion at the news of your twin. Not even an embrace for the newest member of the family? For shame . . . I guess some beings never change. You're just as cold and monstrous as ever."

"What did you say?" Sean asked. His voice was not tainted by anger as I would have expected it to be, given the warning I had received about his temper. Despite Oz's taunting, Sean's tone held nothing but disbelief.

"I said you're just as cold and—"

"I heard that part," Sean interrupted. The hostility that had been absent a second earlier found its way into his words.

"Oh . . ." Oz replied, a smug look of satisfaction overtaking his face. "You guys really don't know anything, do you?" His eyes drifted from Sean to me and then back again, scrutinizing us. "I'd say it's pretty clear you're siblings, but just how many angels do you think Ares has bedded? Do you think that's an easy task? He may have his charms, but I know for a fact that he has only screwed one in his lifetime, and she managed to only let that happen once. Not twice. So . . . that would make you twins, would it not? I'm surprised you couldn't tell, Sean; you like to think your powers of observation are above reproach. I guess you two lack that 'twin bond' thing that the boys have."

"How could you possibly know such a thing?" Drew asked, unable to wrap his head around this revelation. Judging by the brief silence Sean and I shared, we, too, seemed disarmed by the claim Oz had made.

"Because I'm as old as time," Oz sneered. "Older than any of you and privy to knowledge that you are not." He scanned the room, his eyes eventually falling on Sean. "Even you."

"If you know so much, then why did you not know of her existence?" Sean countered heatedly.

"Because even I do not know everything. I knew of their mating. I knew it produced a child—Ares' invincible pet." Oz spat his words as though the information they held had soured in his mouth. "But what I did not know—what none of us could have known—is that somehow your mother hid Khara away. For the life of me, I cannot imagine how she was able to accomplish such a task without being exposed."

"That is something we need to ascertain as soon as possible," Sean grudgingly added. "But there is still something off about this—something that does not add up." Sean's brow furrowed at something while he spoke, as if he couldn't quite piece the mystery together. "If it is true that Khara and I are twins, then she should be dead. Ares would have seen to that."

"That is what the others have said," I concurred, trying to assess Sean's expertly masked expression. "They said that if Ares had laid eyes on me, I would not have been permitted to survive."

A loud, hollow sound rang out through the living room when Sean slammed his hand through the wall.

"That lying bastard," he enigmatically growled, running his other hand through his dark waves. Agitation drove his movements, though I felt at a loss as to why.

"What is it, Sean?" Drew asked, stepping toward Sean, his body creating a barrier between my twin and me.

"Ares has always maintained that the second I left my mother's womb, she thrust my unwanted body into his arms. That she was horrified by what she had birthed. I may not have fully believed his story at the time, but any alternative scenario I conceived in my mind was just unfounded speculation. But now," he started, eyes fully fixed on mine. "He was lying. I know that because Khara is irrefutable proof of it. What she said is true: If Ares had laid eyes on her, she'd be dead."

"What is your point?" Pierson asked, moving toward us.

"My point is that Ares was not at my birth—he couldn't have been. The circumstances under which my mother left me with him were most certainly not as he said."

"Which then supports our theory that Khara's existence is completely unknown to him," Pierson added, his apparent interest in the conversation growing. His analytical nature could not resist the puzzle that Sean and my birth provided.

"Precisely."

"But necessitated the help of others to keep it that way," Casey called out from the couch.

"Perhaps," Oz added. "But wouldn't the simplest way to keep her safe have been to not tell anyone else about her at all and stash her away unaided? Why risk telling even one other living soul—trusted or otherwise? And why abandon her to whatever fate would befall her? Does that make sense? Are those the actions of a loving mother?"

"For most, going against the likes of Ares alone would be insanity under even the best of circumstances. To do so when you're a target in his sights would be suicide. A Light One would not stand a chance against such a maniacal individual."

Oz's eyes narrowed tightly at Sean's words.

"And why do you assume that she was of the Light, *Sean*?" he asked, saying his name like it was poison on his tongue. Either Oz's tone or the sentiments it suggested earned him Sean's hand wrapped tightly around his throat.

"Don't you dare question her purity, *Ozereus*. I let you live once; I will not be so generous a second time."

"You flatter yourself, old friend. My survival then was never in question."

"Then let us now consider it officially debatable . . ."

"You think she was a Dark One," I said quietly while the two postured before me. The thought had only just crossed my mind. Father had long said that I was not built for the darkness of his realm, but perhaps he had been mistaken. Maybe that was precisely where I belonged.

"She wasn't," Sean snapped.

"And you are certain of that how? You never knew her, and Ares has always alluded to that fact, has he not?"

"I know because Ares is the greatest manipulator this world has ever seen. I know because if she had been Dark, there would be no goodness in me. And I know because, if she had been what you dare accuse her of being, I would have turned out just as my father had wanted—a soulless killing machine."

"That isn't what you are?" Oz prodded. "Strange. That's all I seem to remember."

"I've changed," Sean snarled.

Oz smiled widely, though his throat was still being crushed by Sean's ever-tightening grip.

"So I see."

"Listen," Casey called out as he lazily pushed off the couch. "As much as I would enjoy the bloodbath your epic fight would surely bring, I feel like this tangent isn't going to go anywhere productive and I'm over it. Can we get back to the issue at hand? If not, I'm going out to kill something."

"I agree, Casey," Drew interjected. "At least about getting back to the major problem here. We need to know as much as possible about

Khara's current status, and quickly. If her life is in even greater danger because of what she is, rectifying that should be our top priority."

"How does the knowledge of what I am put me in any more danger than I have been in since I arrived?" I asked, uncertain as to how that distinction had been made.

"Because there are perils beyond those that accompany being on the wrong side of Ares, new girl. The Unborn are susceptible to evil," Oz said calmly, his throat still held captive, though Sean's grip had loosened slightly. "Highly susceptible."

"Nonsense. I would never have survived the Underworld if that were true." I dismissed his words easily, questioning how Oz could be so naïve.

"Not all evil is attracted to the Unborn. Most wouldn't recognize what you were. In fact, the Underworld may have been one of the safest places for you to be. Even if the right kind of evil was present there, they would not be there of their own volition. They would be prisoners—the damned—making them powerless, and, beyond that, Hades would never have allowed them near you, from what you have said. You likely would have never been exposed to them."

"And now?" Sean prompted, his eyes still dark and foreboding. It was apparent that he did not wish to receive any kind of aid from Oz, but knew no other option.

"And now she does not have that luxury. She is vulnerable here. Especially *here*."

"Why?" Kierson asked, stepping in to flank me on my other side. It was an act of protection, though from what I was uncertain. "We can keep her safe from whatever comes our way. Nothing in this city would dare challenge us."

"Wouldn't they?" Oz volleyed back at him. Sean seemed less than pleased by his question and slammed him against the wall, Oz's throat still firmly in his grip. "Haven't they already?" Kierson looked thoughtful for a moment, taking in Oz's implication. "I would not

rest on your authority being enough to dissuade an attack on her—
another attack, that is. The second you become the least bit compla-
cent, she will fall. It's that simple."

"Attack?" Sean rumbled. "What attack?"

Drew sighed heavily.

"There was an incident two nights ago while Kierson was on
patrol. A Breather went rogue."

"Interesting. Please tell me how that turns into an attack on
Khara." Though his words were well-mannered, there was nothing
polite about his tone. Fury was building deep within Sean, and, if not
soon appeased, it would be unleashed on us all. I had borne witness
to it many times when in the presence of the powerful ones that my
father employed. A pretty sight it was not.

"We wanted to be sure it was an isolated incident, so we took to
the streets to do some investigating. Kierson came up with a tip. We
followed it . . ."

"To an old building full of Breathers poised to go rogue," Kierson
added. "There had to be about three hundred of them."

"Try eight hundred," Pierson corrected. "I counted the corpses
before I disposed of them."

"Of course you did," Kierson sighed.

"Three hundred or eight hundred, I don't care; what I do care
about is how all of them congregating in a shitty, old building equates
to a battle," Sean growled, his anger thinly contained while he looked
over his shoulder to stare our brothers down.

"Casey got there first and got them riled up," Kierson explained.
"When the rest of us got to the floor where they were all hiding out,
it seemed like a battle was inevitable."

"I think you're forgetting one small detail, brother," Pierson interjected. "At the time, we did not put it together—the violence escalated
far too quickly to take stock of what initially set it off. In hindsight,
we think there was a clear trigger for their actions."

His eyes drifted to me in an accusatory fashion. Sean's eyes followed.

"She was there?" His expression contained a strange combination of disbelief and rage.

"Had we known that she had anything to do with what was going on, we would never have brought her," Drew told him, his tone guilt-ridden.

"She should never have been there in the first place!" Sean roared, the volume of his voice shaking the glass vase on the mantel. He released Oz to turn and face Drew, allowing the full brunt of his anger to assail him.

"She is a born warrior, same as you," Drew countered. "How else could she be trained? We thought we were walking her into a controlled situation that would amount to little more than a Q&A session with a handful of strung-out Breathers. We could not have foreseen what took place."

Sean was in Drew's face before I could process his movement.

"The message I was sent by our mother was abundantly clear. Her life is in imminent danger. And you decided to walk her into the enemy's lair and serve her up on a platter for them."

"Had you shared the information from that message with the rest of us, perhaps this could have been avoided," Drew said, his voice soft but defensive.

"And if you had shared your information regarding her existence with me, it would have been." Sean's black eyes were swallowing Drew whole, and I had no doubt that his wrath would soon be upon him. Looking on, I felt a strange, growing need to intercede. I did not wish to see harm come to Drew for his actions.

"I insisted they take me," I informed Sean, stepping forward to steal his gaze away from the brother I'd known to be both loyal and noble. "I was adamant. They did all they could to prepare me before we embarked on the mission. They sheltered me from all they could when things took a turn for the worse. Drew told me to run, but I was insubordinate. I chose to stay."

Sean's menacing demeanor softened for a moment, his black eyes speckled with flecks of emerald.

"Why?" he asked, his voice only a whisper.

"I did not wish to abandon them. If death was destined to find me, it would. I chose to fight it on my own terms."

"So you stayed and fought?"

"Yes. I killed one Breather. Oz interrupted my attempts to kill several others."

The mention of Oz's name erased any shade of green from his piercing eyes, which quickly shot up and across the room to where Oz remained, standing against the wall Sean had pinned him to only moments earlier.

"You were there?"

"I showed up late to the party, but I wasn't properly invited in the first place, so it was really more of a party-crashing."

"And yet you had no idea that she was the cause of this. You let one of your own kind—your most precious—walk into a den of those primed to turn her?"

"I did not know what she was at that time." Oz ground his response out through gritted teeth.

"Liar," Sean spat as he coiled to attack Oz again.

"I am many things, Sean, but a liar is not one. I did not know what she was," he maintained, steadying himself for the attack he knew he was destined for. "Had I known, I would have taken her from this city the second I saw her, but I couldn't."

"And why not?" Sean demanded.

"Because Light Ones—fallen or not—cannot sense the Unborn. That ability was long ago taken from us." Something flashed through Oz's eyes as he said those final words to Sean. Regret? Sadness? I could not tell. "The fastest way for evil to obtain that which they sought was to use a veritable divining rod. That's what we were. Our ability to recognize the Unborn was the very reason so many were lost." The distant look in his eyes faded back to a hateful stare in an instant. "As I said a moment ago, there is evil scattered about this city that would love nothing more than to corrupt her in one way or another. Keeping her safe will be difficult, if not impossible, in the long term. The margin for error is miniscule."

"Then we won't slack off. That's not a problem," Kierson stated as though his response was the obvious solution.

"Says the man who can't keep his dick in his pants long enough to finish a sentence," Oz mocked.

I could feel Kierson tense beside me, his fist clenching violently.

"Nothing will happen to her on my watch. You can bank on that."

"Nothing will happen to her on any of your watches," Sean quickly corrected. "Because she isn't staying here. I'm taking her somewhere safe." He moved to take my arm, and I took a step back. The movement shocked everyone, most of all me.

"I want to stay."

"Khara," Sean started, his eyes as green as the grass I had longed to see in person. "You can't see that as a logical option. Your mother—our mother—said you had to be found. That you weren't safe. Her words could not be more true."

"Your concern is appreciated, brother, but I am as safe here as I will be anywhere," I protested diplomatically. "Unless you can get me to the Underworld to my father, this is where I wish to stay." I felt the words "with my family" press against the tip of my tongue, begging to be released. I did not let them pass my lips. My choice to stay had been shocking to everyone present, their expressions betraying them all. Surely these unspoken words would have only added to their shock.

"Khara—" he started, his tone soft before I cut it off entirely.

"On this, I will not bend. If you should choose to try and remove me by force, you will succeed only in the short term. I will find my way back. I am far more resourceful than any of you give me credit for."

"Sean is right about this," Drew added, supporting his brother's decision.

"Perhaps he is, but I am willing to take my chances."

"She really is bat-shit crazy, isn't she?" Casey declared from his post. "I think she might be growing on me."

Sean exhaled heavily before muttering something under his breath about stubborn women being the death of him. It made me question exactly what other female would be brazen enough to go against his orders. Sean hardly seemed the type that would tolerate dissension well. Perhaps because I was his sister he afforded me latitude that he might not allow others.

"You really do want to stay here, don't you?" he asked me, rubbing his forehead between his thumb and forefinger. "Then you may stay. For now. There is less danger for you on the seacoast, but the boys are so bogged down with other dilemmas that keeping proper watch over you might fall lower on the priority list than I would like. At least here, attention to the urgency of the situation will not wane anytime soon. You guys will guard her accordingly. And that includes you, too, Oz."

"And why is she suddenly my responsibility?" he asked, his expression the epitome of annoyance.

"Because she is one of *your* kind, Ozereus," Sean boomed. "And because I say she is your responsibility."

"Your words mean nothing to me; neither do your orders. I am not one of your lackeys to command."

"Do not push me, Ozereus," Sean rumbled in warning.

"Your threats are tiring, and I have somewhere to be," Oz said dismissively, walking toward the front door. "You guys can figure out how to clean up this fucking mess while I'm gone. Let me know when you find a solution."

The slamming of the front door as Oz exited echoed through the living room where my brothers and I stood, staring at one another. They looked a mixture of confused, concerned, and, in Casey's case, entertained. It was not until Oz was long gone that the most simple yet obvious question came to me. Silence still permeating the air around us, I broke it with a single inquiry.

"If the concern is that the Unborn are susceptible to evil, and I am still Unborn, then would it not be easiest to make it so I was no longer one of them?"

Pierson caught my eye, his gaze narrowing as he contemplated the scenario put forth.

"What are you getting at, exactly?"

"Simply put, if the Light Ones are angels who have been made or born, as Oz earlier implied, should we not seek the solution to the problem there? Have me become one of them?"

"Could it be that simple?" Pierson murmured.

"It could be, but I'm pretty sure that even you and all your brainpower wouldn't know how to do it," Kierson said condescendingly.

"I may not know, but I'm quite sure that a Light One would. Perhaps even our very own Light One, who is inconveniently not here at the moment," Pierson retorted.

"Casey," Sean snapped. "Hunt Oz down. Bring him back here. Now." His eyes narrowed at Casey before he delivered his final order. "And don't return without him. Khara is not leaving this house until we know the way to correct this situation."

"With pleasure," Casey replied, brushing past me on his way to the door. Just before he closed it behind him, he stuck his harshly angled face back into the house. "And Sean? I'm assuming you don't care what condition he's in when I bring him back, do you?"

"As long as he can still talk, I don't care one bit," Sean replied, a cruel smile creeping across his face as he did.

Casey wore one to match.

"Then I won't be long."

I wondered if Oz was as predictable as I expected him to be. Would Casey only have to go as far as the Tenth Circle to find him? Undoubtedly draped with the barely clothed women desperate to give him anything he desired and more? If that were true, Casey would be back as quickly as he intended to be. Somehow, though, I could not escape the feeling that we were wrong, and it perplexed me. I had never had such a feeling in the depths of me seek to overthrow the thoughts in my head. For reasons I could not fathom, I knew that Oz was up to something. I just didn't know what or why.

"Don't worry, Khara," Kierson whispered, wrapping his long arm around my shoulders. "Oz is wrong. We *can* keep you safe—from anything."

"I feel as though I am the only one here unafraid for my well-being."

"That's because you are," Drew replied in earnest.

"And I feel as though the few women in my life are hell-bent on getting themselves killed," Sean added, the hard line of his brow softening slightly as he spoke. "I don't suppose I could be lucky enough for you to have also been born with my invincible nature?"

I looked at him incredulously, making him aware with that single glance that my situation was not that fortunate. I'd been harmed badly enough in my time to know that I was far from invincible.

"I see," he replied tightly. "I did not hold much hope for that to be the case. It seems that we have not evolved into the same beings. You do not appear to harbor my dual nature, and I have not the wings that you possess—or will possess, once they emerge."

"I am accepting of whatever fate befalls me, brother. Come what may, I still have no fear."

I continued to study him as his face released a tiny bit of the tension it had continually held from the moment he walked into the house. A weight appeared to be suddenly lifting from him, though I could not understand why.

"I think I shall enjoy getting to know you, sister," he told me as a Drew-like smile tugged at his lips. "I think I shall enjoy it immensely."

\\

In the early morning hours, we awaited Casey's return while the brothers debated courses of action in the event that Oz would be less than cooperative or ignorant of how to fix my status altogether. From what I could glean, Sean and Oz had a rather long and complicated past that involved violence, resentment, and quite possibly an assassination attempt. I sat quietly, absorbing all that I could. "Knowledge is power," Hades often told me. Father seldom proved to be wrong.

I watched how they interacted, what their strengths and weaknesses appeared to be in regards to communication and problem solving, as well as battle preparation. Because it was a battle they expected if Oz was unable or unwilling to deliver what they hoped he was capable of. Quite possibly a war.

15

"Are you sure about that, Jay?" Sean spoke into the phone, fighting to maintain his composure. "Dammit! Fine, yes. I'll leave now. But you make sure nothing else goes wrong until I get there, understood?"

He hung up so abruptly that I doubted he even heard the caller's response. It seemed as though, to him, his question didn't require one.

"What's going on?" Drew asked, a look of concern overtaking his countenance.

"A crisis. On the seacoast. I have to leave immediately."

He turned his hardened black eyes to me, and I watched them morph into the green shade of my own. The instant change was fascinating.

"Khara, I have to leave sooner than planned. I would not go unless it was necessary."

"I know," I said plainly, assured that his words were true.

"This crisis . . . it wouldn't happen to have a name, would it?" Kierson taunted from the safety of the kitchen, having gone in there for his third meal of the evening.

"It does indeed," Sean grumbled under his breath.

"You'd think a couple of millennia would teach you how to pick 'em," Kierson teased, coming to rejoin us in the living room, a plate piled high with an obscene amount of food in his hand. He walked over to me, elbowing my side conspiratorially before taking a massive bite of bread. "Sean just can't take the easy route when it comes to the ladies."

"Another word, Kierson, and I'll remove your teeth from your face so I no longer have to stare down that ridiculous grin you so enjoy wearing," Sean countered. His appearance was calm, but his words were menacing. I never doubted their veracity for a moment.

"We'll keep working on solutions to this problem until you can return," Drew reassured him. "Go home. And tell Jay that he still owes me a rematch. That little bastard is a filthy cheat when it comes to poker."

Sean's frustration seemed to subside minutely at Drew's statement, and he gave me a brisk nod before heading out the front door. The sadness that he was incapable of keeping from his eyes made that unfamiliar part of me, deep inside, awaken ever so slightly. I did not like that expression on his face.

"Soooo," Kierson drawled between bites. His nerves appeared to calm with Sean's departure. It also appeared that his teeth would remain intact for the interim. "Sean's gone and Oz is AWOL. Anyone have ideas as to where we go from here?"

"We'll do the only thing we can do—what we've essentially done since she arrived. We never leave her side," Drew stated with authority. In Sean's absence, he was back in command, as much as anyone other than Sean could be when it came to my brothers. I knew he did not want anything to happen to me, regardless of the potential cost to himself, but I could tell by the reactions of the twins that neither of them would want to answer to Sean if harm were to find me. And I did not wish that for them—any of them.

"Am I to be accompanied to the bathroom as well?" I asked for clarification, seeing that the minute amount of privacy I had still been privilege to was soon to disappear in its entirety.

"If we see fit to, then yes. This is serious, and you need to treat it as such, Khara. With all the new revelations, we seemed to have forgotten our initial concerns. Ares is no laughing matter and not someone we want showing up here unannounced to find you. He may not know you exist now, but he's been known to drop in on occasion when situations regarding the balance get out of hand. If we can't get this potential debacle locked down, and fast, he might very well come here. That is certainly a problem we don't need. And to make matters worse, we still have the myriad creatures inhabiting this city to deal with, too. Whichever they are, if they know about you, they'll be gunning for you. We need to keep you away from all potential threats."

Before I was afforded the opportunity to rebut, Oz stormed through the front door, a scowl tainting his expression. Casey did not accompany him. He stalked through the living room like none of us were even there, heading toward the staircase before Drew stepped into his path.

"You're not going anywhere until you give me the answers I want," Drew demanded. That same curious tone to his voice I had heard before filled the room.

"Your parlor tricks don't work on me. You should know that by now," Oz retorted, pushing past him.

"Come here now!" Drew boomed, and suddenly all my brothers and I were standing beside him while Oz just looked over his shoulder and smiled deviously, continuing up to his room.

"Another time, maybe," he mocked as he disappeared into the hallway above, his footsteps fading into the stillness. I could not be certain, due to the dark color of his clothing, but there appeared to be stains on his pants and jacket—muddy, red-colored stains.

"That mother—"

"Drew!" Kierson snapped, clapping his hands loudly for emphasis. "You wanna maybe put us at ease or something?"

"Right," Drew replied absentmindedly. "As you were."

Again, the strange sensation of increasing pressure in the room settled in around us, and we all returned to our previous positions. It was fascinating. I'd never witnessed anything like it. Father easily commanded his domain, but never had I seen his words carry such weight with those that served him or were enslaved by him as Drew's did over our brothers.

"You know I hate that shit," Casey snarled from behind us. "Be more specific next time. It fucks with my head when you do it."

"Sorry. I was irritated. I didn't choose my words well," Drew apologized. "When did you get here? I didn't even hear you come in."

Casey shot a murderous glance in Drew's direction.

"I'm a tracker. You're not supposed to hear me." Casey's stealth was truly remarkable. None of us had the slightest inkling that he had returned until he announced his presence. I could imagine how such a trait would be valuable to the PC and wondered if it was what he had been bred for.

"So you did find Oz," Drew clarified, looking curiously back up the stairs that Oz had just employed to escape us. "When he came in alone, I assumed you had not."

"He conveniently was headed this way when I did hunt him down. I just followed to be sure this was where he was intending to go."

"He did look a little too intact for you to have encountered him directly," Kierson teased.

"Yeah," Casey growled. "I was looking forward to that, too."

When silence fell over us, I looked to Drew, wanting to know more about what he had just done, calling us to him as he had.

"Drew, what powers are these that you hold?"

"He is able to compel those that serve with him," Pierson explained, taking it upon himself to speak on Drew's behalf. "He is also able to do the same with virtually any supernatural he chooses."

"Yeah, everyone but Oz," Kierson added. Pierson's cold expression led me to believe he was not appreciative of the interruption.

"He is born of both the god and goddess of war. It comes with certain . . . bonuses, one might say."

"So, your abilities are unique?" I asked, taken by the possibility that each child Ares reared would possess some quality akin in extremity to that of Drew's persuasion.

"Of sorts," Pierson said with an ambivalent shrug. "Kierson told you what he and I can do. Some of the PC have physical powers, some mental, and others are highly specialized. Those powers tend to go unseen for the most part, making them greater weapons than one may think, judging by their appearance alone."

"Intriguing. Should I not then have some exceptional ability also?"

"Perhaps." His tone was as indifferent as my attitude. "But I have yet to see anything that would lead me to believe you do. Your so-called defensive abilities seemed greatly lacking against the Breathers. Perhaps Ares took out his daughters because he knew they would possess nothing useful to serve the PC."

"Pierson," Drew chastised. "Try a little tact next time." He then turned his warm and friendly eyes to me. "I don't think that's why Ares did that. We already spoke about Eos—"

"Yes, but the Original Three were highly exceptional, Drew. Comparing Khara to Eos is ridiculous. She and her brothers—Deimos and Phobos—were like nothing else created, and have not been re-created since their incarnation. While I do believe that Ares would see another female born of him as an abomination and an affront to Eos' memory, I think it is for reasons other than what rumor has led us to believe over the centuries that his daughters have not been permitted to live. That is my contention. You can do with it what you will."

"You think me unexceptional then?" I asked him before he could turn away and disappear into one of his many books that lay about the living room.

"Yes."

"Then your logic is flawed, brother. Oz said himself that I am an impossibility. By definition, that would make me exceptional." I walked over to him, a flush in my cheeks that warmed slowly. "I will show you that I am worthy of my title—worthy of being PC. When I do, you will acknowledge that without hesitation."

"Ooooooh!" Kierson yelled, before doubling over with laughter. "She totally schooled the scholar. Looks like she's got your number, Pierson."

Pierson met our words with a scowl before grabbing a tome off the narrow table against the wall and heading upstairs to his room.

"That was awesome, Khara," Kierson declared, walking toward me with his arm in the air, his hand turned so its palm faced me. "High five, girl." I looked at him utterly perplexed, which caused him to deflate slightly, dropping his arm to his side. "You have a lot to learn. Guess we should start now."

He reached for my right hand with his left and held it up above my shoulder, then slapped it with his right hand.

"That's a high five. Learn it. Love it," he said with an impish grin. "And be sure to bust it out whenever you succeed in making Pierson look like the ass he tends to be."

I did not know how to respond to him, so I looked away, finding Casey still lurking near the staircase.

"What of you, Casey? What is your ability?"

Kierson and Drew both sharply inhaled at my question.

"What is my ability?" Casey repeated, his expression more surly and foreboding than normal. "I'm a tracker. Or haven't you been listening?"

"That is a label that only vaguely describes what you can do. I would like to know what ability makes you so gifted as a tracker."

"Too bad for you. Tracker is all you get to know."

He turned away, taking the staircase at his leisure to escape my prying questions. His response was not entirely unexpected. He was guarded and abrasive at the best of times—not the forthcoming type. That aside, there was something about his reactions to me that seemed personal. Whenever there was mention of the Underworld or my time there, it seemed to heighten his aggressive tendencies.

"Yeah, you might want to make a note of this: Casey does *not* like to talk about himself much," Kierson warned. "And for the love of the gods, do *not* ask about his mother. Ever. Like under any circumstances. Do you understand? Never."

"Who is—"

"Shhh!" Kierson scolded, placing his finger against his lips as he rushed toward me. "Don't even ask us about it. If he hears you, he will flip his shit, and you don't want that. Trust me. I know."

"Flip his shit?"

"Snap. Lose his mind. Go postal. Start fucking up everything in his path, breathing or otherwise."

"I see," I replied, finally understanding what Kierson was saying. "I shall not inquire again."

"It's late . . . or early, depending on how you look at it. I think now would be a good time for us all to get some sleep," Drew decreed. "I'm going to talk to Pierson about a few things before I turn in. Kierson, do a perimeter check just to be sure. Khara, head downstairs. We will see you in the morning."

I nodded before turning and making my way toward the basement door. By the time I reached for the knob, Drew and Kierson had already disappeared to accomplish their assignments. They were diligent, if nothing else.

In the darkened silence of my bedroom, I lay on the cot, my mind unsettled. Thoughts nagged at me, preventing me from sleep, not the least of which was the memory of my actions at the club, which had led to all the new and ominous revelations: Sean, my mother, the Breathers, and a pervasive evil determined to kill or corrupt me. The last thought seemed ridiculous to me, and I wanted to write it off, but the vehemence with which Oz professed it gave me pause. Though I did not fear death, a point I had made abundantly clear, I did not wish to be made into something I was not. I was neither good nor evil. I did not desire alterations that I did not require.

I tried to sleep as Drew ordered, but my mind continually wandered back to the Tenth Circle and the feeling it had awakened within me. The memory of it caused a resurgence of that sense of freedom that had coursed through me like Acheron through the Underworld:

wild and raging with reckless abandon. I could not afford to be wild, but my body craved it, desperately.

All I wanted to do was appease this desire.

When I could no longer contain the residual urge that had exposed me in the first place, I let the restlessness drive me from my bed. I wanted to feel unburdened, naked—*free*. That need consumed me, burning me from the inside out, driving me from my room, up two flights of stairs, and into the room of another. Without any recollection of my journey there, I soon found myself standing next to Oz while he slept.

Once again finding it offensive, my clothing was off in seconds. My thoughts inelegantly scrambled to keep up with my actions, but it was apparent on a visceral level what I needed. I would satisfy that craving at any cost.

And with Oz, there would always be a cost.

I climbed atop him as he slumbered, straddling his waist as I had so often seen his whores do. That night, I would be one of them. Unfazed by that reality, I reached down to remove the clothes he still wore from that evening. I wanted darkness, rawness, and craved the emptiness that his touch would surely bring. I wanted to feel hollow, bottomless—soulless.

My body worked quickly while my mind numbed further to what was transpiring. Nothing registered as it should have; I was all feeling, without rationale. It was only when Oz shot up, shackling my wrists with his hands, that I became slightly more aware of what I was doing.

I still cared not.

"Khara," he cautioned, his voice lower and huskier than usual. Hearing him say my name cleared my head slightly, giving me pause, though it was short-lived.

"I will be finished in a moment," I countered, struggling against his hold to continue my quest. My growing desire was unrelenting.

"You will be finished now." His words were commanding, nearly penetrating the wall of need that surrounded me.

"No," I argued, writhing against him.

"Khara . . ." he quietly growled, drawing my name out intently. I heeded his unspoken warning. "Get dressed and meet me downstairs. You don't want to do this." Without another word, he abruptly threw me from both him and his bed. His words were a frown, a disapproval that slapped me hard. They, too, helped me to my senses.

When his bedroom door slammed behind him as he exited, the punctuating sound broke what was left of the spell I'd so clearly been under. It had to have been an external force driving me to Oz's room. What else would have made me go to the one I loathed most to seek what I so desperately needed? Those were not the actions of a sane person, fully in possession of her mind. I was not myself.

When I was certain my mind and body had cleared of the dark fog that had rolled in and clouded my judgment, I did as Oz bade me and dressed quickly. Coming down the stairs with as much indifference as I could gather, I found Oz awaiting me, his expression grim. I may have been unimpressed by his dismissal, but I was far more unimpressed with my actions. He appeared to share my sentiments.

"Why did you do that?" he pried, staring into my eyes as though they would reveal my thoughts if he concentrated hard enough.

"Why do you care?" I retorted, thinking that he was hardly able to come from a place of judgment.

"Answer the question."

"I am going to bed," I said, heading toward the basement door. In an instant, he was standing before me, blocking the way. "You may attempt to bully your way into getting what you want, but you will not succeed." I tilted my head to stare up at him. His expression was unreadable.

When he said nothing in response, I moved to step around him, wanting nothing more than to return to my room and attempt once again to find the sleep that had eluded me—preferably before the sun rose. I was met with his arm across my chest, his hand grabbing my shoulder to keep me where I was. Only minutes earlier, I had wanted that hand all over me. At that moment, I wanted to tear it off.

"You don't seem to be yourself," he said matter-of-factly, still searching for confirmation of something.

"I am not myself, Oz—you said so yourself. I am an Unborn. I am also the twin sister of Sean, who leads the PC, and a warrior without skill or ability," I spat, staring him down with my most murderous expression, the one I reserved for the most loathsome beings that roamed in my father's domain. "Nothing about me is 'me' any longer. I have lost all sense of who and what I was. In a matter of days, everything has changed." He said nothing, his eyes still fiercely pinned on me. The silence between us compelled me to continue. "You seem so interested in why I sought you out, wanting to know why I did it, but answer me this: Why did you not give me what I wanted?"

The room around us was lit only with the waning moonlight that streamed through the wall of windows in the back of the living room. That light cast harsh shadows along the planes of Oz's face, emphasizing the anger in his expression.

"Because I have standards, new girl," he started, leaning his face in so close to mine that we breathed the same air. "And even I won't take advantage of someone exercising a complete lack of judgment."

"I am glad that we can agree that my judgment this evening was in err."

"That we can."

"Rest assured, it will not happen again."

I looked at his hand that still held me in place and then turned my impassive gaze back to his face. With a moment's hesitation, he let go of me, taking a small step back to allow me passage. As I walked around his imposing form, he muttered something under his breath so low that I almost could not make it out.

"What did you say?" I asked, seeking clarification. I was having great difficulty believing that what I thought he had said was correct.

"I said I want to show you something." The repetition of his statement confirmed my suspicion. "Are you coming or not?"

I assessed him, wondering what he could possibly have that I would want to see.

"Where are we going?"

"You'll find out when we get there." He started making his way toward the front entrance, but I did not follow. After only a few steps, he turned to see me eyeing him dubiously, unmoving from my position. "You don't trust me," he said, somewhat amused by the revelation.

"You show me nothing to trust."

"Well, that's too bad, new girl, because this is a one-time-only offer. You either trust me and come, or don't and stay. Which will it be?"

"Drew said that I am not to leave," I argued, citing my brother's earlier orders. The ones I found so offensive at the club.

"Well, well . . . it seems you're at a bit of a crossroads then, aren't you?" he mocked, extending his hand toward me. "Which path will you choose?"

I looked at his hand for what it was: an offering, though of what I could not be certain. What I was certain of was Oz's knowledge of my mother. It was plain in his earlier dealings with Sean that he knew something, if not a lot, about her, and I wanted to be privy to that information as well. She was potentially the key to unlocking so much about my past; balking at the potential opportunity to learn all that I could about her seemed lunacy. Father would not have approved. "Tedious alliances," he called them, but he had many of his own.

Perhaps I needed to form one with Oz.

Never taking my eyes off his, I took his hand, accepting both the gesture and his offer. I said nothing as I did.

"You're just full of surprises, aren't you, new girl?" he purred, before turning to lead me away. "And as for Drew: What he doesn't know won't kill him." He stopped to look down at me, winking wickedly. "But it might just kill you."

16

"Precisely how is it that we are getting to the top of this?" I asked, looking up at the skyscraper Oz had taken me to. It was still dark outside, though the sun was threatening to rise far off on the horizon. I could not fathom why he had brought us there.

Oz threw a smug glance my way before replying.

"How do you think?"

"I will not fly up there with you."

He laughed at my defiance.

"Good, because we're taking the stairs." He pulled two small metal implements out of his pocket and began fiddling with them in the lock of the door in the alleyway. He smiled mischievously once the heavy metal door swung open and gestured for me to enter. I did not oblige him. "Still with the trust issues, eh?" he asked, looking at me curiously. "Fair enough. I'll go first."

I followed behind him, up an eternally climbing staircase, until we finally reached our destination: the roof.

"Watch your step," he warned, looking over the ledge. "It's a long way down."

"But if I could fly, that would remedy such a hazard in the future, would it not?" I baited, hoping it would lead to a discussion on how to force my wings to emerge and put an end to the worries of Drew, Kierson, and Sean. I was not so certain that Pierson or Casey cared about what end I met.

"I suppose it would." He looked down at me with a condescending grin and said no more.

"So this is what you wanted to show me? The rooftop of an old art deco building?"

"Interesting," he replied, drawing the word out dramatically. "Subterranean girl knows her architecture."

"I was not raised solely in the Underworld, Oz, nor was I without an education. Contrary to what you may believe, my father's home is not devoid of books and other forms of teaching. And, more recently, in the past few decades I spent with Demeter, I occasionally was provided with a television, though I detested it. Books are far more companionable."

"You really are full of surprises tonight," he muttered under his breath. "Tell me something then: If you are so educated on all things earthly, why do you seem so out of your element here?"

I shrugged ambivalently, uncertain of the answer.

"Facts are not reality. What I saw in pictures or read about in periodicals were facts. They had no context. No meaning. They were not experiences. One may see a photo of a 1920s building, but cannot appreciate the shadows it casts when the sun sets or the three-dimensional details that adorn it." I looked to Oz for a sign of understanding in his expression but found none. Leaning against the concrete ledge, my gaze turned to admire the patinated eagle statue perched beside me. As I continued to explain, I ran my finger down the edge of its copper feathers, rubbing my fingers together lightly after pulling them away. "Take this bird, for instance. You know that its green shade is caused by the oxidation process that copper goes through when exposed to the elements, but you cannot feel its chalky texture or appreciate the minute changes in hue that give it its own identity—its unique fingerprint. Such things need to be experienced, not merely read of, for one to truly know them." I paused for a moment, my eyes still fixed on the statue next to me. "I think I have much in common with this winged one. We have both spent a solitary lifetime observing things from afar."

"Except you don't have wings," Oz countered. It seemed as though this was an attempt at playfulness. My sour expression illustrated his failure, and he tried a different line of observation. "And you weren't alone. Not really. You were surrounded by all those souls." His voice was softer than normal as he spoke, disbelief tainting his words.

I looked at him over my shoulder while my long hair danced wildly in the wind.

"You can be alone even when surrounded by others, Oz. Population does not inherently negate solitude."

His brow furrowed.

"Surely you had those who you befriended over time?"

"Like you have my brothers?"

It was his turn to sour at my retort.

"Fine, but Hades cared for you. You said so yourself."

"And he is the ruler of the Underworld, a job that requires almost constant attention. Do not misunderstand, Hades was good to me, but I was not the center of his world."

"What about your time with Demeter?"

"What about it?" I volleyed his query back at him curtly. "In the beginning, our months were spent together, just her and I. She must have feared that others would find out about my existence. But later on, when she grew bitter and resentful toward me, she would leave me alone in my hidden home, only coming to see me on occasion. She rarely, if ever, spoke, and when she did it was never pleasant."

"Is that why you never really speak of her, only of Hades?"

"I suppose, though I do not do it intentionally. I never truly considered my time spent with her in the woods to be time spent at home. She did not care for me like a mother. Hades, however, cared for me as a father would, and my time in the Underworld felt right," I explained. "I know it must seem counterintuitive to want to be where few beings would choose to be, but it was my home. Lonely or otherwise."

"It shouldn't have been that way," he whispered, looking away from me to the city below.

"Yet it was," I replied. I returned my focus to the buildings surrounding us. "Do you think it would have been different if I had been raised as a Light One?"

"Very." His answer was abrupt but not unfeeling. Something about my past appeared to have reached a part of him that I had not known to exist. "Everything you just described to me is the antithesis of what heaven is."

"It is strange to know that my true home is the extreme opposite of where I was raised. Do you think it would have impacted me so greatly that I would have turned out differently had I grown up there?"

"Who knows?" he replied, his jaw tight and eyes distant. "Better yet, who cares? You are who you are. It's absurd to waste your time contemplating something that inherently can't change."

"Beings cannot change?"

"Oh, they can," he scoffed, "but only when something prompts it. They do not change of their own volition, just because it's the right thing to do. Change is always brought on by external circumstances, which, ninety percent of the time, are unsavory ones. Your mother knew a thing or two about those . . ."

"My mother—"

"Is something I refuse to get into right now," he said sharply, interrupting my chance to learn more about her.

"Fine," I replied tightly, hazarding a glance in his direction. "Then explain your assessment of change; you speak of it as though you have much experience with it."

"In more ways than you could imagine," he said harshly. "And for reasons you shouldn't know."

"You know far more than you let on, and I am not speaking only of my mother," I observed, seeing his tight expression tense even further. "Age can be an enemy when the years are unkind. You are older than me, and I have seen much in my time. Your experience with the unsavory is surely extensive by now."

His dark eyes narrowed at me before a smug grin further tainted his expression.

"I *am* unsavory, remember?"

"Nearly impossible to forget." I let the words hang between us, creating a physical barrier. My response was curt, as it seemed to always be when addressing Oz. However, if my goal was to procure answers from him, that tactic was unlikely to work. It was time to employ a new strategy, just as my father would have. "I find it interesting that Sean was told my mother—"

"*No!*" he shouted, holding his hands up as though to deflect my unfinished query. "I'm serious. I'm not touching that one. You know nothing about her for a reason. And that is how it will stay."

"But you knew her?" I pressed.

He eyed me incredulously.

"Of course. She was an angel."

"A Light One or a Dark One?" I pressed, hoping to clarify what he had said earlier to Sean.

He shrugged in response.

It was my turn to give a dubious look.

"But your contention earlier was that she—"

"What part of 'I'm not touching that one' do you not understand?" he growled. "Don't think you can worm any shred of information out of me that I don't want to freely give. And you can never take anything I say at face value; I specialize in mind fucking. Maybe just fucking in general."

"So what you said to Sean about her was an attempt to anger him?" I continued, ignoring his threats while I stepped closer to him. He glared at me with a look of self-satisfaction. I had hoped to glean something helpful from his answer. My need to know more about my mother was ever increasing.

He shrugged ambivalently.

"Maybe. Or maybe it was true. What you don't seem to understand is that I don't give a shit. I do what I do because it pleases me. I get bored," he replied smugly. "I like to be entertained."

"And is that why we are here now, for your entertainment?" I countered, challenging his bravado. "If you were so bored and in need of entertainment, you should have let me stay in your room and fuck you. You may perceive me as cold and inept at many things, but, I can assure you, fornicating is not one of them."

I watched his eyes widen momentarily. It amused me immensely.

"So very, very full of surprises, new girl," he muttered under his breath while his lids hooded his eyes.

"Something you should remember."

"Oh, I will," he purred, still staring at me.

I broke his heavy gaze to look out over the city and the nearby river that wound its way around and through it, hoping to clear my mind and get our conversation back on track. He was unwilling to tell me about my mother; that was abundantly clear. What was not clear was whether or not he could resolve the issue regarding my Unborn status. I needed to determine that as quickly as possible and convince him to rectify it, providing he could.

No small feat, indeed.

"Tell me something, Oz," I started, my voice as neutral as it normally was. "What are we to do about the fact that I remain Unborn? You said that my wings had not yet been birthed, implying that they will or can still be. How can we achieve this?"

"We?" he scoffed, his surly attitude flaring. "There is no 'we,' new girl."

"Tell me something. Who cared for the Unborn before they became Light Ones?"

"I think that answer is rather obvious, is it not? They were mentored and cared for by appointed Light Ones."

"Did the Light Ones not see them through their metamorphosis then? Could you not be the Light One to do the same for me?"

Again, he shrugged.

"You're assuming a lot of things based on very little," he started while he also looked out over the city as though the rooftops held the answers to my probing questions. "What I will tell you is that I am in no position to help."

"Fine. I will let the others know," I replied, accepting his response. Interrogating him further on the issue would yield no results. Of that I was certain.

"Do that," he said gruffly. "Maybe they'll listen to you. I'm pretty sure I'm on their shit list at the moment. Even more so than usual, if that's even possible."

"I am confident that it is." He spared a sideways glance at me, but my expression was unreadable. The wry smile I felt attempting to break through my façade, however, would have made Kierson proud. "Tell me something, Oz. Are you going to share with me why you brought me here? Your request seemed so pertinent at the time, yet I fail to see why. Why is this somewhere I needed to go?"

"You'll see," he said enigmatically.

All I saw was the slowly disappearing darkness that surrounded us and the lights of the city beneath us.

"What were you like before you fell?"

I saw him tense instantly at my words. The harsh planes of his face seemed even more angular.

"I was a totally different being once," he replied, his gaze drifting off to the heavens. I had seen him do it earlier when we first arrived and wondered if he did it consciously or if it was some internal compass calling him home. I felt no such pull. "Now, I am a shell of what I was." His attention dropped back to me as a lecherous grin distorted his face. "And I like this guy far more. He lives by his own rules. Does as he pleases. I'm bound to no one. True freedom—nothing is sweeter than that."

When he spoke of freedom, his eyes were hypnotic, beckoning me to join him in his euphoria. Before my time in the city of Detroit, I had never known what it was like to be free, but I had never questioned the absence of this feeling. My existence just was. But having enjoyed the slightest taste of that freedom—and seeing the raw pleasure it gave Oz, who had chosen to live his life how he saw fit—made me ruminate over the possibilities. Perhaps his particular brand of freedom was exactly what I needed.

"And how does one procure this 'true freedom' that nothing is sweeter than?" I asked, standing to see the light of the sun begin its ascent into the sky.

I felt him move in close beside me, the warmth of his body a welcome barrier to the cold breeze blowing around us. His breath was soft on my ear, a breeze all its own.

"Simple," he whispered softly. "You take it."

My eyes closed involuntarily. I pictured a life without limits or boundaries or consequences. It was a seductive fantasy indeed.

When the heady feeling subsided, I opened my eyes to see the most glorious fiery glow cresting over the horizon. In that instant, I knew that was why he had brought me there—to remind me of my home. I looked over to him, struggling to understand how someone so self-indulgent could be capable of doing something so generous, but my question went unanswered. Instead, I found myself alone on the roof.

Oz was gone.

17

I surveyed my surroundings but saw nothing. It was only me and the statues of the eagles that adorned the roofline. Having no other reason to remain, I made my way to the exit and descended the numerous stairs before returning to the back alley where Oz and I had entered the building. When I turned to make my way back to the vehicle, I found Oz leaning casually against the brick façade of the building, smiling wildly.

"Took you a while."

"I was not aware it was a race, nor that it had begun."

"I think it's time we get you home before the boys get good and riled up, don't you?"

I stared in response.

"I'll take that as a yes," he replied, turning his back on me to lead the way to his personal vehicle—a Jeep, he had called it. "And you're welcome for the field trip. I'm not sure you'll be getting out much now with the boys knowing what they know."

"I think the greater issue at play here is what they do not know. That is the most important variable in this equation."

"Like I said, what you don't know might kill you," he said as we arrived at the vehicle. "And usually does, although, in your case, it may just steal your soul or turn you evil." His expression tightened as he opened his door, looking at me across the top of the vehicle while his wavy hair danced in the wind. "I suggest you keep that in mind."

"I keep many things in mind, Oz, your warnings included."

He paused before responding.

"Good. That might just keep you alive then."

"Until I am no longer entertaining to you," I retorted as I opened the passenger door.

The gleam in his eyes was undeniable as he stared at me.

"Oh, I wouldn't worry too much about that, new girl. There's never a dull moment when you're around."

The instant we arrived at the Victorian, the fighting began. Kierson was livid, his face an ever-reddening canvas on which he displayed his rage. None of it, however, was directed toward me.

"You fucking bastard," he yelled, charging Oz the second we stepped foot inside the house. "She may mean nothing to you, but she sure as hell means something to me. You could have gotten her killed, or emptied . . . or whatever it is that could happen to her if she falls into the wrong hands. Hell, for all we know, that's exactly what you were *trying* to do!"

"Drew, I suggest you put a leash on him before he gets himself hurt," Oz said, his disinterest in Kierson's anger plain in his tone.

"Where were you?" Kierson demanded, turning to me with worry in his eyes. I remembered that look well. My father wore it the day I was taken from him.

"On a building," I replied calmly. "I am fine."

"Fine," Kierson muttered under his breath. "You're always 'fine.'"

"I could not sleep—I felt strange. Oz offered to take me into the city, and I saw no harm in it. You have all professed that he is a great and capable warrior. I saw him slay the Breathers; I felt that all would be well."

"Well, leave a note next time, would you?" Kierson chastised, walking away from me and toward the staircase. He disappeared without another word. Once he did, I felt something that I had not for centuries—not since Demeter showered me daily with it while Persephone was imprisoned. Guilt.

Drew gave me a disapproving look while Casey and Pierson remained as disinterested as always.

"Did you learn anything productive during your spontaneous outing?" Drew finally asked, his expression sour.

"Nothing that would change my circumstances," I reported. "Oz is unable to help me become what I was born to be. Our solution will not be him. We will have to find another Light One to determine if he or she is able to perform the task, if it can be performed at all, or find a way to return me to the Underworld, where I will be safe."

"Well, this sounds like it's going to be another exciting rehash of stuff I've already heard ten times over, so I'm going to take off. I have more important things to do," Oz announced, not awaiting a response. Instead, he just walked back out the front door without a care. "Glad you're feeling more yourself now, new girl," he tossed over his shoulder just before the door slammed behind him.

"Well, as much as I would like to figure out whatever possessed you to go into the city with Oz, I have other matters to attend to, not the least of which is sorting out this mess with the Breathers. We may have taken out a horde of them, but we can't be certain that is the end of them." Drew called for Kierson, who came down the stairs without looking at me, and demanded Pierson put his research aside to join them. Casey was then ordered to remain home with me. His objections to babysitting fell on deaf ears. "And, Khara?" Drew started, looking at me with clear disappointment in his eyes. "Don't pull a stunt like that ever again."

The three left without further explanation, and I soon found myself standing in the entrance to the living room while Casey assessed me curiously.

"If you weren't on house arrest before, you sure will be now," he purred, slowly peeling himself off the couch to stalk toward me. "Was it worth it?"

"I was to be confined to this house until Drew deemed it safe for me to leave regardless of my impulsive behavior. Their reaction to my excursion with Oz this morning did not have any bearing on that."

"Fair enough," he replied, coming to stand before me. "But was it worth it?"

I contemplated his question.

"Yes. It was."

We engaged in our customary staring contest before I broke my gaze, turning to walk past him to the basement door.

"The boys are going to be gone all day, you know," Casey called after me. "Probably well into the night." His words were a dare of sorts, taunting me as I opened the door to my room. I looked back over my shoulder to humor him. "I don't want to be stuck here any more than you do," he continued. "You're PC, and I think that you should be treated as such. Nobody sits around and holds my fucking hand when shit gets real, nor did they baby those we lost to those fucking *suckers* out there. You were born of Ares like the rest of us. It's time we started letting you act like it."

"What are you suggesting, Casey?"

"I'm suggesting that I have a little recon of my own to do tonight, and I resent not being able to do it because I'm stuck here with you," he explained while a malicious smile spread widely across his often listless face. "So I'm going to take my babysitting gig on the road. You're coming with me."

I eyed him tightly before turning back to the staircase.

"Then I shall get some rest."

"Do that. You're going to need it."

※※※※※※※※※※※※

"Is there a reason that all the foul and shady dealings in this city must be done in some decaying relic of a building?" I asked, surveying the crumbling concrete walls of the structure before me. They, like so many others I had seen in Detroit, were covered with brightly colored, tattoo-like paintings.

Casey turned his cold, black eyes to meet mine and said nothing in response as he advanced into the Masonic temple.

"Come out, come out, wherever you are," he called into the darkness, taunting those he had come to meet. On our way here, he had refused to tell me who or what we were en route to. We progressed into the main room, the only light illuminating our path from the moon above, filtering in through the vast crevices in what had once been a roof. There was a pervasive odor that filled my nostrils—rot and decomposition. The stench of evil surrounded us. "Don't make me have to work harder than I want to, boys."

"To whom are you speaking?" I asked, seeing no one but us.

Again, my question was met with an empty stare.

He stopped walking when we arrived at the middle of the great hall, its vast nature still imposing, even though its structural integrity had waned. I was certain we would be buried alive if the wind outside continued to pick up.

"Have I not made myself clear? Perhaps I should remedy that."

His voice carried, filling the silent, pungent air around us. It was quickly followed by a sound that I had only recently come to know as the pump of a shotgun. I had not seen him slip the firearm out from under his coat.

As the sharp sound of sliding metal echoed through the room, reverberating its way down the halls, I heard a fluttering noise that grew in both strength and volume. I recognized that sound as well— the flapping of wings.

"Yesss," replied a serpent-like voice from the shadows. "You have made yoursssself clear."

A dark, leathery creature emerged, barely visible, from a corner of the room, approaching on all fours. It had a thick, broad build, like that of a massive canine, and its movements were cautious and slow.

Had it not been for its obvious and palpable fear of Casey, I would have thought it—it and all its minions that slowly came at us from every perceivable angle—was stalking us, preparing an attack.

They scaled the walls, crawling down from the roof above and up from the gaping holes in the wood floor beneath our feet, closing in around us. There was an insidious quality to them that I could not place. I had not seen such beastly things in my life, but there was a strange familiarity to them. They reminded me of the demon animals my father commanded.

Suddenly, in the blink of an eye, they were upon us. Completely surrounded by the unfamiliar creatures, my eyes shot over to Casey, who stood stoically, unfazed by their surprising change in advance tactics. Whatever they were, they moved with unnerving speed, which failed to bother Casey at all.

"Who would like to be the first to tell me exactly what the fuck is going on in this city, specifically with the Breathers?" Casey started, his voice low and even, as it always was. "We just took out a nest of them. Funny that we knew nothing about it before one of them went rogue."

"What makesss you think we know anything about—"

A piercing blast tore through the room, nearly deafening me in the process. The screeching sound that the mysterious creatures made in response did nothing to assuage the ringing in my ears, and I clung to the sides of my head in a futile attempt to deflect both the sound and the pain.

"Now," Casey continued, "I will ask again. Who would like to be the first to tell me what the fuck is going on with the Breathers?"

"We don't know exxxactly," replied the beast that had stepped closest to Casey. He was larger than the others and possessed a menacing appearance, the scars carved deeply into his leathery face testifying to his violent past. What struck me most was his offset jaw and his lower canine tooth that was larger than the others, which caused it to project strangely from his mouth. It accounted for his speech impediment.

Casey tsked in a dramatic show of disappointment.

"Wrong answer, Azriel. Must I carve your friend up to get the details I'm looking for, or might we be a tad more civilized and you just tell me everything you know without me having to interrogate you?" Casey inquired, making his way over to the beast he had shot. Instead of the limp mass I expected to see lying on the ground before him, a frozen and statue-like creature stood unmoving. It looked to be made of stone.

It was then that I recognized just what we were dealing with. I had seen one, only days earlier while out with Kierson, perched on one of the towering buildings near the Tenth Circle. A gargoyle, he had called it, though he failed to mention at the time that it was anything more than just a hideous decoration to an otherwise unadorned building.

Casey held the shotgun in such a way that would allow him to club the motionless gargoyle before him with the butt end. I presumed that, if the creature had not been killed by the initial shot, it had incapacitated him on some level. Tapping the stony beast's head tauntingly with the butt of his weapon, Casey trained his eyes on what I assumed to be the leader of the winged ones.

"Shall I start here?" he asked, his tone inquisitive while indicating his target.

"There isss no need for that. I will tell you all I know—all *we* know."

"Excellent, because I was starting to get the notion that you were not going to be very forthcoming with me, which would lead me to all kinds of crazy conclusions . . . like you being on someone else's payroll, perhaps. Someone more important than me. But you and I both know that that would be suicide, don't we?"

"Yesss, it would." The two eyed each other in the darkness for a moment before Azriel continued. "We learned about the uprisssing with the Breathersss only days ago. It appearsss that sssomething brought about a change in them. Sssomething powerful enough for them to no longer sssee reassson."

"Interesting, but I'm not here for what you've deduced about the situation. I'm here for what you *know*," Casey cautioned, stroking the head of the statue lightly, like a favored pet, just before he crashed the butt of his weapon down upon it, shattering it like a thin pane of glass. As the pulverized stone settled on the floor in a layer of dust, Casey snatched Azriel by his thick and muscular throat, then dragged him off the ground. Their faces were dangerously close as Casey's eyes bore threateningly into the gargoyle's. "You are an informant, are you not? And who do you think you are to keep informed?" He stared the beast down as though he was already obtaining answers, even in silence. When he looked faintly satisfied with what information he'd obtained, he leaned in closer. "You've forgotten your place, old one. Mistakes like that are costly."

"There wasss talk," the beast choked out against Casey's crushing grip. "Talk of sssomething in Detroit that ssshould not be."

"I'm listening," Casey replied, still holding the gargoyle's throat.

"The nessst you found . . . they had been trying to track it down."

"What 'it' are you referring to?"

"The Unborn."

Silence hung heavy on Casey's tongue, not allowing him to reply. The mask of darkness that seemed ever-present in his expression shifted slightly, something else flashing in his eyes for the briefest moment. It came and went before I could fully recognize it.

"What did you just say?"

"I sssaid, they were sssearching for the Unborn," Azriel repeated, his wide, inhuman eyes looking to me.

"And what do they want with it?"

"It isss not what they want to do with the Unborn that you ssshould be concerned about." He hesitated slightly before continuing. "It isss who they were to bring the Unborn to that ssshould be feared."

"You are trying my patience with your riddles, Azriel," Casey growled.

"I do not know hisss name or what he isss, but the Unborn callsss to him, a sssweet sssong that cannot be ignored or essscaped."

"Where can I find him?"

"I do not know," he hissed sharply, fearing that Casey would not tolerate his ignorance any longer.

Casey's face twisted in anger as he breathed his orders into Azriel's face, his words little more than a whisper.

"Then you will dispatch your underlings and find out where he is and report back to me and me alone. You will say nothing of the Unborn to anything in this city—with or without a pulse. Insubordination would not be a wise course of action, Azriel. Nor would failure," Casey warned. "I'm in a particularly forgiving mood this evening. I would not count on such generosity in the future." To emphasize his authority, Casey tossed the gargoyle across the room, scattering his minions in the process. "You have until tomorrow night."

We looked on as they dispersed themselves through the room, all climbing down through the various cracks in the floor. I knew that Azriel was lucky to still be breathing.

"Where are they going?" I asked, wondering why creatures with wings would seek escape below the building.

"The sewers." His words were clipped, frustration marring his tone. I did not expect him to elaborate on his response, but he did. "To answer your earlier question, we came to this particular rundown building because underneath it is one of the largest connections to the city's sewer system. That's where they live. This," he said, indicating the room we stood in, "is where I go to find them."

"And they will do as you ordered? They will find this one who seeks me?"

"If they know what's good for them," he replied gruffly. "Gargoyles are good for one thing and one thing only: information. It's their currency." He looked down at me, the light of the moon swallowed whole by the black of his eyes. "And they better pay up."

I followed my brother back out of the building without concern of retaliation from the gargoyles. Casey had made it clear that they were little more than bottom-feeders in the supernatural hierarchy. To attack us would have meant annihilation for them, hence the fear I saw in their eyes when they first approached us. Casey was truly something to behold. He was ruthless, cunning, and perfectly bred to do whatever necessary to carry out his mission.

The thought brought a curiosity to mind. If each of the women Ares bedded was clearly chosen for a purpose, precisely who had he bedded to create Casey? The answer was suddenly of utmost interest to me.

"Fucking goyles," Casey muttered under his breath as we broke out of the building and into the silvery-blue light of the full moon.

"They are little more than a nuisance to you, are they not?"

"Nuisances that have forgotten themselves."

"It seems you have made your point. Assassinating one of their own before their eyes was an excellent strategy and a highly effective motivator. They will not forget again."

For once, he eyed me keenly, as though I had said something interesting for the very first time.

"You have seen this tactic before." His words were not a question.

"Of course. Such strategies are often used to keep order in the Underworld. A necessary evil, as it were."

"You didn't even flinch when I crushed the cretin's skull," he said, stepping closer than was comfortable. "And you had no reaction the other night when we eliminated those Breathers. Just how desensitized to our way of life are you, sister?"

I met his stare as I had the day I met him—with utter indifference.

"I am well adapted to survive violence, Casey," I explained, my tone low and even to match my brother's. "If I was not, I would be dead. The Underworld is no place for a tender, sensitive soul. I do not react to death and brutality because I was steeped in it from such a young age that I know little else. What you perceive as desensitization, or deadening of emotion, is nothing more than who I am. I have lost no part of me, but grown to be a direct expression of my environment, and rightly so. I do not see myself as you do—damaged. Would I have turned out differently had I been raised under the care of someone else? Possibly, but not certainly. I have always seen things for what they are and not what I hope them to be. The world for me is as direct and literal as I am, Casey. What you see as a fault, I view as an asset."

"I said nothing about your indifference being a fault, Khara. Quite the contrary. It might very well be the one thing that kept you alive down there."

"And what of you, brother? Is your callous nature due to your upbringing, or is your soul truly as black as your eyes?"

His dark orbs narrowed tightly in response.

"For me there was never hope of turning out any other way. Ares had that in mind when he fucked my mother." There was a trace of disdain in his voice, which led me to believe that, on some minute level, Casey did not want to be that which he so absolutely was. At that moment, something became clear to me. Casey was a creature of the darkness—a son of the Underworld.

What I was bound to by magic, he was bound to by birth.

"Which one was she?" I asked abruptly, ignoring Kierson's earlier warnings about Casey's mother.

His eyes flashed wide momentarily before he regained composure.

"Which one?" he asked, feigning ignorance. "One of who?"

"Which one of the Underworld's women was she?"

He paused only slightly before answering.

"Hecate, goddess of magic, ghosts, and necromancy."

"I know her well. She is an inescapable fixture in my father's domain and Persephone's personal companion when she returns for her time with Hades."

"She is a whore who spread her legs for another one of Ares' breeding experiments, though it did not yield what he had hoped for.

He realized early on that I was not invincible. It seems that only Sean captured that quality, though I'm not convinced that you have not inherited that trait as well. It seems that no one is willing to test the theory on you as Ares did on me."

"I am not invincible, Casey. It is unnecessary to carry out whatever scheme you have concocted in your mind. I have had more than my share of brushes with death. You need not provide me with another."

"If you insist."

He turned to walk away from me, but my next question stopped him in his tracks.

"You were not raised there, were you? In the Underworld?"

"No," he managed to reply through gritted teeth. "I was not afforded that opportunity like you were." Bitterness laced his words, and I found his response confounding. Most wanted nothing more than to avoid my father's realm at all costs, but Casey seemed slighted because of his inability to stay there.

"You are angry that she gave you up."

"I'm angry that I could not stay where I belonged, *sister*," he snapped, whirling around on me in an instant to cram the harsh angles of his face into mine. "The dead call to me—are a part of me. I feel unbalanced here on Earth. I crave the darkness and depravity that the Underworld surely boasts, and yet I can no more return there than you. Few can traverse that which separates the living from the dead, and, even given my birthright, I am not one of them."

"Then why does Ares keep you here? Surely he would know a way to return you if that is what you wish—"

"He keeps me here for the very reason I want to be in the Underworld—the dead call to me. And Detroit has no shortage of them."

He looked at me with curious eyes, as though assessing whether or not I could put the pieces of the puzzle together. Wondering if I was bred to be as shrewd as he.

"And the Breathers—the Stealers—both are forms of the dead, aren't they?"

"Bravo, sister. Bravo," he replied, his evil smile creeping slowly across his face, though never reaching his eyes. "I was kept here for my ability to find and police them specifically, amongst other reasons. Apparently, I have not done that job very well."

"But up until this point they had done nothing to require such strict regulation, had they? No need to aggressively hunt them?" I countered. "There are so few of you here in a city so large with much ground to cover. I fail to see how any one man could police the Breathers over such a vast area without the possibility of failure. It would take an army."

"I *am* an army," he rumbled, still hovering closer to me than was comfortable.

"Why does this single oversight vex you so? You care for no one, especially not the humans. Protecting them is your charge, not your desire. If their lives are lost, you will not mourn them. Essentially, you have failed at nothing—lost nothing."

Heat from a fire deep within Casey, kindled by his fury, rolled off him and warmed my face. I knew what was to come next. I awaited the blow stoically, not flinching as his jaw flexed wildly and his fists clenched.

But the blow never came. Instead, Casey turned and stormed away from me, muttering something barely intelligible under his breath. *Nothing yet.* I quickly recognized those as the words he spewed into the black night that framed his dark silhouette. It was then that my brother, as soulless and depraved as the worst of the Underworld, showed me that he cared for something.

It appeared that something was me.

~~~~~~~~~~~~~~~~~~~~~~~~

"Drew," Casey barked into his phone from a few paces in front of me. "We've got problems. We need to meet. Where are the others?" He paused momentarily, awaiting the answer to his question. "Yeah, we're down by the Masonic temple . . . yes, Khara is with me. No, don't you fucking start with me. You can be pissed later," he snapped into the phone. "Meet us at the Heidelberg Project. It's close, and it's abandoned. Be there in five." He hung up the phone abruptly and shoved it into his coat, where he had also again concealed his shotgun. "Time for a family meeting, sister. There's a shitstorm heading our way. We need to head it off at the pass."

"We can do nothing until you hear back from your lackeys," I replied, confused as to what could possibly be gained from meeting with the others without any specific information.

He gave me a wary glance before he opened the car door.

"I'm not convinced that we have that long."

18

We pulled into a seemingly vacant neighborhood, full of brightly colored and oddly adorned houses. They were unlike anything I had ever seen. I felt Casey's eyes upon me as I stared out the car window at the bizarre sight.

"Some of the neighborhoods in Detroit became so run-down over time that everyone essentially left," he explained without provocation. "This one has been taken over by artists who seem to think that painting the abandoned homes like clowns and nailing baby doll parts and other tchotchkes to the buildings somehow makes this shithole neighborhood look better. I think it's a fucking joke, but . . . humans are strange beings. If they feel better about their decaying city because they've turned it into a cartoon, so be it."

Unable to find the appropriate words to comment on what I was seeing, I just continued to stare until we pulled up in front of a particularly strange-looking edifice. The entire exterior was covered from the ground up with dots of every shade and size. In the vacant lot beside it was what Casey referred to as the "Vacuum Graveyard," where there were hundreds of those devices lined up in meticulous rows, all bearing a cross of some sort. It was utterly fascinating.

When I finally was able to peel my eyes off the peculiar sight, I saw the others coming toward us from behind the spotted house.

"Explain," Drew demanded as he stormed toward us.

"I got bored. We went out," Casey replied casually, as though Drew wasn't about to flay him alive. "Not important at the moment, though."

"What is so important that it could not wait until we were home?" Drew snarled as he came to stand before us.

"Bad guys, what else?" Casey was unfazed by Drew's hostile tone. "Listen, I paid a little visit to my sewer-dwelling friends."

"And?" Drew pressed, looking uncharacteristically annoyed.

Casey cocked his head as though Drew's agitation was amusing to him.

"And it seems like the Breathers are the least of our worries. Turns out that Pierson was right about them tracking Khara. They want her. Badly. But not for themselves."

"Badly enough to get themselves whacked in the process?" Kierson volleyed, his hand flexing around the hilt of his dagger. "That's a bold move for sure and would require a lot of motivation. Besides, who would use them to get her, especially if that individual wanted her intact? All the Breathers wanted to do when they saw her was feed on her . . . maybe worse."

"Yeah, well, whether or not they were the right henchmen for the job, I have a sneaking suspicion that they aren't the only ones out there that are trying to find her," Casey continued. "Whoever or whatever it is that seeks her knows precisely what she is. Azriel referred to her as the Unborn."

"Fuck," Kierson spat. "So now what? Are you telling me that every questionable supernatural in this city not only knows about her but is also after her? Is there a bounty on her head?"

"That's what I inferred from the gargoyle. He wasn't nearly as forthcoming with his information as I would have liked," Casey said with a downturn of his mouth. "I'm not sure he told me all he knows . . . even after I killed one of his own in front of him. That didn't seem to loosen his lips at all. If I'm wrong about this, then I guess I owe him a fruit basket. If I'm not, then there's someone roaming this city who's after Khara that has Azriel leveraged tightly enough that he would rather face my wrath than give him up."

"Fucking gargoyles . . ." Kierson grumbled. "They're loyal to the highest bidder and no one else."

"Who is powerful or malevolent enough to have them willing to walk into a slaughter rather than talk?" Drew asked, trying to rationalize the gargoyle's seemingly irrational behavior.

"The Dragon is," Kierson offered.

"But the Dragon isn't around," Casey replied with amusement. "He and I had a . . . *discussion* of sorts the last time I saw him. I'm pretty sure he's back in Europe, attempting to find someone to take care of the little problem I gave him." Drew shot Casey a curious look that was met with pure malice. "He won't be back around here for a while. Besides, girls aren't really his thing."

They continued to throw out names and classes of supernatural beings until they appeared to have exhausted their list. Frustrated and without answers, Drew ran his hand through his hair, tugging it roughly. Then he stopped suddenly, frozen in place. Slowly, he turned back toward me, staring at me with fearful eyes.

"There is someone else . . ." His words were quiet and drifted off into the cold night air. He continued to look at me as though his stare was enough to communicate what he was unwilling to say aloud. When enough time had passed, and he realized that I yet again was not following him, he grudgingly and quietly whispered the name that sent chills up my spine.

"Deimos."

The others looked completely bewildered at what appeared to be a random accusation. Judging by the confusion in their expressions, Drew had still not told them of our conversation in the car a few nights earlier.

"Deimos?" Kierson repeated, equally quiet. "Where did you pull that name out of, Drew? He's a scary motherfucker, but he's not exactly lounging around Detroit. Why would you think—"

"Because Khara said that he would come for her once he knew that she had been taken."

A collective silence fell over the group as they processed Drew's words. It was obvious that they too knew enough of Deimos to be wary of him and were not thrilled about the possibility of him being the one who was after their sister.

"Drew," I said calmly. "He would not make a production of my abduction. He would not use lackeys to seek me out. He would come for me himself and take me. There would be no pomp and circumstance. Though he is one that would inspire fear in virtually any being, evil or otherwise, I do not believe he is behind this. It is not his style."

Kierson let his breath out heavily beside me while Pierson and Casey allowed themselves to move for the first time since the mention of Deimos. While living in the Underworld, I knew he was feared by all, including myself, but I had no way of knowing that his reputation in the world above was as terrifying. Regardless, it was warranted.

With the elimination of Deimos from the suspect list, Drew resumed his pacing amid the cemetery of vacuum cleaners.

"So we're essentially no further than we were ten minutes ago," he barked. "All we have to go on is what Azriel said, Casey, and you're not convinced he was even telling the truth."

"I don't trust him, if that's what you're getting at," Casey sneered. "I don't like the feel of this. Something is off."

"The whole fucking thing is off," Kierson shouted, throwing his blade at the adjacent house. It stuck firmly into the bottom half of what had once been a baby doll, affixed to the wooden siding. "I just want something to stab . . . something to kill. I hate all this waiting around. I want to do something now."

"We have to assess what information we do have, brother," Pierson said calmly. "We need to determine precisely what end this being is after. If we knew what the desired result was, we could work back from that to more concretely identify the person who seeks Khara."

"How?" Drew demanded. "She's an unprecedented being, Pierson. There is no book that you can bury your face in to ascertain such information. It doesn't exist. Period."

"I think that if I—"

"Hold on," Drew interrupted, preventing Pierson from expanding on his theory. He reached into his pocket and withdrew his cell phone, giving it a wary look. He pushed a button, then pressed it to his ear. "Oz, what do you—she's right here. Why?" His expression tightened further as he listened. "We're in the Heidelberg Project." Drew pulled the phone away from his ear, looking at it curiously before putting it back into his pocket.

"What the hell did that asshole want?" Kierson snarled as he made his way back to the group, having retrieved his knife. "He never calls us."

"I know," Drew replied soberly. "He said not to go anywhere— that we should be safe where we are—and he needed to meet up with us right away."

"Sounds ominous," Casey growled. The thought seemed to appease him slightly. He, like Kierson, seemed to be itching for a fight.

"We should know momentarily. He said he was only a couple miles away." Drew reflexively surveyed his surroundings, suddenly on high alert. "We need to move inside," he stated calmly, though the tension in his body betrayed him. "We're too exposed here." He pointed to the spotted house beside us and motioned for us to go inside. He no longer spoke, giving directives with hand signals only, his eyes forever tracking something in the distance that did not appear to be there.

Without giving me a choice in the matter, Kierson snatched my arm, ready to drag me to the front porch and inside the house, but Pierson clamped down on my shoulder before he could. His eyes were pinched closed, his body unmoving. Then, only seconds later, Kierson's grip on me tightened, his eyes wide and wild. But it was Casey who broke the silence amongst us, interrupting the vision Pierson and Kierson were sharing. It seemed that he, too, had inside knowledge of what was headed our way.

"It can't be," he whispered, his sharp eyes falling beyond the houses to the east of us. "They're back . . ."

"Casey?" Drew pressed, searching for the impending danger as he quietly demanded an explanation.

But there was no time for one.

All I heard was the drawing of Casey's blades from the leather strap across his chest before Pierson screamed a war cry, signaling the incoming battle. It startled the others into action as well. The word "Stealers" echoed through the abandoned neighborhood until the wall of evil approaching us at inhuman speed swallowed it whole.

The agreement had been most egregiously broken.

19

There was no pause—no plan of attack. The horde raining down upon us allowed for little more than reaction from the brothers, and that was no coincidence. We had most certainly been ambushed.

"Get her in the house!" Drew screamed, but his words were unnecessary. Kierson had already closed the distance between us and the spotted building, throwing me through the front entrance before the order was given. He slammed the door behind him, but only after he tossed me one of his many hidden blades.

"Stab anything that comes in here," he barked before locking me in the darkened quiet, the fight outside muffled by the walls. I looked around quickly, taking in my surroundings before making my way to a broken window. My need to see how the few were faring against the many was uncontrollable.

When I peered out, it was impossible to ascertain which side was winning. A sea of bodies encircled the house, my brothers swallowed by it. And that is when I felt it—the pull. The darkness called again, only this time it was hundredfold. My eyes darted to the front door, the sound of cracking wood and heavy steps on the porch demanding my attention, as did the darkness that the one on the other side of the door possessed.

As if it was weightless, my body glided toward the barrier that kept me from that which I so deeply desired. With every phantom step I took, the intensity rose, stoking the fire that grew within me.

Whatever awaited me, I wanted it and would stop at nothing until I had claimed it. The darkness was mine.

And then the craving subsided.

For a second I felt its absence like a wound, sharp at first, then fading abruptly to a dull and pervasive ache. I lunged for the door-knob, needing to find what silenced the call. But before I could reach it, the door flung open and Oz stormed in, his eyes wild, his body covered in blackened blood.

He stepped toward me, weapons in hand. Without hesitation, I obeyed Kierson's words and stabbed Oz.

He looked down at the dagger embedded in his arm, myriad emotions playing across his face.

"Your aim needs work, new girl," he mocked, plucking the blade from his forearm as though it were a splinter—a nuisance and nothing more.

"Kierson said to stab anything that came in the house."

"Perhaps he and I will have to have a discussion about specificity once we all get out of here alive," he purred, a look of wicked amusement overtaking his hardened expression.

There was something else in it, something beneath the bravado and arrogance, but I was afforded no time to analyze it further. The darkness called again.

"Time to go," he said, scooping me up in his left arm and tucking me inelegantly underneath it. I fought his hold with every step as he retreated from the house, taking to the streets, and, consequently, the ongoing battle within them. All the while, that sweet song of evil sang to me, calling me to join it.

That was all I wished to do.

Oz slashed his way through the melee still engulfing the colorful neighborhood. Then I heard him call to Drew. The only response from him was, "Get her out of here!"

Doing as he was told for presumably the first time in centuries,

Oz wound his way through the bloody brawl, breaking free of it after some time. With incredible speed, he ran down the street toward his Jeep. Unfortunately for him, he was not alone.

The battleground seemed to ebb and flow based on my presence. As soon as it was apparent that I had left, a wave of remaining Stealers followed us, gaining ground as Oz struggled to get me into the vehicle. I would not go willingly.

"For fuck's sake, Khara," he yelled, shoving my head in the door while my arms remained splayed out across the entrance in protest. "This is hardly the time to play hard to get."

At the sound of my name on his tongue, I relaxed, and he took full advantage of that single moment, heaving me through the driver's side door and across the interior to come crashing down on the passenger seat. Jumping in behind me, he turned the ignition, threw the vehicle into gear, and raced down the road, narrowly escaping the approaching mob.

He wove through the streets of Detroit with ease, driving at speeds far greater than those of the other vehicles occupying the road. In a matter of minutes, we arrived in a familiar area. Our house was near.

With growing distance from the Stealers, my head cleared. The call of darkness faded until it was little more than a buzzing sensation in the back of my mind. That, too, eventually disappeared.

As he drove he said nothing, his utmost concentration remaining on the task at hand: carrying out Drew's orders. He had accomplished part of that with our successful escape, though it was through no help of mine—a point that I was most certain he would address once we were inside the home.

The Victorian soon emerged on the horizon, and Oz sped toward it but did not stop. Instead, he drove past it, turning down a side street two blocks away. When the house was fully out of view, he parked his Jeep and got out.

"In case we were followed," he offered as though he knew what I was pondering. I watched him closely as he stood outside the vehicle, staring back at me. "We need to get to the house. Now." Still, I remained unmoving. With a loud, put-upon sigh, he slammed his door and made his way to my side of the vehicle, cursing as he did. "It's like you're trying to get yourself killed," he muttered as he threw my door open and glared at me. "Shall we?" He made a sweeping motion of his arm, bowing slightly to me in a mocking manner.

Tentatively, I emerged from the vehicle, still recovering from the night's events. My clarity of mind was returning slowly, but it did not prove to be fast enough for Oz, who was soon in my face assessing something, his disgruntled expression intact.

"Are you still in their thrall?" he asked pointedly. When I did not immediately answer him, he grabbed my arms and shook me slightly. "*Khara!* Are you still in their thrall?" His words were more urgent and demanding that time, and my gaze wandered up to his fierce and threatening eyes.

"My name," I whispered, my voice sounding distant and detached.

"Yes, I said your name. Can we go now?"

"Something happens when you say it . . ." I continued, ignoring his reply. "At the car . . ." For a moment I paused, trying to make sense of what I remembered. "You said my name and I hesitated." With a clearer mind, I thought back to the few instances when Oz had used my given name to address me. Every time it had some sort of effect on me. "Why?"

He looked at me strangely, as though he were preparing to argue with me, then stopped. His lips pressed together tightly in a grim expression.

"If it helps you make better decisions while trying to escape a horde of soul-sucking savages, does it matter? Can we go now, *Khara?*"

Without responding, I stepped out of the vehicle to stand in front of Oz, who was looking over me, into the distance. My skin prickled. His eyes narrowed.

"Definitely time to go," he said, grabbing my arm as he started running in the direction of the Victorian. His speed was impossible to match, and he once again snatched me up, throwing me over his shoulder as he hastened toward the safety of the wards.

With only a few houses left to pass, he came to a halt, snarling under his breath at something before him that I could not see. But I did not need to. My soul recognized the beautiful song instantly.

"So good of you to collect her for us, Ozereus," a melodic voice called out. It sounded vaguely familiar.

"Is that what I'm doing?" he replied venomously.

"You know she will be ours," the man said calmly, his words falling on my ears like sweet music. "Hand her over now, fallen one, and this can all be over. No need for further bloodshed."

"Speaking of bloodshed, how did you manage to escape it? I saw you with the others, and they weren't faring so well when I stole her from under your noses."

"The PC brothers, though skilled, are not infallible. They have lost in battle before, Oz. They will lose again. Do not overestimate the abilities of those you have allied yourself with."

"I ally with no one," Oz corrected as he dropped me to my feet beside him. The second I was free, I turned to see whose voice beckoned me. Under the spell of his darkness, I showed no surprise when I saw the man I had shared drinks with at the Tenth Circle looking back at me. The one who presumably set this entire plan in motion.

Though I should have wanted to flee him, I instead felt my body drifting toward him—him and the army of his kind that blocked us from the protection of the warded Victorian. Oz held me back, his arm a tether around my waist. I wanted to stab him again to get free.

"I am well aware of where your loyalties lie, or, better yet, where they do not. Funny, though, that you fight for one of your own who doesn't want you. Look at her strain to escape your grasp," he said, then turned his attention to me. "You want to come to me, don't you, Unborn?"

And I did. With every fiber of my being, I wanted to float toward him, riding on the haunting chorus that sang only to me. His deep-set, dark eyes could see it in my expression, and he extended his lithe arm, further beckoning me to him.

"*Khara,*" Oz said calmly, his tone even and unfaltering. Again, my head cleared just enough to let his words permeate the haze that threatened to permanently overtake my mind and deliver me to the vacuous creature before me. "Do you know where the house is?"

"Yes," I replied, wondering why he would ask such an inane question. I looked beyond the wall of hungry Stealers standing between me and the safety of the warded Victorian. I realized then that his question was less about my knowledge of where I lived and more a test of my lucidity at that moment. "Do you remember what Kierson told you? Back in Heidelberg Project?"

"Of course."

"That rule still applies," he said with a slight smile in his voice. "With the exception of me this time."

I stole a glance up at his expression, but got nothing in return. Whatever humor had tinged his response was gone. His harsh, cold eyes were all for the enemy before him. It was a sight to behold indeed.

"Where can she go, Oz?" the presumed leader of the Stealers asked, his voice condescendingly diplomatic. "There is no hope of her escaping, with or without your aid. We are too many and the pull is too strong. Even now, I can feel the draw, however muted. She wants to come to us."

I could not dispute his claim.

"*Khara,*" Oz cautioned, tightening his hold on my waist. He leaned in close, whispering something in my ear. His lips brushed against me while a low rumbling of foreign words echoed through my consciousness. When he finished, he stole a glance at me to be certain that, on some level, I had understood what he had said. Much to my surprise, a part of me did.

Drawing my borrowed blade, I stood beside Oz, awaiting his directive. The air prickled around us, the energy nearly electric between the two parties. Between evil and not.

"Time to see exactly what you're made of, new girl," Oz purred, his body coiled to strike the congregation before us.

I mimicked his stance. With a cleared mind and able body, I, too, was ready to see just what I could do against those that sought to steal my light. I would not be remade into something else. My soul, tainted though it may have been, was mine.

And I would fight to preserve it.

20

Whatever ancient words Oz had spoken, they awakened something in me. Something that had always been there. I felt the shift deep within me.

The second Oz lunged at the slew of Stealers facing off against us, I followed. They were many and we were not, but it took only one to rule the evil of the Underworld, and I had studied him for centuries. Surely I had learned something of value in that time.

My feet felt light and swift beneath me, moving with a speed previously unknown to them. I fell upon the darkness before me, slashing at the Stealers as they reached for me, trying to pull me into their web of emptiness. But I would not be theirs to take.

Oz at my side, we fought in unison until nearly half the Stealers had been disposed of. As they fell, I felt our chances were good, not only for escape but also for the total annihilation of those attacking us. Imminent victory was a heady feeling—and my arrogance may have been my undoing.

The very moment I allowed myself to be distracted, the tables turned.

Oz was glorious to watch, fighting with an ease and grace befitting his kind—*our* kind. But he, unlike me, had centuries of practice and unfaltering focus. In that single second when my attention waned, I was grabbed from behind. Whatever good Oz's words had done evaporated in an instant. The darkness took its place.

"So sweet . . ." my assailant whispered in my ear. My head turned of its own accord to seek the lips of he who spoke. I did not struggle. I did not call for help.

I did nothing but anticipate what was to come.

"Khara!" Oz screamed, breaking the psychological hold the Stealer had on me. I quickly broke his physical hold as well, piercing his throat with Kierson's blade. I watched him shrivel as I withdrew it before returning my focus to the task at hand.

Somehow, despite how hard we fought and how many we killed, it appeared as though their numbers were increasing. Instead of seeing a few Stealers left to dispose of, an entirely new crop had replaced those that had been slain. I knew not where they were coming from.

"Khara!" Oz shouted again as we attempted to slash our way through the formidable mass of enemies. "The wards . . . get to the house." Though my arm sawed through the evil before me as if possessed, I knew that we were succumbing to the numbers amassing around us. "I can't watch you and kill at the same time," he shouted when I refused to leave. "Go! Now!"

So I did as he bade me, taking out as many Stealers as I could on my way. After a path was cleared, I ran for the home just down the street with a foreign and lightning speed. I knew I would make it. I knew I could not be caught.

I crashed upon the front door in a blur of motion, yanking it open without care and slamming it behind me. The second I did, I heard a cry from the battle that rattled my very core.

"Oz!"

Unthinking, I threw open the door that had just shut out the ongoing war in the street, needing to see what had caused him to make such a sound.

That carelessness was the reason I soon found myself in the entrance of our once-grand home being courted by death.

My life had been spent around evil, learning its every move, its inner workings. "Know your enemy," Father said often, his words now echoing through my mind while the one who would drain my soul stood in front of me, beckoning me to him. I would have choked on the irony of it all, wondering if I had any soul left at all to steal, but I was too preoccupied with the darkness to acknowledge anything else.

My time had come, and I welcomed it.

The leader's voice caressed my skin softly as his lips neared mine, whispering of wondrous pleasures that would soon be upon me. I awaited them with bated breath. It felt as though he had seen something in me that I had not seen myself and called to it deliciously, coaxing it to the surface with every look, every movement, every word. I was soothingly lulled into a trance, rendering me vulnerable in every possible way, and I delighted in the feeling—the escape. I craved it.

The second his lips touched mine, everything changed.

What had just seemed so tempting and sweet soured in an instant. Gone was the promise of joy beyond my wildest dreams; pain and horror quickly replaced it, and I frantically fought to escape.

He forced me deeper into the house while I clawed at him wildly, wanting nothing more than to separate us. In the short time it took to reach the living room, I felt the futility of my fight. The longer we were connected the more my desire to combat him dissipated. I could feel him searching through me, looking for the light he so desperately sought—the sweet sustenance he required. Things I had long forgotten were brought to the forefront of my mind to be relived as he scoured my mind and body for what he had come to claim.

"There is so little left in you," he muttered as he held my face to his. "Such a hard life. So much pain. I shall end it soon . . . you will thank me for that."

My mind began begging him to make good on his word, wanting anything but to relive the centuries of physical pain that had surfaced simultaneously while he endeavored to steal the essence of my being. It was intolerable. Death or emptiness seemed a far more favorable option.

Instead, I was delivered from my fate in an entirely different way.

The sound that the Stealer made when the blade sunk deeply into his throat was something I had heard before, though I had not expected to hear it anywhere apart from the Underworld. His shrill but garbled cry was the same sound that those brought to Father under false pretense would make. There was a certain agony to their tone when their sentence was carried out. He told me it was because they were taken against their will—that their souls cried out for justice. I did not presume to know if Stealers had souls of their own, but I wondered if it was the souls he had stolen that cried out instead. If so, their cries were heard.

Justice was swift.

When its body fell to the floor, shriveling into a desiccated mass, it revealed who had been standing behind it. The one who saved me from my pain—saved me from my doom. Oz stood inches away from me, the blade still in his hand. He appeared to be talking to me, but I heard nothing, just the call of the damned and the dark voices in my head.

"Cold . . ." I whispered, uncertain if he could hear me. "I am so cold."

He lunged at me, taking my chin in his hand. He stared at me, long and fiercely—all the while rambling on about something, the details of which I still could not comprehend. His eyes dropped to my throat, and he tilted my head back to gain a better view of it. Brutal heat seared my skin when his fingers danced along my neck quickly, and I screamed from the pain.

Collapsing to the ground, I shook violently. He darted away from me, only to return in an instant with bandages and tape.

"Try to hold still." I heard his voice as only a whisper, though I could tell by the strain in his features that he was clearly yelling his order at me. I did my best to submit to his command, but I could not quell the systemic tremors that coursed throughout my body. "Dammit," he yelled, the veins in his neck bulging grotesquely. "I have to cleanse and close this. Your body cannot tolerate his blood—it's poison. This is going to hurt."

With his trailing words, he pinned his knee firmly against my chest, pressing the weight of his body down onto it. Again the fiery burn was upon my neck and, though I tried desperately to contain them, my screams escaped instantaneously. Then they stopped.

My hearing returned in full, which was greatly demonstrated by the assaulting volume of Oz's voice. Along with my hearing came the cold.

"Khara!" he snarled, thrusting his face into mine. "Snap out of it!" With his words, the clarity of my thoughts returned, however slightly.

"What happened?" I whispered shakily as my body continued to revolt against my mind. "Why do I feel this way?"

"Because you almost let that evil bastard suck you soulless, that's why." His expression was furious and condescending. "He was just getting started, but if I'd arrived a minute or two later . . ."

"So cold," I said softly, trying to focus on what he was saying. I could not. The only thing I could bring attention to was the frozen emptiness I felt and how to abate it. It was as if the frigidness I had endured my entire existence had been multiplied exponentially. "I need to warm myself."

I tried to push up off the floor with little success, my body continually betraying my every attempt.

"Here," Oz mumbled, lifting me into his arms abruptly. "Where are you trying to go?"

"The bathroom . . . the shower," I started, raising a feeble and shaky arm to point in that direction. It was the most logical place I could think of to lessen the iciness consuming me. He whisked me in there and sat me down before he turned the water on as hot as he could tolerate, then helped me undress.

My skin was ghostly white—deathly pale. Oz ushered me into the blistering spray of the shower without a word, though he stared at me intently. He looked pained in his silence, as though holding his tongue was the greatest challenge he had faced that night. I stood awkwardly, bent in on myself from the incessant contracting of my muscles, and let the water pelt me, burning my exterior while my insides remained frozen to the core.

My plan was not working.

"I can't stop shaking," I uttered through chattering teeth.

"I know," he said, eying me tightly. "The cold you feel has nothing to do with temperature. It is the start of the emptiness."

"I have always been cold . . . this is far worse," I whispered shakily.

He stared at me momentarily, then reached in without my suggestion and turned off the water, wrapping me immediately afterward in a towel. His hands worked furiously to dry me before he scooped me up yet again and carried me downstairs to my room.

"I don't know what to do for you," he said angrily, "but something must be done. He may not have succeeded in taking your soul, but he took something nonetheless. Something that needs to be replaced."

"He said I had so little left," I whispered faintly. It was becoming increasingly arduous to talk while my body constricted against my lungs. "What did he mean?"

"Light," Oz replied with his back to me. "He meant you have little light left in your soul. It had already been overcome by darkness, or maybe it was never very light to begin with. Either way, the irony of that is it may have been your saving grace. Souls are not easily taken. Apparently yours was harder to steal than most."

"I felt the evil . . ."

"It's not hard to when it's sucking on your face." His voice was harsh, but when he looked up at me, his eyes falling heavy on mine, there was something in them—pain. "Don't worry about that . . . it's not important now," he said, getting up to search for warm clothing to give me. He handed me what he could find, then continued. "Do you remember anything? Anything about what happened?"

"My memories," I whispered, shuddering at the pain I had relived.

"What about them?" he pressed, squatting before me. There was urgency in his expression as he leaned in closer to me.

"It was as though he was sifting through them, selecting certain ones and leaving me to relive others."

"Do you remember what he tried to take?"

"No," I whispered. "All I remember were the things I had long ago forgotten. Things I had not wanted to recall. Whatever he found while rummaging through my memories, he kept."

Oz cursed loudly as he helped to layer the clothing he found onto my body.

"Your father—Hades—you love him, right?"

I considered his question for a moment.

"I do," I answered, confusion evident in my expression. "But I cannot remember why. I feel that I cared for him, but I cannot think of anything that would warrant that emotion toward him."

"Shit!" Oz shouted, throwing something heavy across the room. "Can you think of anything that ever made you happy? That brought you joy of any sort, no matter how little?" I shook my head in negation. "Fine," he replied, his eyes darting around as though searching the room we occupied for the answers he sought. "What if you could replace what was taken?" His words were spoken aloud, though they sounded like a thought that he had accidentally allowed to escape. After a moment of silence, he focused on my eyes, leaning against my legs as he moved in so close that our noses nearly brushed. "What if you could fill the emptiness, Khara? What if you could fill it with memories like those that were stolen?"

"More memories?" I replied, not following his train of thought.

"Memories . . . feelings. But new ones. Lighter ones." He captured my face in his hands, gently demanding my attention. "Khara—"

The smashing of the front door interrupted him, the start of a ruckus breaking out upstairs. My brothers had returned.

"Think, Khara," Oz growled, grabbing my face more fiercely. My mind momentarily cleared. "Does nothing bring you happiness? Is there nothing that could fill this void?"

I stared into his deep brown eyes, wondering if anything could replace what light was stolen. The desperation I found in them was startling. His dark expression accurately portrayed his hopelessness, which implied that he, for once in the time I had known him, felt something other than anger, bitterness, or entitlement. He dropped his hands to my shoulders, sliding them down my arms while we continued to stare at each other in silence. My shaking quieted in his grip.

"Khara!" Casey rumbled from the floor above, reminding me that they, too, had been embroiled in battle that night. Until that moment, I had not known what the outcome was. At least Casey had survived.

I looked back to Oz, only to find his formerly panicked face masked by its normal arrogance.

"I am all right," I called loudly enough to be heard both through the door and over the commotion above.

The basement door nearly flew off its hinges before Casey descended the stairs while two others followed him down. They quickly consumed the space around Oz and me.

"What happened to her, Oz?" Drew asked, his tone threatening. "Explain."

"I think, Drew, that the body upstairs along with the ones littering the street outside should be explanation enough, don't you?" he replied, coming to stand nose-to-nose with my brother.

"Do not trifle with me on this, Ozereus. Not this time. I want answers. Now."

"Then it is Khara who you should interrogate," Oz said casually as he stared Drew down. "I simply walked in on a Stealer making out with her. I stabbed him through the throat, as was needed. The rest is Khara's story to tell."

"Did he take anything?" Pierson asked, pushing past them to hover over me slightly.

"I do not know for sure. Memories, I think," I replied faintly. "But I felt the emptiness . . . and the cold."

"You are lucky she's okay," Drew threatened, still posturing with Oz. Pierson eyed me intently, looking me over before asking his next question.

"That has yet to be determined." He examined me as best he could as the others came to crowd around him. "And now? Do you feel the cold now?"

"No," I whispered, looking down at my previously shaking limbs. "I do not." He looked as surprised as I felt. It had been only moments before that I wished for the cold to cease, yet somehow, in my dealings with Oz, I had missed its disappearance entirely.

Oz ripped his gaze from Drew's long enough to look down at me strangely before he pushed his way past him, heading up the stairs.

Drew whispered something to Pierson before following after Oz. Casey, who must have retreated from the initial chaos surrounding me, approached slowly from the shadows of the basement. Rounding the foot of the bed, he stopped just in front of me, silently staring me down. I returned his glare with equal force. That had become our standard form of communication. When he seemed satisfied with my response, he gave a brisk nod of his head and laid his hand on my shoulder, ever so slightly squeezing it once.

He indicated to Pierson that they should join Drew upstairs, presumably to deal with the shell of the Stealer still lying on the living room rug—along with those strewn about the street. Just as Pierson started to argue, claiming I was in need of further attention, there was another outbreak of noise from the first floor. One far louder than before. The two of them raced up the staircase, and I found myself leaping off the bed to follow closely behind them. For no reason that I could explain, I felt a tightening in my chest.

Something was amiss.

"Where is she?" an unfamiliar voice roared, echoing off the walls.

Before an explanation was given, I broke into the living room to see a staggering sight. The shredded body of the Stealer danced through the air beautifully, the tiny flakes showering down on all who stood there, covering the room with a macabre layer of snow-like matter.

I looked through squinted eyes to see a nearly unrecognizable Kierson, covered in blood and breathing heavily. He clutched daggers fiercely in both of his hands. As the pieces of the petrified body settled throughout the room, I was able to see him more clearly. His eyes were black as night, his hair disheveled. He looked at me as though he would attack and kill at any moment.

"I am here," I said quietly.

"Did he touch you?" he asked between sharp inhales.

"Yes."

He threw his head back violently and let loose a sound so penetrating and sharp that the entire room, including its occupants, shook while the mirror behind me shattered. When he stopped, he brought his gaze back slowly to meet mine. His eyes had lightened and the fierceness in them had left. A familiar sadness replaced it.

"Are you okay?"

"I am fine," I replied softly. "From what can be ascertained."

He dropped his weapons to the floor and slowly made his way toward me. Pierson stepped into his path, stopping him momentarily. The two had a silent conversation, staring at one another before Kierson nodded once in agreement to whatever message Pierson had relayed to him. Picking up his pace as he neared me, Kierson's arms spread wide. The second I was within reach, he snatched me up tightly, crushing my body into his embrace and smothering me with his chest.

His heart beat wildly.

"Don't ever make me think something happened to you again,"

he whispered, his breath tickling the top of my head. "I could not survive your loss. None of us could."

I felt as though my arms had taken on a life of their own as they drifted up, unaided, to the small of his back. They wanted to comfort him. The gesture felt alien to me, as did the sentiment that drove it, and they stopped just shy of their goal, slowly sinking back down to my sides. For the first time in my life, or at least the life I could remember, I had wanted to hold another as they held me.

"I will not cause you to worry again," I said, my words muffled by his body. "But you would survive my loss, Kierson, as would the others, because it is part of who you are. The strong go on. The weak perish."

"You," he said with a growl as he pushed me far enough away from his body to see my face, "are *not* weak." He looked around at the other faces in the room, seeking their confirmation of his assessment. Much to my surprise, they appeared to agree.

Then Kierson's gaze fell upon Oz, whose expression was completely devoid of emotion.

"You saved her." His words were not a question but an accusation, his tone conflicted. It was more than apparent that my death would have caused Kierson inescapable pain, but to be in Oz's debt yet again appeared to weigh on him more than even he likely expected it to.

"She had been saving herself just fine until she lost all sense and practically delivered herself to the Stealer who's currently decorating this room." Oz's eyes quickly fell on Pierson. "Want to explain how that asshat got in here in the first place?" he sneered. "I thought your high-and-mighty self had this place on magical lockdown." Pierson's expression soured, but he did not respond. "I won't ask twice," Oz growled.

With a heavy sigh, Pierson answered his question.

"He got in here because the house was not warded against his kind."

The silence in the room was oppressive as my other brothers and Oz stared at Pierson incredulously.

"What do you mean 'not warded against his kind'?" Oz rumbled, stepping toward Pierson, who did nothing to retreat.

"Simply put, the house was not warded against Stealers. And why should it have been? They were no longer," he offered in his defense, though none appeared to be accepting his reasoning. "Magic takes energy to maintain and comes at a cost. There was no logic in spending that which I have so little of on something that posed no threat."

"But that's exactly who we needed to protect her from," Kierson cried, a sense of sadness and disbelief in his tone. He revered his twin—possibly envied him. For Pierson to have fallen so short of his expectations was just shy of inconceivable to him.

"A fact that has only recently been brought to my attention, Kierson," Pierson countered, his mask of superiority intact, but wavering slightly. "Had I known that they were a present threat before this evening, I would have taken the appropriate measures to fortify the wards."

His response, though reasonable, did little to appease Kierson, who was still on edge from the scene he had walked in on moments earlier.

"Pierson is not to blame, Kierson," I said softly. "It is illogical to protect against something that you know to no longer exist. I would have made that same oversight had it been my responsibility to guard the house and those in it." I looked across the room to Pierson. He would not meet my gaze. "Had there been a way to know that the Stealers had reemerged, then blame could be cast his direction. Since there was not, no guilt should fall upon him."

At my words, Pierson slowly turned his eyes to mine. For the first time, they held something other than arrogance and wisdom.

"Which brings about the bigger issue here, that somehow those fuckers managed to not only re-create themselves but also multiply like rabbits right under our noses," Kierson observed. "I think it's now abundantly clear that the rogue Breather I found the other night wasn't the first one to slip up. That's the only way for the Stealers to have been reborn. And somehow I don't think it's a coincidence that this is all occurring around the same time as Khara's arrival here. I mean . . . they had that picture of her . . ." His eyes narrowed slightly as he came to his final deduction. "And why do I have the sneaking suspicion that we didn't face the full force of the Stealers tonight? We couldn't possibly be that lucky. If I'm right, just how screwed are we?" Kierson's expression was grim while he spoke. Behind it was a story. "I mean . . . last time, we had all the others . . ."

"Yeah," Casey barked, cutting him off. "And they're dead now. We're the ones that survived the war. We can handle this."

"You've done a bang-up job of handling them up until now, haven't you, Casey? Aren't you the great and mighty tracker? The one who can sense the dead?" Kierson, fueled by fear and rage, stuck his face directly into Casey's as he spewed forth accusations. "The Stealers showed up on your watch, Casey, and they almost killed Khara. How well did you deal with that?"

"I will deal with it now," he replied, stepping closer to Kierson, whose hands were drawn back, ready to throw the first punch.

"Enough!" Drew roared. "Neither of you move!" Like trained pets, they obeyed his command—frozen in place, only inches from one another. "We're not going to be especially helpful to Khara, or anyone in this city for that matter, if we don't stop fighting amongst ourselves and start figuring out just what the fuck happened tonight and how we're going to fix it." His eyes were glowing with anger as he stalked around the room. "Can you two get it together enough to focus on the task at hand?" he asked, his anger still palpable. Kierson quickly agreed, and, in true form, Casey took his time to respond. Once Drew appeared confident that they could behave, he released them. "Now, Casey, is it possible for the Stealers to have been here long without you finding them?"

"No," Casey rumbled. "No way."

"Good, so that means this is something new . . . a new development.

With any luck, they haven't been able to amass numbers that are outside of our ability to eradicate."

"That's a bold statement there, Casey," Oz drawled from his perch on the stairs where he sat. I had nearly failed to notice he was there. "You're really willing to make that assumption based on your skills alone?"

"What the fuck do you care?" Casey spat.

"I don't," he replied, his eyes firmly fixed on my brother. "It's just an observation."

"Yeah, well, you can shove your observations up your ass. We don't need your help."

"And yet you did, just tonight, in fact."

"About that," Drew interjected, his eyes narrowing slightly. "What was so important that you called me in the middle of the night—during your prime mating hours—to see where we were? What we were doing?" He moved slowly toward Oz, his thoughts made plain by the scowl on his face. "You made sure to check on Khara's whereabouts as well. Care to tell me why?"

It was Oz's turn to harden his stare, training it on Drew while he remained silent.

"Son of a bitch," Casey roared. "You knew. You knew about them, and that's what you came to tell us. That's why you were concerned enough to drop whatever ass you were hitting and run over to the fucking Heidelberg Project. You knew they were after her."

"Yes. I knew," Oz muttered, slowly uncurling his body to stand on the staircase before us all.

"How?" Casey asked, his voice so low it was virtually inaudible. "How could you possibly have known?"

"I think the question you would be better suited to ask here, Casey, is, 'How could you possibly have known when I did not?'" Casey slowly drew his favored blade from the harness across his chest, making a show of it as he did. "That would be unwise," Oz cautioned. "For several reasons, not the least of which is that you need me."

"Why?" Drew asked, doing nothing to stop Casey this time as he slowly stalked toward Oz. "Why do we need you?"

"To find them." Oz's cavalier attitude only enraged Casey further.

"The dead call to me!" Casey snarled, lunging for Oz. Seeing the inevitable, Drew halted him with his words, once again leaving Casey only a breath away from his target, straining against the command that held him so firmly in place.

"The dead may in fact call to you, Casey, but you know as well as I do that your proximity to them limits that ability. Unless you are close enough to feel their presence, or there is a veritable army of them, they go undetected." Oz leaned forward slightly, taunting Casey further. "They were practically in your lap before you felt them tonight, weren't they?"

Every muscle in Casey's body tensed.

"I'd go easy on the insults, Oz," Drew warned. "If you piss him off enough, I'll let him loose, and when the brawl breaks out I won't have any intention of intervening." Oz scoffed haughtily at Drew's threat. "You still haven't answered my question yet, Oz. Why is it that we need you?"

"If you want to find them, then I'm your best asset in that endeavor. The dead may call to Casey, but they scream for me," Oz purred; the air of violence circulating around him delighted him. "I couldn't escape their call if I traveled to the farthest ends of the earth. It's a part of who I am—imprinted on my soul."

"You have no soul," Casey observed, his words not a slur of character but a statement of fact.

"My soul is very much intact, Casey," Oz growled. "The fact that I choose to ignore it is hardly an issue of importance at the moment. Only Dark Ones are without the ability to feel the presence of the Stealers, and I am hardly that." When there was no response from the others, his arrogance took over, and he began taunting Casey even further. "I'm also rather skilled at eliminating them, in case you didn't notice."

"At ease, Casey," Drew ordered, that strange crackle in the air as he said it. Grudgingly, Casey lowered his weapon, sheathing it in his chest strap. "It seems we may need him after all, presuming that he can be trusted to do what needs to be done, when it needs to be done." Drew stared Oz down, seeking a sign that his conditions were understood, but received nothing in return. "I'm thrilled to know that you have some semblance of a soul, Oz, but I'm curious as to how you came to realize the Stealers were back. That detail seems a bit fuzzy still, and I'd like to clarify it because, as you well know, the return of an evil force like that is something you should have most certainly shared with us—immediately. And I'm not sure that's what you did, unless your contention is that you only found out about them this evening . . ."

Oz's gaze fell on me for the first time since I'd entered the living room. His stare was cold and hardened—everything I'd known him to be. There was no shred of the angel who had fought beside me.

"I had my suspicions at the club last night . . . especially when she stripped down and nearly swan-dived off the balcony," he said, his eyes returning to Drew. "But it had been a long time since I'd felt the presence of a Stealer. And, with all the other evil dwelling in that place, I couldn't be sure. I just knew something was wrong." He paused for a moment, returning his gaze to me. His eyes softened, if only for a second. "Then later that night Khara came to me. That's when I knew that what I had felt that night was a Stealer. That is why she acted so strangely."

"She came to you? How is that confirmation of anything?" Drew pressed, his frustration mounting. "I don't understand how those two things coincide, but I sure as hell better in a hurry."

Drew's indirect threat had no effect on Oz.

"For whatever reason, their darkness calls to her—influences her," Oz struggled to explain. "I saw it that night in the club. I saw it tonight when we fought the Stealers in the street outside the house. And I saw it last night when she came for me, needing flesh in a way that she surely never has before. That alone would have been all the proof I needed. The night she exposed herself, the Stealer's effect had been lasting and strong—his thrall all-consuming." Again he paused, a brief look of sadness marring his standard haughty expression. "She inherently sought out any form of darkness she could find to satiate it."

"Meaning?" Drew asked, sounding less irritated and far more angry. Oz gritted his teeth violently.

"Meaning she tried to get me to fuck her brains out."

Drew faltered for a moment, blindsided by the crude phrasing of Oz's response.

"And did you manage not to stick your dick in her before that realization?" Casey asked, his hand reaching for the hilt of his dagger. His words were a test. Had Oz failed it, blood would have been shed.

"Of course," he scoffed, his trademark arrogance tainting his reply. "She's not exactly my type, in case you hadn't noticed. I prefer mine a little less uptight and a tad more compliant." A wide, satisfied smile spread across his face—a show for those who looked on. Oddly, as he stared the others down, his eyes strategically never settled on mine.

"Then you get to live," Casey said, taking his hand away from his weapon of choice.

"Which is really for the best, given that *you* didn't have any knowledge of his presence that night in the club. Like it or not, Casey, you need me."

Drew ignored the posturing that was starting again to address me directly.

"Did this happen as he claims?" Drew asked, looking far more composed than he had when Oz first informed him of my near indiscretion the previous night.

"It did. I cannot explain what occurred, or why it did. My body demanded things that my mind would never have sanctioned, had it been in control. I believe it was the darkness. It seems that I have few defenses against my attraction to it."

"I will see what I can find," Pierson declared. "There must be a way to shield you from it, if only temporarily."

"Good idea, Pierson," Drew concurred. "Now, can we get back to the part where you explain precisely how you knew they were after her, Oz?"

"I thought that's what I just did," he replied, annoyance polluting his tone. "Do you think it was a coincidence that there was a Stealer at the Tenth Circle? I'm pretty certain that your reputation is widespread enough for any and all the supernatural beings in this city to know that you frequent it. Why would something that is not permitted to exist put itself in the line of fire just to play a little grab ass and drink?" He stared Drew down, willing him to see the wisdom that was plain in his words. "He knew. It's the only explanation that makes sense in retrospect."

Drew's eyes assessed Oz carefully while he mulled over the explanation he had been given. He appeared loath to admit that Oz had an exceedingly valid point.

"Fine," he conceded, looking to the rest of us. "In the meantime, I'm going to hash out a plan of attack for the morning. I've already called Sean; he is coming tomorrow. And we are all going to do whatever it takes to get as much of this situation sorted out as possible before he arrives, because I for one do not wish to expose yet another area of our failure to him."

"Is that all?" Oz asked, heading for the stairs. "Because if we're finished here for the night I'll be retiring, if that's acceptable." His words were mocking, knowing that Drew could do little to stop him, even if he had still required his presence.

"Are there more?" I called after him, the words escaping me before they had registered fully in my mind. Oz halted, looking back over his shoulder at me with an impassive expression.

"When it comes to evil, new girl, there will always be more."

With that, he disappeared into the darkness of the hallway above, not to be heard from again that evening. When I turned my attention back to my brothers, I was met with a mix of emotions. Kierson was still riddled with worry. Pierson was pensive. Casey was brooding. And Drew looked weary, exhausted from what had happened and what was yet to come. I did not envy his position. Knowing that the situation had gotten further out of hand meant one thing for him: explaining to Sean upon his arrival why things were spiraling downward yet again.

"Khara," Drew said softly as he approached me, coming to a stop with his hand upon my shoulder. The other reached up to the gauze on my neck, brushing it lightly with his fingertip. "You need to rest and heal. We have a mess on our hands, as you well know, but most of it can keep until tomorrow. Pierson will be up until he fortifies the wards, and, in the meantime, we will all take shifts to be sure that you are well guarded."

I nodded once in response, turning to leave without any further production. Drew had made his point abundantly clear, though it was unnecessary. I was already aware of what we were facing. It had nearly taken my soul that night.

When I opened the door to the basement, I found myself hesitating slightly. Somehow, our interaction felt unfinished, and, though I was unclear on exactly how to proceed, I needed a better sense of closure after all that had happened that evening.

"Thank you," I said firmly, still facing the direction of my retreat. "For everything."

Before any of them had a chance to respond, I closed the door behind me, sealing myself off from the residual emotions still swirling throughout the first floor. I immediately descended the stairs and crawled into bed, burying myself deep under the covers. So much had happened that night, more than I could gain perspective on by filtering it through my past experiences.

The sense of freedom I had only just acquired was threatened by the very beings that could enslave my soul, and Oz, the one who had proved to be the bane of my existence from the moment I arrived in

Detroit, was the principal entity needed to prevent that from occurring. I could not make sense of the dichotomy and struggled against the pressure that mounted in my head as a result of it.

Knowing that Oz's presence had somehow aided in abating the cold of the emptiness did nothing to help.

My mind had always been a tangle of absolutes, amassed over a lifetime of trial by fire. Every turn that evening took had unraveled another of my truths, until all I was left with was a series of unknowns. The discomfort I felt tormented me as I lay awake, wanting nothing more than to be able to see things as they were—as they had always been.

I did not like change.

In a weak attempt to derail my mind, I replayed the events of the evening leading up to my near demise. It only served to make me feel like a fool. In all my dealings with evil, I'd thought myself capable, if not masterful, at the fine game of evade and conquer. I had argued that my survival skills were a defensive tool in and of themselves, but that night had illuminated gaping holes in my belief. I proved to be not only vulnerable to the darkness but easily seduced by it as well. I had practically fallen into its arms willingly, ready to waltz off into oblivion with a smile on my face—my blood ran cold at the thought. In one evening, I had managed to disgrace myself, my lineage, and my father, all while being saved by the one individual I was loath to admit I needed.

Oz's displeasure at my stupidity had been plain in his initial reaction. He resented my weakness nearly as much as I did. The anger that coursed through me helped to clear my head, giving me something more tangible to focus on. Anger was a far more useful and palatable emotion than shame or embarrassment. I wrapped myself up in that anger and tried to sleep. The next day I would have to deal with my shortcomings. That night, I wanted to dream of anything but.

21

I knew my brothers would be up early to further prepare for Sean's arrival and the war against the Stealers. In the clarity of the morning, my shame had returned, replacing my anger of the previous night. My ineptitude still thoroughly disgusted me.

I remained in my room until I heard my brothers depart. Their inevitably piteous expressions were unwelcome and unwarranted, and I wished to avoid them entirely. Their sympathy would do nothing to allay my feelings.

I even ignored Kierson when he called to inform me that Oz would remain behind for my safety, causing him to come down to check on me, worried that something had happened. I pretended that I was too asleep to answer. My irritation with myself had only grown as the night progressed, and by morning it had reached a fever pitch.

When I was certain they had departed, I crept up the stairs silently and passed through the door, quickly making my way into the kitchen. My plan had been to collect enough provisions so that I could stay in my room alone all day and avoid those who were so willing to fight my battle for me once they returned. I loathed the idea that they needed to. My brothers were warriors. I, however, clearly was not.

I rummaged through the pantry for anything palatable, coming up with only a few items. When I closed the cabinet door, prepared to retreat to the basement, I found Oz standing steadfastly behind it.

I startled momentarily, cursing myself internally for confirming what I had already decided.

Definitely not a warrior.

"Does almost getting your soul sucked out of you make you hungry?" he asked, leaning against the wall casually, though there was nothing casual about his gaze. His eyes burned with an unmistakable intensity. Anger filled them.

"Must you skulk around while I make my breakfast? Do you have no other useful employment?" I asked, turning my back on him abruptly. I did not want to meet his gaze.

"I seemed pretty busy last night when I was saving your ass. Is keeping you alive and intact not useful enough employment for you?"

"That," I said to the sink before me, "is an entirely subjective question."

"Is it now?" he asked, moving about behind me. His footsteps fell lightly as he crossed to the opposite side of the kitchen, blocking the exit. "Explain the subjectivity."

"It depends heavily on whether or not having me as I am is viewed as beneficial or not."

"And what is your answer?" he asked, advancing two steps toward me. From the sound they made, they were slow and calculated. Knowing a face-off between us was imminent, I forced myself to turn and address him directly.

"Given the circumstances, I would say no," I replied, looking past him to assess my most viable exit. Standing before him, his formidable form looming only feet away from me, made my nerve endings prickle most uncomfortably. I wanted little more than to escape the feeling. "Unless my brothers are in need of mindless bait, which is all I have proven to be thus far, I really provide little service—or value—to them. Whatever skills I was to acquire when born into the PC have not fallen my way. All I seem capable of is attracting those that they seek to destroy. That may be of use to them, but it is not a service that will stand the test of time. You yourself said it—that I could not survive the evil indefinitely."

"Did you not fight beside me last night?"

"Yes," I replied flatly. "However, I think that was only facilitated by the words you spoke to me before we attacked. Had you not said them, I believe I would have delivered myself to them willingly."

"Those words," he said, his voice so low I could scarcely hear him, "are the words spoken by our kind in preparation for battle. That tradition is older than time itself. You seem to forget that you are more than just the daughter of Ares. You are also your mother's daughter, and she was one of the greatest warriors I have ever seen."

"But I am not like her," I countered, frustration coursing through me. "I am an Unborn—vulnerable, weak, and without purpose."

His jaw flexed furiously in his effort to keep his mouth closed. He opened it only slightly once, then snapped it shut, grinding his teeth while he calmed himself. Once he regained his normal air of ambivalence, he spoke.

"Since you are so convinced that you are useless to yourself and your brothers, what would you have me do differently next time, just in case the situation should present itself again?" He crossed his arms tightly over his chest, sidestepping a pace to prop his shoulder against the wall. He was a master of illusions—his calm façade still concealing the storm that inexplicably brewed beneath it. I awaited his eruption without angst.

"The most logical response would be to let the Stealer finish. If I cannot survive on my own in this world, then I do not wish to suffer it," I replied, coming to stand defiantly in front of him. "I am my own being now, with the ability to exercise my will for the first time in my existence. I can choose to live or die on my own terms, regrettable though they may prove to be. If I can see the logic in this course of action, then surely you can oblige it."

A sudden breeze rustled my hair as I was whipped toward and firmly affixed to the wall behind me. Oz's grasp was fierce, and when he finally released it his arms straddled my head, pressing so heavily into the decaying wall that I could hear it giving way beneath the pressure. He leaned in close, his breathing shallow and quick. Pinning murderous eyes on me, he analyzed my expression just as intently as I did his.

"I oblige *nobody* but myself." His words tickled my ear when he whispered them directly into it. My nerve endings lit up yet again. "And, even if I were willing to forgo that truth, there is no wisdom to be seen in your course of action."

He then pulled away only enough to return his raging gaze to me, his eyes slowly raking over my body, examining my state further. His proximity was disagreeable, and I longed to escape to my room and away from his interrogation. My pulse raced uncontrollably in my flustered state, and the tiny curl at the corner of his mouth illustrated his amusement with it.

"Am I frightening you?" he asked, his voice dangerously playful.

"Do you wish to?" I countered.

"Do you wish me to?"

"I wish for you to leave me be."

"Are you certain of that?" he asked, his eyes landing heavily on my chest. "*I* don't think you're certain of that." His face advanced slowly to mine until his nose was only a hair's breadth away from my own. "I also don't think you're so certain about your choices. Your bravado, though admirable, is gravely misdirected. The death you would face, should you choose not to become the evil that attacked you, would be slow, grueling, and excruciating. And there would be nothing your brothers, or even I, could do for you."

"And why does this concern you so?" I asked, my voice low and breathy. "I am nothing to you."

"That," he said, pressing his body against mine, "is entirely subjective."

I pressed my palm to his chest, forcing him away from me just enough to gain some breathing room. We stared at each other in silence as a tension built slowly between us. Completely enthralled by our stand-off, neither of us heard my brothers when they returned to the Victorian.

"Is there a problem here?" Casey asked, rounding the corner to find the two of us embroiled in our silent battle. His voice was low and threatening as always.

"Is there?" Oz repeated, looking at me intently. "Or do we understand one another?"

"I believe we do," I purred in response. "Subjectivity notwithstanding."

His devilish smile spread wide.

"Excellent. I'd hate to think we'd have to revisit this topic again."

"As would I."

He turned and brushed past Casey without an ounce of concern, making his way to the living room. I watched as he did, questioning his antics, his motives, and the strange chill I felt in his absence.

It vexed me greatly.

"What's the word on the street, kids?" Oz asked the others, who were still filing in through the front entrance. After I collected my thoughts, I joined them, leaving Casey to follow behind me.

"Pierson is certain that he has the ward situation under control for now," Drew announced.

"Yes. And in light of what Drew mentioned last night regarding Deimos, I went ahead and worked him into the wards as well," he said, his eyes genuflecting slightly. "I did not wish to be ambushed again by my own oversight or have you suffer an unenviable fate because of it."

"I'm sure you have been more than thorough, Pierson. Thank you," I replied.

"Sean has been delayed," Drew continued, "but he is coming. Whatever is going on at the seacoast has him stressed, but he assured me that he wants to be present for the retribution the Stealers are going to face tonight. He plans to be here just before sunset."

"You make his arrival sound so dramatic," Oz scoffed as he meandered through the room.

"It will be, and, quite frankly, I think a little drama is warranted given our current situation," Drew replied, heat building in his eyes. "Speaking of which, I told Sean that you were going to give your complete cooperation in the search and eradication of the Stealers. Sean would have been here sooner otherwise. But I wouldn't get too comfortable, if I were you. He sounded remarkably calm on the phone. Nothing good ever happens when he sounds like that."

"I'm aware of that, Drew," Oz lamented. "More aware than you can possibly imagine."

A silence stretched awkwardly throughout the room, begging for someone to fill it. Ignoring the tension brewing between Oz and Drew, Pierson changed the subject.

"How are you feeling today, Khara?" he called from the far side of the room. He stood just before the vast wall of windows, the light billowing in through them highlighting him in a pleasant manner, softening his typically shrewd expression.

"I feel well, brother."

"No residual effects from the incident last night?"

"None that I am aware of, though I have not regained the memories that were taken. All I feel is a nagging sensation in my brain when I try to recall certain events or focus on certain individuals. It's as if there is a mental fog that won't clear, clouding certain parts of my mind. I do not hold out much hope for improvement."

He nodded briskly.

"And your neck?"

I reached up and pulled the gauze off my wound, exposing it. Tracing my hand lightly over it, I could feel the disruption in my skin, the scab dry and sharp against my touch.

"It feels fine."

"We shall have Sean take care of what remains when he returns,"

Pierson replied. "He has some healing skills that he has used on more than one occasion, especially as of late. His mate appears to have a penchant for danger."

"If you feel it's best."

"I do." He paused for a moment, his brow furrowing slightly; then he took a step toward me. "Khara, I've been up all night researching, trying to make more sense of all of this. And after many hours and myriad texts, the single obstacle I repeatedly find myself against is that you are an Unborn but also PC. There are no instances of such a being in history, and, because of this, there is no way to know just what they are after or what will become of you if they succeed."

"They won't succeed," Kierson growled from his station by the fireplace.

"If there was some way to know . . ." Pierson continued, ignoring his twin's outburst.

"There are only two outcomes she will face if they get hold of her," said Oz, interrupting Pierson's ruminations. "Option one: She dies, as nearly all Light Ones who fall to the Stealers do. It is a slow and painful fading, but it is the choice they make, given the alternative."

"Which is?" Drew pressed, irritation lacing his tone.

"Becoming a Dark One."

"But I thought—"

"Yes, yes," Oz interrupted, dismissing Drew's objection with a cavalier wave of his hand. "I know what you're going to say, and the answer is yes. Dark Ones are made when the Light are corrupted, but that is not how they initially came to be, nor is it the only way to create them." He paused momentarily, allowing the reality of his words to settle before he continued. "But really, what better way to corrupt a soul than to have it sucked out by those leeches, leaving the Light One empty to then fill with the very darkness that created them?"

"That's all well and good, Oz, but Khara isn't technically a Light One yet. She is still an Unborn," Drew protested.

"Which only proves my earlier point," Pierson cut in, stepping into the center of the room. "From all I could find, the Unborn were simply killed by the Stealers. Their pureness was their undoing, is that not true, Oz?"

"Yes," Oz replied, his voice tight with anger. "Which is why we no longer allowed them to be earthbound."

"But Khara isn't pure. Far from it, I imagine," Pierson continued, his words an inference, not an allegation. "So, if she is not the delicacy that they were once used to and she is not a Light One who can be turned Dark, what is it that they want from her?"

"Who the fuck cares?" Kierson cursed, his irritation with the conversation plain. "Even if there is a door number three, does it matter? I'm pretty sure there won't be sunshine and rainbows and tutu-wearing unicorns behind it. Why put energy into figuring something out that can't be solved instead of channeling it into something we can do—namely, annihilate those fuckers from this city and any other corner of the world they might be hiding in?"

"Agreed," said Casey, looking excited at the promise of violence.

"Which brings us to the plan: draw those sons of bitches out and kill them before they have a chance to force either of those options upon Khara. However, there's work to do before any of us will be killing 'those fuckers,' as Kierson so eloquently put it," Drew announced, turning his attention to Oz, who had again seated himself on the staircase to the second floor. His gaze still refused to fall upon mine. "Oz, since you're so adept at finding them, I'm going to need you to track down where they're hiding out. I need numbers, locations—everything you can get me that might make this task easier. And don't you dare think of pulling a Casey and go after them on your own."

"Not an issue," he yawned, stretching his arms high above his head. "I'm too tired for that today."

"Sean isn't bringing an army with him; there's too much going down out east for that. We need to be organized and prepared, two things we haven't been thus far. We're likely to only get one shot at this. We can't afford to waste any of our resources."

Drew's eyes narrowed harshly at Oz.

"Fine," Oz grunted in response. "You'll have the information you need by sunset."

"Casey," he continued, directing his attention away from Oz. "You need to track Azriel down and find out just what the hell happened last night. If you are convinced by the end of it that he did indeed sell us out, you need to send a message. A big one. Understood?"

"Loud and clear," Casey replied with a killer smile.

"If he didn't, then you need to find out everything he knows, and I mean everything. Employ your usual charm to make sure that happens," he commanded. "Pierson, you get to work on protecting Khara from the draw of the Stealers. If there's something that can be done there, you need to do it. We can't protect her very well if we can't keep her from going to them willingly."

"I'll be upstairs," he replied, heading in that direction before he even finished his thought. Stepping around Oz, he ascended the stairs and disappeared to his favorite companions: his books.

Drew then shot a curious look to Kierson.

"What do you need me to do?" Kierson asked, his enthusiasm for retribution plain.

"Someone needs to stay behind with Khara."

"But Pierson will be here—"

"And he will be occupied."

"What about you? Where are you going?" Kierson's interrogation nearly sounded like that of a petulant child.

Drew's gaze shot over to Oz.

"I'm going with him."

Oz launched to his feet, agitated at Drew's plan.

"The hell you are."

"I need to see that you're doing what you say you will," Drew explained unapologetically.

"You're just going to slow me down," argued Oz.

"I'm confidant I can keep up."

"Listen, I said I would get you the information you need, and I will."

"Great. Then you won't mind me tagging along for peace of mind," Drew pressured. "Consider it my insurance plan."

Oz's eyes narrowed.

"You don't trust me . . ."

Drew shrugged.

"Trust is a funny thing, Oz. It's not freely given; it's earned. You haven't done a lot to do so in the time I've known you. And I have known you many lifetimes," he said, slowly approaching Oz. "You have always and will always suit yourself, which has never been an issue for us, but, in this situation, it is. Khara's life, or soul, or whatever it may be that they are after, likely hangs in the balance, and I am not willing to hand that over to your minimally invested ass. If you want to take my lack of confidence as a personal slight, so be it. I've never questioned your ability in battle, Oz. But I do question your loyalty."

"I work alone or I don't work at all," Oz rumbled, his defiance dominating both his tone and posture. It was clear that there was no middle ground to be found between the two of them.

"Drew," I said softly. "Let him go. He has said he will do it. Let him prove his loyalty to you." I turned to face Oz, deliberately waiting until his eyes met mine before I continued. "He proved his loyalty to me last night. In the context of battle, he is exactly what you told me: fiercely effective. He did not have to warn us of the Stealers, nor did he have to come to our aid. Is that not loyalty? I am well aware that he enjoys violence as much as Casey, but he left the battle and promise of bloodshed, only moments after showing up, with the express purpose of getting me home to the safety of the wards. Oz has proven to be selfish, arrogant, abrasive, and even vile at times, but one thing he has never proven himself to be is a liar. I do not suspect he will do so today."

Oz's mouth pressed into a straight line, trepidation overtaking his expression. Something was stirring behind his eyes, though I could not determine what it was.

"I've got some shit to do," he declared, heading to the front entrance. "I'll let you know what I find out when I get back." He stopped abruptly just before the front door, looking back over his shoulder directly at me. "Try not to do anything crazy while I'm gone, will you, new girl? I'd hate to go to all this effort for nothing."

I stared at him silently—I could not muster a response. How could one promise such a thing when my ability to make rational decisions all but disappeared in the face of the Stealers? His words had proven to be the only thing to clear my mind in their presence, and he was leaving. I was left solely reliant upon Pierson's skill with magic to prevent their call from getting the better of me.

And to fight off that darkness required mighty skill indeed.

22

While the others worked on their assignments, Kierson and I sat around the house, the hours passing in slow monotony. It was a tedious way to await the inevitable. Kierson was so agitated by late afternoon that he nearly stabbed Pierson when he came down the stairs, throwing a blade that narrowly missed him. Perhaps their twin connection kept Pierson safe from the otherwise deadly strike.

I inquired about the battle in the Heidelberg Project, having not been present for the majority of it. They told me that things had taken a turn for the interesting upon my departure. They were aware that we were followed initially but were certain that Oz was capable of handling whomever showed up, if they even made it that far. However, the atypical aspects of the fight seemed to arise only minutes after that. Pierson said that they had thought the dwindling numbers of Stealers had been due to the losses they had taken, but, when he hazarded a glance at the amassing bodies, there were not nearly enough to account for the numbers the enemy had presented with at the outset of the fight. It was at that point that Pierson had retreated to the house to quickly observe what he had become convinced was true: the Stealers were strategically escaping the battle, but were not headed in the direction they had come from. They were headed toward the distant Victorian in numbers far surpassing those that he had expected.

Their explanation made sense of what I remembered from my more lucid moments of the battle Oz and I had fought outside the house. And it served to only further confirm what Oz had claimed: The Stealers truly were after me and were willing to suffer countless losses during their elaborate ruse to ensure they got me.

When I shared my thoughts on the matter, the twins wore the same expression. It was not an inspiring one.

"I've performed the ceremony for what I think should protect you from their thrall, Khara, but I cannot guarantee it," he admitted. "I have no reference for a spell like this. I had to improvise."

"I'm sure it is better than the alternative," I reassured him, knowing that the alternative was nothing at all.

"What's taking them so long?" Kierson grumbled, pacing laps around the living room furniture. "I hate all this waiting. It makes me edgy."

"I had not noticed," I replied dryly. When he turned his bloodshot eyes to meet mine, he saw something in them that made him smile.

"I didn't know you had it in you, sis," he proclaimed in admiration. "Sarcasm . . . it works for you. You should try it out more often."

"If I survive the evening, I shall try my best."

His smile immediately fell.

"If that was another attempt at humor, it sucked." The sadness in his eyes kept any response I had at bay. He was still hurting from the previous attack, which could have left me dead or unrecognizable. Neither fate seemed to sit well with him. He was a sensitive soul indeed.

"When will Sean be arriving?" I asked, directing my question to Pierson.

"I'm not sure. He will alert Drew with the details soon, I imagine," he said plainly. "Sean is rarely, if ever, late."

As we spoke, Pierson's phone made a buzzing sound, and he quickly retrieved it from his pocket.

"Speak of the devil," he mumbled, staring at the screen.

"Is it from Drew? What'd he say?" Kierson asked, coming to stand behind Pierson. He peered over his shoulder to see whatever Pierson was looking at, a gesture that seemed to instantly infuriate his twin.

"Drew is on his way back now, and Sean has reported to him that he will be arriving very shortly."

"And having Sean present for this is a good thing, I presume?"

"Khara," Kierson started, his face the very definition of gravity, "Sean is seriously badass. He can't be killed, for fuck's sake! You think you might want that kind of manpower on your side?" I started to reply when he threw up his hand to deflect my response. "That was a rhetorical question, Khara, because the answer is now, and will always be, yes. When shit gets serious, you want Sean on your side. Period. End of story."

"Just as you would want Oz on your side?" I prodded, hoping to gain some insight into why they despised one another.

The twins shared a look at one another before returning their gazes to me.

"Something like that," Kierson said tightly.

"Agreed," Pierson added. "Though it might be best if you kept that analogy to yourself after Sean arrives."

"If they detest each other so much, how can they be capable of fighting alongside one another?"

"That's simple," Pierson replied, his expression every bit as haughty and condescending as I had ever seen it. "You." I felt my brow furrow at his words, unable to mask my incomprehension. Pierson sighed at the realization that further explanation was required. "You are why they are willing to fight on the same side, Khara. They have a mutual interest in the outcome." My expression remained unchanged. "I would think that Sean's attachment to the outcome would be fairly obvious. Oz's is less so, but it is apparent nonetheless."

"How so?"

"I have studied his behavior since your arrival. It has been perplexing, indeed, but my theory is that somehow, on some level, you are what has made his current lifestyle . . . less comfortable."

I found his words fascinating.

"I have never met someone more comfortable with who they are and what they do," I countered. "And yet you are telling me that he is not because of me? I do not understand this."

He shrugged ambivalently.

"I don't profess to know the inner workings of our not-so-angelic squatter, but my powers of observation are unmatched. He has changed. Of that, I am sure."

"And how do you view his current behavior? Is it an improvement or a devolution?"

"It is different. I'm not sure how to qualify it beyond that."

It was quiet for a moment while I processed Pierson's words, until Kierson decided to make an observation all his own.

"All I know is he's still a raging asshole."

"Agreed," Pierson chimed in, his expression still severe.

I could not help but see the humor in Kierson's response.

The abrupt opening of the front door jarred the three of us to attention. Our momentary distraction had let us all forget what was headed our way. Thankfully, all that found us in that second was Drew.

"Casey back yet?" he asked as he walked into the living room. "I've been trying to reach him."

"If he is looking for the gargoyles, he will most likely be in the sewers. I can't imagine that the service there is at all foolproof."

"Good point," Drew replied, but something in his eyes said that he wasn't fully convinced of the veracity of Pierson's claim. "I just can't imagine it's taken him this long to hunt them down."

"Well, if they did sell him out, I highly doubt they would hide in their normal places," Kierson offered. "I mean, do you want a pissed-off Casey hunting your ass down?"

Drew's look of skepticism disappeared with Kierson's observation.

"Better point still," he said with a smile. "He beat you to that one, Pierson."

"That's because he has copious experience pissing Casey off and hiding from him."

Kierson, appearing bested, did nothing to defend himself from Pierson's allegation.

He would not have had a chance to, even if he had sought one. Seconds later, Casey stormed through the front door, slamming it violently in his wake.

"Azriel's dead," he blurted out before entering the room.

"So, I guess you decided he did sell us out then?" Drew asked cautiously.

"No. I mean I've been looking for him for hours, but it's hard to find a gargoyle during the day, especially when he's already dead."

"Already dead? You didn't kill him?"

"Didn't need to," Casey growled. "I'm not sure which pisses me off more: not getting answers or not getting to kill him myself."

"That can't mean anything good," Kierson noted, tightening his grip on the dagger that hung at his waist.

"No shit," Casey snarled in response. "I knew he was holding out on me, but I guess I won't know why now."

"Someone is cleaning up their loose ends," Pierson stated matter-of-factly. "There is no possibility that this is a coincidence. Azriel has lived too many lifetimes to fall easily."

"Yeah, well, if you'd seen what was left of his corpse, you wouldn't think that. He was so mangled I hardly recognized him as a once-living being. It was only after I rooted around in his virtually liquefied remains that I found his lower jaw. His one canine never did look right. It was nearly twice the size of the others."

"And he was alone? You didn't see any of the others?" Drew pressed, trying to piece together what little information he could to better grasp the meaning of what Casey had found.

"There was no sign of any other gargoyles to be found in all of the greater Detroit area. That's the main reason I've been gone so long.

After locating what was left of Azriel, I've been trying to find a single one of them," Casey explained, his typical demeanor traded in momentarily for one of confusion. "It's like they just vanished."

"Jesus Christ . . ." Drew uttered in disbelief.

"You called?" Oz shouted from the foyer of the Victorian, punctuating his remark with a slam of the front door. He strode in, looking every bit his arrogant self, but it belied a tension that I could not ignore. I did not know why I sensed this, but I did. The second his eyes met mine, I was certain. "Never mind with the pleasantries, boys. Our little situation has been upgraded to a big fucking catastrophe."

"What did you find out?" Drew demanded, striding across the room to meet Oz.

"I found out that there are more Stealers than you could possibly imagine. I found out that they aren't working alone—that other supernaturals are working alongside them. And, most importantly," he started, hazarding a glance at me, "I found out who's behind their uprising."

"Who?" Drew pressed, anxiously awaiting his response. Oz, however, looked uneasy, not wanting to divulge his secret.

With a heavy breath, he finally did.

"Deimos. He's one of the—"

"We are well aware of who he is, Oz," Drew snapped, cutting him off. A brief silence then filled the room just before chaos overtook it. "But what you're saying doesn't make any sense." He looked to me for confirmation. "Khara said herself that if Deimos were aware of her whereabouts, he would just come for her."

"I must agree with Drew. Your information is false. If Deimos were here, I would know it," I said calmly, though the mere mention of his name sent a shiver down my spine.

"Oh, really?" Oz retorted, his condescension plain. "How could you possibly know that?"

"Because he plagued my time in the Underworld since I was a child," I reminded them, my words more heated than I expected them to be. "He views me as a long sought-after prize, and if Deimos were here I no longer would be. He would have stolen me right out from under your noses and taken me back to the Underworld to resume his demented form of courtship without giving a second thought about it. He is not an elaborate schemer, Oz. He is a taker. And when he wants something badly enough, that is precisely what he does."

Oz's eyes narrowed harshly at me.

"You are his?" he asked, unable to disguise the disgust in his voice.

"I am no one's." I stared back at him, my eyes devoid of the emotion that brewed within me. It was strange and inexplicable. "And you are wrong. Deimos is not behind this."

His eyes widened with rage momentarily before he contained it.

"Who told you about Deimos?" Drew asked, still standing between Oz and me.

"That's not really important now, is it?" Oz snarled. "What's important is that we figure something out, and really fucking quick, because I don't know about you but I don't know how to kill that bastard. So, unless you want to wait until he shows up on your doorstep to try a few things out, we need to move. Now."

But the brothers did not. In complete contradiction to the night at the Tenth Circle, when they whisked me away from perceived danger on Oz's command, they stood defiantly, unwilling to take him at his word. Something was amiss, and I was in the dark as to what.

Clearly seeing their lack of cooperation, Oz's anger rose to a level that even his well-manufactured façade could not contain.

"Of all the times you could question my judgment, you choose now?" he roared. "Listen to the words coming out of my mouth: Deimos is here. He is coming for her with an army of soulless bastards. You need to get her out of here now!"

"Maybe that's exactly what you want us to do," Drew shrewdly observed. "You know more than you're saying, and until I know what that is, we're not going anywhere."

"Have you lost your fucking mind?" Oz shouted.

"I don't think I have," Drew replied, maintaining an eerie level of calm. It was a complete contradiction of Oz's fury.

"Drew," Kierson piped up from behind us. "If he's right, then we need to go. I don't know what you think is going on but—"

"It's not what I think, Kierson; it's what I know," he said, addressing his brother with a glance over his shoulder. Then he pinned hateful eyes back on Oz. "What do you think I've been doing all day? Khara may have thought you were to be trusted, Oz, but I didn't. There were too many red flags to be ignored." Oz's body twitched with anger. "So I followed you. Your arrogance clouded your focus, thinking that you had once again wriggled off the hook. But you hadn't."

"What happened?" Kierson asked, his voice a ghost of a whisper.

"Do you want to tell them, or should I?" Drew posed the question to Oz, but received no answer. "Fine. I'll do it." He turned to address the rest of us, his eyes fierce and sharp. "I followed him down to the old shipping district on the outskirts of the city. He never faltered once, as though he had always known where they were—like he'd been there before." He paused dramatically, allowing the implication to settle fully in our minds before continuing. "I looked on as he entered the building without hesitation, even though there were guards at the door. They never made a move to stop him."

"And why would they?" Oz snapped, no longer able to contain his rage. "They knew instantly who and what I am. They knew I slaughtered a hundred of their own last night without even breaking a sweat. Do you think they wanted to die?"

"Last night, in the street," I started, recalling our battle. "The one that tried to take me called you by name." I looked at Oz curiously. "He knew you."

"Of course he did," Oz snapped. "I'm what legends are made of. Do you think there are many supernaturals in this world who don't know me by name?"

"That's a convenient excuse," Drew retorted, his eyes burning with distrust.

"The truth usually is, Drew. But, please, feel free to continue wasting time. Time that we don't have."

Ignoring both Oz's attempt to defend himself and his warning, Drew continued his incrimination.

"I sat outside that building for an hour or two, waiting for any sign of distress or sound of a fight, but there were none," Drew explained, continuing to ignore Oz. "Eventually, you walked out just as easily as you went in. No problems at all. I wonder why that is?"

"You asked me to find them, and I did. You asked me to get the information you wanted, and I did. And now you're fucking around about semantics when you need to get her the fuck out of Dodge, Drew," Oz shouted. "Put your petty shit aside for right now. You can be pissed at me later—when she's safe from Deimos!"

"You're really pushing hard for us to leave here, Oz. I can't help but wonder why you want us to flee from the one place she is most safe," Drew pondered aloud, baiting Oz with every word. "She's protected here, not only by us but also the wards. Leaving here would remove the latter obstacle for the enemy. It also removes Sean from the equation, too, because he's due to show up any time now, but you know that already, don't you? And who else would better know the warring abilities of Sean than you, who has been on the receiving end of them before?" Oz silently scowled, allowing Drew to arrive at his conclusion, which everyone—including myself—could now see coming. "You are hardly a novice in the art of war, Ozereus. You are as cunning and shrewd as any I have ever fought beside, and you of all people would know that the simplest way to take a target out is to drive it away from its optimal place of defense."

"True," replied Oz, clipping that single word so short it was barely audible.

"Drew," Pierson called, directing attention away from Oz. "Where is all of this coming from? I agree that it is no coincidence that Oz so easily tracked the Stealers down, but it is quite a leap from questioning Oz's previous knowledge of the Stealers to purposely trying to put Khara in harm's way." Pierson assessed Drew's expression for a moment, reading something in it that I could not see. "Your argument, though logical in a sense, seems largely unfounded. You have never doubted Oz's judgment in battle before. Why now? What has changed your mind?"

"Because I saw something in Oz the night that Khara was attacked that I have never seen in him before—*guilt*." His eyes wandered back to Oz. "And, at the time, I could not place what you would have to feel guilty about. At first, I thought that maybe you felt badly that one of your own was attacked because of what she was and that you could not change that for her, but then, really, if you lack that power, is it really your fault? You can do no more for her in that regard than the rest of us. And you, more than anyone I know, would not feel guilty about something you could not control. So I knew that could not be the reason."

Drew strode slowly toward Oz, who maintained his remarkable silence, despite being slandered.

"The more I thought about it, the more I realized that your behavior had not made sense. Your reaction at the club when she exposed herself, your call to us in the Heidelberg Project, and your insistence to track down the Stealers alone today," he continued, pressing closer and closer to Oz, blade drawn. "I wonder how you can stand here and face us after lying and scheming the way you have. You may have felt guilt for what you've done, but it has done nothing to stifle your deceitful ways, has it? You're setting Khara up, and I want to know why. What price was high enough to make you willing to send her to slaughter with little more than a pang of guilt?"

"She's going to be taken if we stay here," Oz countered, maintaining his original story.

"Oh, yes . . . because Deimos is coming for her," Drew replied sardonically. "You might have tried to find a better reason than that, since even Khara does not believe your lie." Oz looked to me, a rare pain in his expression that could not be ignored. "See!" Drew shouted. "That is what I saw the other night. Deny that what I'm saying is true, Oz."

Those pain-filled eyes stayed fixed on mine as Oz addressed me and me alone.

"We have to go, Khara. They are coming for you," he said softly. "You believed I was not a liar only hours ago. Believe that still. I never lied to you, and I am not lying about this."

"You betrayed us," Drew spat, cutting off Oz's line of sight. "You betrayed us all."

"*No!*" Oz shouted, cracking under the pressure of Drew's words. "I betrayed you and your brothers." He thrust his finger into Drew's chest, shoving him backward. "You want to know why I knew what I knew and did what I did? Because the Stealers have been paying me off, that's why. They've been back for longer than you'll care to know, and my job was to make sure you didn't know about it." His face contorted into a smug smile as he turned to address the brothers. "Seems like I'm better at my job than you are at yours."

"You motherfucker," Kierson snarled.

"Helloooo . . . fallen, remember?" Oz mocked, sweeping his arms wide in a grand gesture. "I never claimed to be loyal. And I certainly don't have the unlimited financial resources that the PC has. I saw an opportunity, and I took it. You can hardly fault me for that."

"Wanna bet?" Casey growled, launching himself across the room at Oz. I stepped before him just as he raised his blade to slice down upon his intended victim. He looked at me curiously through fiery eyes. I was certain that I had only further solidified his thoughts about me being a "crazy bitch."

"Let him finish," I said softly, holding Casey back weakly with my outstretched arm. When I knew he would not advance, I turned to face Oz, my expression remaining impassive.

"I betrayed them, that much is true. But I have never betrayed you." Again his sad eyes found mine and held them captive. "I went to the Stealers today to try and find a way to stop this by offering them something else in trade, but there was no deal to be had. Deimos was behind the Heidelberg fight, and, I assure you, he is coming for you now. I don't know when he came into the picture or what he wants. They weren't overly forthcoming with that information, and I didn't want to waste any more time to try and force it out of them. Khara, we can't protect you from Deimos. The only way to escape is to run. You need to do this," he pressured, quickly looking off to the west through the walls of the house. "There's no more time."

Not awaiting a response, he grabbed my hand and started up the stairs, dragging me behind him. Just as we crested the landing of the second floor, Pierson let out a shrill cry that stopped me cold. Yanking my hand out of Oz's grasp, I descended the steps as quickly as I could until I saw Pierson lying on the ground, his hands clamped violently around his skull. Kierson was by his side, trying to determine what was attacking his twin. Helplessness overtook him, and he looked up to me for some shred of an answer.

At that very moment, I realized that I had one for him, though it was not one that I wanted to share. The familiar tremors that I felt whenever Deimos was present started up my spine before I could stifle them. He was near. Oz had not lied.

Pierson grabbed Kierson's wrist while he continued to writhe on the floor. The second they touched, Kierson joined his brother, fighting the unseen alongside him. Oz came down to join me, observing the twins to assess what was causing their identical behavior.

"The wards," he finally said frantically, rushing past me to Drew. "How does Pierson feed them?"

"I don't know," Drew replied tightly, running over to Pierson. "Is it the wards? Are they falling?" His words were a plea. I could hear the desperation in them, begging for Oz to be wrong.

"Can't . . . hold them," Pierson panted before his and Kierson's pain ended, the two laboring to catch their breath.

"Incoming!" Casey shouted, looking out the back windows. From where I stood, I could not see what he did, nor was I permitted the chance. Grabbing my hand again, Oz rushed me up the stairs and down the hall. He ran with purpose, whispering the same words he had the night we fought the Stealers in the street.

"Khara," he called over his shoulder once he had completed his chant. "We may be too late." The look on his face was one I had seen before, though not on him. His expression was coated with the same fear my father wore when I was taken from the Underworld, though the danger that advanced upon us now was far greater than a single Dark One. It was far greater than I, or any of my brothers, had expected. Oz, however, had not underestimated it.

He had a plan.

Whipping me up the final set of stairs to his room, he dragged me through the door, then paused for a moment to look at me. His jaw worked furiously, doing its best to contain the thoughts he was struggling with. I stood steadfast, awaiting his directive, though none ever came. Instead, he shoved me toward the spiraling staircase, forcing me up the steps and through the window that led onto the third-floor rooftop. He followed close behind. I wasn't certain how being on an exposed rooftop was an improvement to our situation, but I trusted that his plan had accounted for this risk.

When he stepped onto the roof behind me, his eyes immediately turned to the sky, a scowl overtaking his strained expression. I followed his gaze up to the heavens, only to find them blocked out entirely. A black, leathery, swirling sky converged upon us. The missing gargoyles had been found.

"I guess those fuckers really wanted to cover all their bases," he scoffed under his breath.

"Am I to assume that we won't be flying out of here then?" I queried, watching him as he stalked to each edge of the roof, peeking over to see if there was an acceptable alternative. The look in his eyes when he turned to me told me that none existed.

"We weren't flying out of here in the first place," he muttered, walking back to me. "Seems like nobody around here really understands what 'fallen' means. It's hard to fly when you no longer have wings."

A shot of electricity arced between my shoulder blades, behind my markings, as though somewhere deep inside me understood what the potential absence of my wings might feel like. I may not yet have birthed them, but I had not lost them either, a distinction that was now painfully clear.

"Oz—"

"There's no way out," he said softly, cutting me off. "They've got the whole house surrounded." His eyes were heavily weighted with an emotion I had only recently come to recognize—sadness.

"Then we will stay and fight," I told him. "I will fight alongside my brothers, as is my birthright." I started for the window, but he intercepted me.

"No," he boomed. "I told you what will happen if they get you, and neither option presents a pleasant outcome. Pierson's magic has fallen, don't you see? There's nothing to protect you from their pull . . . the darkness. And I cannot protect you from yourself and fight them at the same time. There are too many, and the risk too great. Letting you anywhere near the Stealers in this war would be madness."

In a rare moment, I felt my mouth lift ever so slightly at its corner, mimicking an expression I had so often seen Oz wear. A so-called smirk assumed its place upon my face.

"Is that not one of your specialties, Oz? Madness?"

"This is no time for you to find your sense of humor!" he yelled, snatching my arms up violently in his hands. His grip was harsh and punishing. "They cannot have you. Do you understand me? They cannot have you!" His attention snapped back toward the house, a commotion coming from deep inside. I pulled my arms from his hands and drew my blade, turning to go and aid my own. As I strode toward the window, I heard him mutter under his breath, a plea to someone I did not know.

"You failed her once, Celia. I pray your choices do not fail her again."

Then, from behind me, a great wind blew, carrying words not unlike the call to battle he had spoken earlier—words as old as time. Oz was chanting something that called to me, but in a way quite different from the call of the darkness that was upon me. A softness characterized it. A caress.

I looked back to see him in the most glorious light. Though it burned my eyes, it felt like home, willing me to it. I was of the Light, and they wanted me back.

Suddenly, I saw what made Oz so powerful. His formidable silhouette was highlighted by the glow that emanated from all around him, and I stood in awe. Slowly, he approached me, still shrouded in the burning light.

"Khara," he said, his voice carrying a divine power. "I tried to keep you from this fate. I did not wish for it to come to this." I looked at him as if he was the world. "But I see no other way. I have no choice."

With his aura of godliness surrounding him, he muttered hypnotically in that same ancient tongue, but this time his words were discernibly different than those he had spoken before. As his melodic chanting surrounded me, lulling me softly into a state of calm, I felt a nagging sensation as something sought to interrupt it.

Darkness. It was coming for me.

I turned to look back to the window behind me, but the second I did I felt the markings on my back rage in protest, burning violently. I wanted to cry out against the pain as my skin protested the awakening it withheld, but I could not. No sooner had Oz finished his own call—the call to the Light One within me—when his lips fell upon mine, strong and brutal. He held me tightly while my knees threatened to give out from the pain stabbing through my back, but his intentions never faltered. He kissed me with the desperation of one who truly saw no means of escape. I tasted the fear on his lips as mine met his, and that is when I sensed what he was doing.

He was saying good-bye.

Seconds later, the window behind us shattered into pieces, spraying us with glass. The enemy had announced its presence. Oz sheltered me with his massive body, turning me and forcing me backward toward the roof's edge. But there still was no escape.

One by one, the Stealers stepped onto the roof, wielding a power of their own—the power of the dead. A power that rivaled Oz's own. He held me behind him as I struggled against him, but with a whisper of my name he calmed my protestations ever so slightly.

"You will not take her alive," Oz shouted, his voice deep and threatening.

"It need not come to that," the newest leader of the Stealers purred in response, stepping cautiously forward. "Death is not part of his plan. He has . . . loftier aspirations for her."

I felt Oz tense before me, and I fought to peer around him, at what was happening. Surely, I had missed something terrible for it to have elicited such a physical response from him.

"I'll kill her myself if I have to," Oz countered harshly.

Finally able to gaze around his arm, I saw the Stealer who spoke to Oz looking at him incredulously.

"I think we both know that you are unwilling to do that, Ozereus," he replied patronizingly. "The reason why is written all over your face." He hazarded another step toward us, which tripped something in Oz. He reached around to me, snatching me up in his grasp and pinning me tightly against his chest. Overwhelmed by the alluring call of darkness, which pressed down upon us, I fought his hold, bucking wildly to escape it. My body was betraying me.

"This ends now," Oz boomed, drawing his weapon.

"This is her destiny," the Stealer roared, his features twisted into an ugly expression. "You cannot stop it!"

"I am her destiny, and she is my charge," Oz bellowed, stepping closer to the roof's edge. "And I *can* stop you." Oz growled four final words in his ancient tongue, the rumble of his chest vibrating fiercely against my back.

And then he released me from his grasp.

Before I could take advantage of my newly obtained freedom and run to the Stealer who continued to beckon to me, I felt Oz's massive arm strike me, knocking me over the roof's ledge. Falling through the air backward, my hair rushed over my face to obscure my last view of him. Even through that veil, I could see how pained his expression was when he looked down at me. Then the enemy fell upon him, engulfing him and stealing him from my view. He shouted something to me as they did, but I never heard his words. Instead, I closed my eyes and thought of my father, knowing that, once the awaiting Stealers found me and either had their way with me or delivered me to Deimos, I was going to see him soon. Given the way Oz had explained that situation, it appeared that all roads would lead to Hades, no matter which path was chosen for me.

But if I were lucky enough to just die from the impact of the fall, which seemed to be what Oz had intended, I prayed there would be enough evil within me to demand my soul's presence in the Underworld with Hades.

I missed him.

I was ready to go home.

23

But I did not go to my father; I did something else entirely surprising instead.

Just before I crashed to the ground below, another searing pain tore through my back, and my shirt shredded to pieces as large, mottled-gray wings unfurled. I swooped up into the sky, a survival instinct propelling me upward, for I had no conscious control over my newly developed appendages. It felt right having them behind me, spread wide for the winds to carry me. It felt as if I had had them my entire life. However, making them do exactly as I commanded seemed to be an acquired skill that I lacked entirely at first.

I may have avoided crashing into the ground and the Stealers that occupied it, but my control over the massive wings was minimal at best, and I soon found myself smashing into a brick wall only blocks away from the Victorian. I crumpled to the ground, the awkwardness of my wings making me clumsy as I fought to stand, staggering to find my balance. Looking around to get my bearings, I realized I was in an alley of sorts, not unlike the one I had found myself in when I first arrived in Detroit, though the buildings that bound this alley were far more residential in nature.

Before I could better assess my escape options, a strategy the brothers had taught me, I turned to find myself being stared down by the very enemy Oz had sought for me to avoid—the Stealer that had been on the roof with us only moments earlier. And the smile he wore was wicked.

"Oz has taken you from me, Unborn," he said enigmatically, the anger behind his smile seeping through in his tone. "You were to be my sweet prize, but now you are ruined. You are little more than a feast of revenge. But that matters not. Feast, I shall."

"And what of Deimos?" I asked, my tone laced with an authority I had never before possessed.

True amusement lit his smile, his teeth gleaming in the scant light of the alleyway.

"Deimos . . ." he delighted, stepping toward me slowly. "I'm surprised your fallen one never told you."

"My fallen one told me Deimos was coming for me and nothing more. But you will tell me," I said, an equally wicked grin overtaking my face. "You will tell me now."

"He has a plan for you. That's why I am here," he replied, sweeping his hands wide.

"And what are you to do, Stealer? Deimos is not one for minions. I see no reason why he has involved your kind at all. To do so seems so beneath him."

"He requires my skills, our skills—skills that he lacks," he continued, inching toward me as he spoke. As he neared, I realized that I felt no pull, no need to go to him. I truly was no longer an Unborn. But I felt the darkness of his presence, just as Oz had said I would. It screamed at my soul. "I am to change you. He wants you purged of whatever lightness keeps you from going to him willingly."

"He has taken me before," I said coldly. "What would stop him from doing so again?"

"He may be able to take your body, but he cannot take your mind. His inability to do so vexes him greatly. He thinks that the solution to this lies with me. And we are going to find out."

"But I am of the Light, and with that comes a choice," I reminded him, holding steadfast in my position. "And I will choose death. I will not become what he plans for me."

"Oh, sweet girl . . . so, so sweet," he whispered, approaching me still. "Don't you see? Either way, he wins. In that death, you will become a slave in the Underworld. You will beg for his protection—his favor. You will run to him willingly, and he will own you."

"Hades maintains that I don't belong in the Underworld. That my soul is destined for a lighter place," I countered.

"And that would be true," he replied, his smile impossibly wider, "if you had been born of a Light One. But your mother . . . your poor, poor mother, she was not. She chose the ways of the Dark long ago. You were born while her black wings spread out wide behind her."

"You lie," I refuted, knowing that he could not possibly have such knowledge. Oz had implied that my mother was a Dark One, but had done so only to agitate Sean, or so it had seemed. When later confronted, he did not confirm the veracity of his claim.

Though he did not deny it either.

The Stealer standing before me leaned in close, whispering to me in a conspiratorial fashion.

"You are not as much a secret as you would like to think, sweet girl. How else could Deimos have come to such a plan in the first place?"

He was right. Deimos' plan could never have come into being had he not known the very reason I had been hidden away for centuries in the first place. The hiding that had eventually placed me in the Underworld with him and in his sights. He knew whom I was born of, and it was apparent that he also knew what I was—what I had only minutes earlier been. I could not dispute the Stealer's logic.

So, instead, I would fight it.

"There is only one flaw to your plan," I whispered back, brushing my lips along his earlobe. "You have to succeed in taking my soul. And I do not wish to part with it."

He turned wide eyes upon me, staring in disbelief, as though he could not fathom one so new to the Light fighting him off. He lunged for my face, not bothering to try his enchantments on me any longer. It was clear that he had little interest in making this experience pleasant for me. He was recruited to do a job, and anger now fueled him. Oz had stolen something truly precious from him.

He seemed obliged to do the same in return.

With lips locked violently onto mine, a familiar sensation started to pull at something—my essence—from deep within me, a dark and burning pain accompanying it. But then, suddenly, the sensation stopped. Inexplicably, his attempt to take that which he sought had no effect on me. He pulled away, looking at me in utter disbelief as he did. His plan was not working as he had hoped—my soul was not to be his.

And we were both about to see why.

I felt my eyebrow cock as evil started to flow into me. I wasn't aware of where it was coming from until the mighty Stealer before me started to writhe in pain, collapsing to the ground as he slowly withered. The tables had been turned.

No being could survive without that which sustained them, and he proved no exception. In a surprising twist of fate, I had taken into me all those tormented souls that he had fed on, forcing him to painfully fade. By the time I was done freeing him of them, the Stealer was little more than a shell, a sloughed-off casing that had once looked human—for it harbored no soul of its own.

The grossly disfigured expression staring up at me from its unmoving countenance gave me no pause. I felt nothing about what I had done to him. Nothing at all. His life had long ago been forfeit; I just carried out his overdue punishment, though I had no idea how I had managed it.

As I hovered over his corpse, I suddenly realized that I was not alone. Without the distraction of the Stealer to occupy me, that familiar fear shot up my spine. I looked down the narrow way to find Deimos, in all his terrible glory, staring at me. His distaste for what I had done was plain in his expression.

"Your plan has failed," I called to him. "You can send as many of them as you wish after me. They, too, will fall."

His chest heaved furiously and his nostrils flared. His exterior, normally a calm yet terrifying façade, was marred by raw fury, all of which was aimed toward me.

"You're coming with me," he roared, charging me. I did not move. I had expected him to take me at some point. At least I would return to the Underworld as a winged version of myself, though I would pay dearly for spoiling his plans. His retribution would not be immediate, though. He would wait, toying with me until he felt it was safe to unleash his retribution. He may have wanted me for his own, but that did not mean I was exempt from his evil machinations.

"She goes nowhere," a voice growled from far behind me. Sean's presence stopped Deimos in his tracks. His brow furrowed heavily as he stared at the man behind me. My brother. My twin. At that moment, I experienced the connection that Kierson had spoken of.

Sean murmured something in Greek as he neared me—something I could understand. A spell. A banishing spell.

I looked on stoically as Deimos began to dissipate, his once-corporeal form slowly becoming transparent and dispersing into the air around us. With one final word, the small remainder of Deimos that was still visible disappeared in a flash, a loud popping sound accompanying his exit.

I turned to find Sean standing right behind me, his eyes wide as he took in my winged form. Something about the intensity of his gaze made me want to escape, but, when he reached out and ran his finger along one of the delicate gray feathers, I could see the sad reverence in his eyes. He was not disgusted by them. He was envious.

"The others?" I asked, a flash of the impending battle ricocheting through my mind suddenly. "We have to help them!"

I turned in the direction I had come from and ran as quickly as I could, my wings eventually taking action of their own accord and lofting me into the air. When I saw the rooftop of the Victorian, I was relieved. Oz and the Stealers were no longer there. Flying directly over the property, I looked down to locate my brothers.

I saw nothing.

They were gone—all of them—and that knowledge, combined with Oz's absence, created a tension in my chest, causing my breathing to become tight and shallow. In a burst of speed, I soared over the neighborhood, searching for any sign of the battle, the dead or the survivors.

Still, I found nothing.

Fear. I felt abundant fear in that moment, but not of the kind driven by Deimos' presence. My brothers were gone, and Oz was nowhere to be found. That unwanted emotion threatened to take me over, and I retreated back to the house, praying to the gods that my brothers were the warriors I knew them to be and had easily slain the enemy while I was eliminating the Stealer that sought to prepare me for Deimos. It was all I could do.

Landing on the roof, I raced to the shattered window of Oz's room. My bulky wings refused to retract fully, making the task of entering infinitely more difficult than expected. Annoyance was all I felt, and I cursed aloud, forcing my newfound appendages through the sharp opening. I felt a surge of pain in retribution for my efforts.

Glancing back at the damage I had caused, I was met with something unexpected. The downy appendages that had been gray only moments earlier in the alley with Sean had inexplicably turned as black as night.

It was true.

I was my mother's daughter.

With no time to dwell on that reality, I made my way down the spiral stairs quickly, calling for the others.

"Oz! Drew! Casey! Are you here? Kierson? Pierson?"

My calls were met with silence.

I ran through Oz's room, then descended the stairs to the second floor, painting the tattered walls red in my wake with my bloodied wings. All the while, I kept shouting for my brothers. By the time I started down the final flight of stairs to the first floor, I heard a familiar voice.

"We are here, Khara." It was Drew. A weight lifted instantly from my chest. With my final steps into the living room, the scene that awaited me there unfolded. I took in the faces that stared at me, undoubtedly assessing the implications of what I had only recently morphed into. I felt an awkward smile take over my face in response.

"It cannot be as bad as you think," I told them, rushing toward the five of them standing side by side in front of the couch. Then I stopped abruptly.

Five. Only five.

My eyes made their way down the line taking each of them in. Sean was there, having returned from the alley in haste. Casey. Drew. A very bloody Kierson, and Pierson.

Before I could ask where Oz was, my eyes fell on a pair of limp and deathly pale feet dangling over the arm of the sofa just beyond Pierson's rigid stance.

"Oh, no," I whispered, running toward them. The brothers yielded their positions, allowing me full view of what I was not certain I wanted to behold. There, on the sofa, lay a broken and barely alive Oz. The power he had emanated earlier that night was gone. What was left was only a remnant of the greatness he had possessed. He was fading, and painfully at that, just as he said he would. However, in contradiction to his word, it did not look like it would take long. He did not have much time. Death was something I was well schooled in; I recognized it easily.

"Oz?" I called, kneeling beside him while my heart seized in my chest. I reached to touch his face, but found my hand intercepted on its course.

"You mustn't touch him," Sean said sternly. "He has been compromised."

"Compromised how?" I asked, coming to stand in a challenging posture before him. "What has happened to him?"

Sean sighed heavily.

"Deimos. He is to blame for this," he started, stealing a glance at Oz, who lay silent and suffering on the couch beside us. "From what Kierson saw, Deimos held Oz hostage, allowing the Stealers to do their worst." His expression turned even more grim. "And that they did."

His eyes remained black and cold while he relayed his message, not allowing even the slightest emotion to bleed through. He truly was every bit my equal.

"I tried to get to him to help, Khara," Kierson said softly. "I really did . . . I just couldn't get to him fast enough. By the time I did, Deimos had scattered, and Oz was . . ."

"As he is now," Pierson finished the sentence for his twin, who could not. "I foresaw it. I knew what was to happen to him . . ."

"So he will die?" I asked, looking down at his weak and vulnerable state. Oz vulnerable was a sight I never thought I would see.

I did not wish to ever see it again.

"His choices are death or darkness, just as they would have been for you," Pierson gently reminded me, remorse bleeding into his tone. "And I do not think even Oz would choose the latter."

"I'm so sorry, Khara," Kierson said weakly. "I didn't want this for him . . . or you. I had a debt to repay, and I came up short. I failed you both."

I nodded at him tightly before returning my gaze to Oz.

"What can we do? There must be something. Surely you do not mean to let him lie here and suffer until he fades?" I asked incredulously. I could feel emotions storming within me, rising slowly. There were more of them—and of a greater intensity—than I had ever felt in my lifetime, and they threatened to escape.

"I have nothing to offer," Pierson said softly.

"And I see no other course to take," Sean replied, his midnight orbs allowing a green as light as mine to bleed through. "For what it is worth, I am sorry this has happened. He was a warrior worthy of a far more dignified death than this."

"But . . . there was talk of your healing abilities? Did you not save your mate?"

"That was different, Khara."

"Different in what way? That he is not my mate, or that he is not worth saving as she was?"

"I have already tried . . ." His voice trailed off, leaving the words "and failed" unsaid. He truly believed nothing else could be done.

"But if those powers came from our mother, then perhaps I, too, possess them?" I speculated, hearing the desperation creep into my tone.

"It took me centuries to hone those skills, Khara, and there is no guarantee that you have them at all."

"Does that mean I should not try? Would you not even afford me that chance?" He said nothing in response, his now-green eyes firmly fixed on mine. I leaned in close to him, my anger fueling my actions. "Could I keep you from trying to save the one you love if it were her that lay dying?"

With every word that passed my lips, a rage grew. My life had been spent obeying the rules of others. My actions, my learning, my surroundings—all were dictated to me, and I had accepted. But I would accept no longer. Oz had taught me about freedom, and I owed it to him to exercise it, if for no other reason than to try and save him.

"You and I are not the same, Khara," Sean said, a heavy sorrow in his voice. "I feel that may be both a blessing and a curse."

The emotion behind his words soon permeated me. In that fraction of a second, an awareness leapt forth. I thought of the emptiness, the cold—the vacuous, emotionless being that I had grown to be. I had long thought it was just an adaptation to my surroundings, but what if it was not? What if I had always been that way for a reason? A purpose. Maybe there was a reason why I remained frozen in the land of the damned, and it had nothing to do with the light inside me. What if it was the emptiness—the constant call of the evil surrounding me?

There were none like me in existence, leaving no opportunity for a comparison to be made, but it was clear that I had stolen something from the Stealer who had sought my soul in the alley. I had killed him easily, without thought or effort. It was as if that emptiness in me wanted to take those souls from him—to unburden him—and in doing so, I felt that void fill up inside me.

If I was truly able to extract complete souls as the Stealers had, could I not also be selective in what pieces I stole, just as the Breathers were? And, if so, could I not take from Oz that evil which had caused his fate? Could I not undo what had so grievously been done? His fate was sealed if I could not, and that fact made blood rush through me, filling my face in a hot flush. The barrage of foreign emotions I fought to contain defeated me, leaving me abraded and raw. With no other outlet for them, my temper flared.

"If you do not let me try and save him, Sean, you will know no forgiveness from me," I said resoundingly. "I cannot comprehend all that I am feeling right now, but I know that I cannot let him die like this—not with me sitting idly by. I will fix this . . . my mind refuses to accept anything less."

Not awaiting Sean's reply or permission, I leaned over Oz's limp form.

It had been the connection between Oz and me that had helped to fill the void the Stealer had originally left the night I was attacked, potentially allowing me to survive something that I might not otherwise have. With growing conviction, I placed my lips atop his, holding his face firmly in my hands.

"This may burn a little," I whispered, hoping that he could still hear me—that he could still be reached. Then, with a tenderness I had never previously been capable of, I kissed him, coaxing whatever darkness I could find to the surface.

But he would not let it go.

Instead, I felt the overwhelming darkness that I had drained out of the Stealer flowing from me into him. I closed my eyes, feeling a sweet release at first until my mind became fully aware of what he was doing.

Oz had made his choice.

"No!" I cried, pulling away from him, but it was too late. I knew because the emptiness of my existence had returned.

I looked on as his eyes shot open. They had once held a cruel warmth to them, but I watched helplessly as that morphed into an empty shade of evil that I could not quite put into words. They were blacker than black—devoid of life. Empty.

And they were firmly fixed on me.

He rose from the couch, uncurling his body to stand for all of us to behold. The setting sun provided the perfect backdrop to his frighteningly beautiful form. And, as the rays broke through the windows behind him, he spread his wings. They were black as the ravens of hell. He was what I had been told to fear most and what I thought I had become.

A Dark One.

"I'm afraid I can't stay," he purred, staring down the boys who surrounded me. "Looks like I'm running with a new crowd now." His wings fluttered slightly while he grinned in a way that made my heart sink. The fallen one had fallen further still. "Thanks for getting these back for me. They're not quite the shade I'm used to, but they'll do for now." His eyes bored a hole through my heart as he looked right through me. "Freedom sometimes requires sacrifice, new girl. It seems you know all too well about that now."

Without another word, he ran and crashed through the wall of glass behind him at an incredible speed, taking flight the second he could. I watched as he darkened the horizon in the distance, his giant wings blocking out the orange sky. Had I known that what I was would have led to his transformation, I never would have interfered. Dead or Dark, he was lost either way—and I much preferred the thought of him dead to the alternative.

"You could not have known," Drew offered in placation, precariously winding his arm around my shoulders. He seemed uncomfortable with how to negotiate my cumbersome appendages. He seemed uncomfortable in general, really. His words were meant to console me, but there was something unspoken in them—a knowledge. An empathy. An understanding of something I had yet to grasp.

"Your wings," Pierson started, moving toward me. "They are gray, not black as they were when you arrived. They've changed."

"They were gray when they emerged. They only changed after I killed the Stealer. I stole from him what he had stolen from so many," I explained. "I think that is what I just unknowingly fed to Oz."

"But—"

"I am tired," I declared, pulling away from Drew's consoling embrace and Pierson's impending interrogation. "I would like to be alone." With eyes downcast, I made my way to the basement door. I could not hold my brothers' gazes.

"Khara," Kierson said tentatively. "Don't worry. It'll be okay."

"Will it?" I asked as emotions I had never felt before attacked my insides from every angle. "I am not certain you are right, Kierson."

"We must discuss what happened to you," Sean called after me. "And your wings." His tone was softer than usual, but it held an unyielding edge to it. He would want answers to that which he could not understand—that which I had become.

"Tomorrow . . . please," I pleaded softly, the doorknob to solitude grasped tightly in my hand.

With only a momentary pause, he conceded to my request. "Tomorrow."

Turning the knob, I opened the door to my subterranean refuge, seeking the comfort and familiarity the shadows and cold offered. I heard my brothers upstairs speaking while I climbed into my bed, awkwardly tucking my wings behind me. Concern for my welfare seemed their highest priority. There was much conjecture as to what happened on that rooftop before Oz threw me to my potential death and then nearly met his own as a result. Only he knew what had been said and done before Kierson arrived, and my suspicion was that he would not feel especially forthcoming anymore.

If only the Dark Ones answered to Father like so many others did.

There were things I wanted to know—things that involved our time on the rooftop, but not what happened after I was thrown from it. The before was far more interesting in my estimation.

After much time, I heard my brothers retire, one by one. There was apparently no reason to patrol the city. The Stealers had been eradicated, from what I could surmise. Whatever other beings existed in the city could be left alone for one evening. The thought of my brothers getting to truly rest for once made me smile.

My emotions were offering me a crash course in all things unfamiliar and uncomfortable. Though they had increased slightly at the introduction to my brothers, the bond between us somehow unlocking them, that evening pushed them to another level of intensity altogether. Strangely, the bizarreness of it made me laugh. Laughter, smiling, happiness. Those were not things of my previous world—my previous life. But my birth had created a gateway to things I could have never expected. The questions left in its wake ambled through my mind as I drifted off to sleep. *How much darkness did I have left? Was I a vessel for it? Could I both remove it from and inject it into others? And, most importantly, could I unmake that which had been made?*

That would be the only way to truly save Oz.

Retrieving the answers I needed threatened to be the very definition of impossible. I knew of only one individual rumored to possess the knowledge that I sought, or the ability to procure it, and the task of reaching her would prove virtually insurmountable. I felt defeated by the irony of my situation. The Underworld was where I would find her.

And I could not go there on my own.

24

I could feel his presence.

The emptiness cried for me to go to him.

Deep in the night, when the air lay low and silent, I heard him call to me. I leapt from my bed, trying to silently climb the wooden stairs that led up from the basement, which did their best to sabotage my effort with every step. When I emerged from my underground sanctuary, I found the window restored in the living room and a very dark angel standing just on the other side. Pressing his forehead against it, he drummed his fingers lightly upon the glass while he whispered my name over and over again. His call, though soft, screamed so loudly in my mind that I clamped my head in my hands in an effort to protect it.

"Khara . . ." he continued, his eerie song drawing me to him. "Khaaaaraaaaa . . ."

Step by cautious step, I made my way to join him, pressing my body against the thin, fragile barrier that kept us apart.

"I will have you," he chanted softly, moving against the glass as though it were me he was touching. "You will know no other . . . only me."

He was the answer to the problem I faced. I stared at him, keeping my emotions that rose within me far from my expression. He was my ticket into the Underworld. All I needed was his compliance to get me there.

"You will have nothing," I said, my voice low and seductive, "unless you give me what I want."

"You would make demands of me?" he replied in mock indignation. Then he laughed, causing every hair on my body to stand at attention—some out of fear, others out of lust. "I can take what I want. You know this." His tone was cautionary, reminding me of that which I needed no reminder of. The Dark Ones did as they wished, whenever it pleased them. They answered to nobody—or nobody that I was aware of. Their behavior embodied everything that Oz had become after he fell, only amplified.

"I need to get into the Underworld. You will take me," I said, my expression as indifferent as the day we had met. "When I get what I have gone there for, you can have what you so clearly want."

I felt the window bow ever so slightly under his weight as he ground himself against it to be closer to me.

"I will do this," he said abruptly. "And you will do as you promise. Be ready; I will come for you shortly. There is something I must do first." He peeled himself from the clear divider and stepped backward so that I could see the evil majesty he held. "And Khara?" My nerve endings delighted in the sound of my name on his tongue—just as they had before his transformation. "Do not tell the others. I would hate for our first trip together to be cut short—Sean can be so meddlesome."

"They will not know."

"Excellent," he breathed, his words like sweet poison. "I'll see you soon."

He disappeared into the night sky in seconds, leaving me alone and conflicted in the living room. I knew my brothers would worry at my disappearance, and I did not wish for that. It was, therefore, imperative that I find a way to get word to them without affording them time to interfere with my ill-conceived plan.

As I made my way back to the basement to prepare a few things for the journey, I saw a notepad lying on the console table. I picked it and the pen lying next to it up and made my way downstairs. I sat on the edge of my bed, worrying the pen over and over in my hand. I knew not what to write, but I owed them an explanation. Knowing that time was of the essence, I settled for a short message that highlighted the gist of what I was about to do. However, I left out the pertinent information regarding the how and why of my journey. The brothers were keen enough to put that bit together on their own.

I hoped I would be far away when that time came.

EPILOGUE

Expectations prove dangerous.

I had never had any before that moment, but it was plain to see why they cause so much turmoil. A nervous hum coursed through my body while I stood at the gates of the Underworld, my terror-inspiring escort beside me. True to his word, Oz had returned to the Victorian, prepared to steal me away from my brothers. A small pang of guilt tugged at my heart when he led me away, but I knew I had to go.

I wanted to see my father.

I wanted to go home.

I wanted answers.

But with those intense desires rose a fear far greater; doubt plagued me, giving me pause. To accomplish the task of returning to the Underworld required me to make a deal with the devil, a phrase I had learned from Kierson. I did not doubt for a moment that my deal would come at a high price. With Oz, there always was.

And what of Oz? His motives for returning me were surely inscrutable—his purpose far from noble. The Dark Ones, from all I had ever known, were little more than mercenaries. For him to come for me at all implied a bounty had been paid. His casual compliance with my demand only made me further question his motivations. However, I could not shake the words he had spoken that night when he pressed against the window, their echo forever plaguing my thoughts. *You will know no other . . .* That sentiment laid claim to me in a way that threatened to override my skepticism. He wanted me for his own.

To what end, I could not be sure.

And yet, he was not the only one who sought to own me. Deimos was a threat that had neither been eliminated nor deterred, his fixation on me surely amplified in the face of his temporary defeat. Sean had succeeded in banishing Deimos' earthly form back to the Underworld—back to the very place I was destined for—but there would be consequences for that action. The wrath that would certainly await me could not be ignored. Whether or not it could be stopped remained to be seen.

Deimos would not easily be denied.

The shining light in all that darkness was Hades. He was surely to be my salvation on more levels than I had initially anticipated. He could not only shield me from Deimos, should he sense the danger, but I hoped he could also shed light on the shadows of my past, providing he knew precisely what they were. My plan weighed heavily on his ability to do so.

After meeting my brothers and hearing of Ares, I had no doubt that my mother's choice to abandon me had been for my safety. What I needed Hades to do was fill in the cracks and fissures that remained in her story—my story—filling it out until whole. That demand sounded benign when I repeated the questions that required explanation over and over again in my mind. However, I was not so certain that, once they were answered, I would think them so harmless. Some secrets were meant to persist.

Perhaps hers were.

With a heavy breath, I steadied myself, preparing for the harsh journey home. I glanced beside me, taking in Oz's formidable silhouette, his obsidian wings stretched ominously around us. It was by a Dark One that I had returned to Earth, and it would be by a Dark One that I would return home. Stepping in front of him, I allowed him to snake his arm around my waist, pulling me against his naked chest. Adrenaline surged within me at the contact, but I stifled it immediately. Oz no longer held the promise that he once had, which only reminded me of the final reason I was going back to the Underworld and the uncertain circumstances it promised. I needed to find out if what had been created could be unmade. Right or wrong, I was going to find a solution to his dark predicament, even if it killed me.

And, if the fates were against me, my journey might prove to do just that.

//

ACKNOWLEDGMENTS

I want to keep this simple and brief, so here it goes . . .

I would not be able to accomplish all that I do without my amazing team of authors, bloggers, editors, and friends. Shannon Morton, Amy Bartol, Jennifer Ryan, Kristy Bronner, Virginia Nicholas, Cristina Suarez-Muñoz, Jena Gregoire, and Denise Grover-Swank, you guys kick ass. My husband, who might just be the most patient man alive, is a saint for running interference with children, helping me with my computer that eats things, and making dinner while I tune the world out so that I can write about the craziness going on in my head. I would be lost without you, Bry. Lastly, I want to thank my 47North family, both authors and staff. Getting this novel published has been a wild ride. I'm glad I found a group of equally wild people to accompany me on the journey.

ABOUT THE AUTHOR

Amber Lynn Natusch is the author of the bestselling *Caged*, as well as the Light and Shadow series with Shannon Morton. She was born and raised in Winnipeg, and speaks sarcasm fluently because of her Canadian roots. She loves to dance and sing in her kitchen—much to the detriment of those near her—but spends most of her time running a practice with her husband, raising two small children, and attempting to write when she can lock herself in the bathroom for ten minutes of peace and quiet. She has many hidden talents, most of which should not be mentioned but include putting her foot in her mouth, acting inappropriately when nervous, swearing like a sailor when provoked, and not listening when she should. She's obsessed with home renovation shows, should never be caffeinated, and loves snow. Amber has a deep-seated fear of clowns and deep water . . . especially clowns swimming in deep water.

Made in the USA
Middletown, DE
13 July 2019